F

D1795581

6-9

# NICKNAMES ONLY

WILLIAM DONALDSON

# NICKNAMES ONLY

Macdonald

A Macdonald Book

Copyright © William Donaldson 1978

First published in Great Britain in 1978
by Methuen & Co Ltd, London, under the title
*The Balloons in the Black Bag*

This edition published in Great Britain in 1985
by Macdonald & Co (Publishers) Ltd
London & Sydney

823′.914[F]      PR6054.O4/
ISBN 0–356–10984–4

Printed in Great Britain by
Redwood Burn Limited, Trowbridge, Wiltshire
Bound at the Dorstel Press

Macdonald & Co (Publishers) Ltd
Maxwell House
74 Worship Street
London EC2A 2EN
A BPCC plc Company

Toby Danvers the Impresario has escaped from the lunatic asylum to which his various wives, acting in unison for once, tried to commit him last October. He took off in his pyjamas in the middle of the night and secured a job on the Greenwich telephone exchange. Here he's happy for the first time in years, since it's manned entirely by struck-off persons like himself, who dream continuously of spectacular returns to the professions they once adorned. This, he explains, is why we the public so rarely get satisfaction. We dial 100 and hang on helplessly while a discredited entrepreneur of one sort or another finishes the article he's reading in *The Stock Exchange Gazette*, *Variety* or *The Journal of the Law Society*.

He still keeps his ear to the ground, however, and was thus able to give me a frightful shock last week by phoning to say that Ken the Australian Horse Player was back in town and was coming after me, what's more, with a gun.

'He seems to think,' said Danvers, 'that your refusal to pay the police on his behalf was un-Australian.'

For some time, in fact, I'd been feeling guilty about my failure in this respect. A year before, Ken had been extradited to Australia to face charges concerning the sale to unwary Aborigines of shares in a marmalade mine, and the arresting officers in London had offered certain favours in return for two hundred pounds. For some reason my solicitor at the

1

time had advised me not to hand the money over. I'd changed solicitors since then, of course, but the damage had been done.

'He plans to shoot your ears off,' continued Danvers.

'Hell.'

'Yes. He's staying with his brother, the Professor. It was the Professor, in fact, who gave me the news. I bumped into him last night at the Star Tavern.'

I had no one with whom to discuss this depressing turn of events, because Emma Jane – ever a source of strength in times of adversity – was out with Dawn Upstairs doing a trick for the Foreign Office. I sat in a funk for some hours staring at nothing in particular. When Emma Jane at last got home, she said:

'Hullo, my dear! What's up? Why aren't you watching television?'

'I've had a shock.'

'I can see that. You're missing *Hawaii Five-O.*'

'Ken the Australian Horse Player's going to shoot my ears off.'

'Good gracious! I thought he was in the boob in Australia.'

'So did I. It seems he was acquitted on all charges. He's back in London and, according to Toby Danvers the Impresario, blames me for not bribing the police here in the first place. What shall I do?'

'Tricky,' said Emma Jane. She pondered the matter for a while and then, as usual, came up with a solution. 'I know. Take the initiative! No point in being a sitting duck. Draw his fire, as it were, by arranging a meeting yourself.'

'Wouldn't that be a trifle dangerous?'

'Not if *you* choose the place. Pick somewhere *ultra*-respectable: a place where unbridled hooliganism is simply unimaginable. The restaurant at Harvey Nichols, for instance.'

This was a good idea. The favoured rendezvous of well-behaved ladies up for the day seemed an unlikely setting for anything even vaguely sensational. Newspaper headlines such as 'OUTRAGE IN BROAD DAYLIGHT! AUSTRALIAN HORSE PLAYER SHOOTS EARS OFF ENGLISH GENTLEMAN IN HARVEY NICHOLS!' had never featured much in the past

2

and it seemed reasonable to suppose that the same state of
affairs might hold good in future.

❀ ❀ ❀

The meeting took place today. I got to Harvey Nichols first
and when Ken the Australian Horse Player arrived I
embraced him theatrically. This show of affection was to
enable me to frisk him, albeit unprofessionally. It also served,
I think, to take some of the wind out of his sails, and after
a matter of minutes we were old pals again, shoulder to
shoulder against the Responsible Society. We discussed his
miraculous escape from the clutches of the Australian authorities and then he asked me what I'd been up to during the
past year.

'This and that. Scratching around, you know.'

'Emily Jane still keeping you? Eh? Eh?' He chortled
roguishly and then struck out with a playful left hook to the
jaw which would have spun me off my seat had I not drawn
back in time.

'Well, more or less. But not for much longer, I'm happy
to say.'

'What! You've taken her off the game? You're going back
to *orn*treprenerring?'

Good God, what was that? Was he referring to my time
as a presenter of West End entertainments?

'Certainly not.'

'You *are*, you rascal! You know what they say: "Once a
man of the theatre, always a man of the theatre." I knew it!
You've got a musical up your sleeve!'

'Far from it. I've written a book, in fact.'

'A *book*?' He couldn't have been more surprised. 'A *book*?
You scoundrel! Is it in the shops?'

'Any minute now. It's excellent. It's called *Both the Ladies
and the Gentlemen*. You particularly will relish the sly borrow-
ing from Auden.'

'The ladies and the fucking gentlemen! Well, well, well.
You rascal!'

'Thank you.'

Ken pondered this for a while, then he narrowed his eyes, leaned forward until our noses were almost touching and began to speak out of the side of his mouth in a low conspiratorial tone, like Eric Morecambe in a spy sketch.

'Here, it's not about – er –' He broke off and carried out a quick security check on the silent majority from the home counties peaceably eating their *goujons* of sole to our left and right. 'It's not about – er – you know what?' He tapped the side of his nose and winked.

He was alluding, I supposed, to my life of shame living off the artistic earnings of Emma Jane.

'It is, as it happens, yes.'

'Go on! You scoundrel! What name have you used?'

'My own. That seemed simplest.'

'Your *own*? Don't come the raw prawn with me, old pal! Come on, what name have you really used?'

'My *own*, honestly. William Donaldson.'

'Oh dear, oh dear.' He was astounded. Since Australians, as a matter of policy, use an assumed name to cross the street or pick up the dry cleaning, his amazement at my bravado was to be expected. 'Rather putting yourself on offer, aren't you, old pal?'

'I like to think so, yes.'

'Here, you haven't mentioned me I hope?'

'*You?* Good heavens, no! I'm cool.'

Ken was silent for a while in contemplation, then:

'FUCK ME DEAD!' he suddenly bellowed, bringing his fist down on the table with such a crack that the well-born ladies lunching quietly on either side of us shot upright in their seats as though their haemorrhoids had caught fire. 'PECKINPAH!'

'What's it got to do with him?'

'What's it got to do with him? We sell him the film rights, that's what it's got to do with him! But not for peanuts, mind. No sir, not for fucking peanuts! Sam's as tight as a fish's bum, but he'll have to pay for this one! Yes sir! Have

4

you any idea, *have you any fucking idea*, how much Niven got for *Jaws*?'

'They were hanging an innocent man.'

'No. Four million! And I don't mean pounds! No sir! *Dollars!* Film rights are the name of the game, baby! Now, you leave everything to me. We don't want Peckinpah to screw us.'

'God forbid. I'll leave the arrangements to you entirely.'

'We'll need a watertight contract.'

'We certainly will.'

'Fucking WATERTIGHT!' he bellowed in fury, and once again the proper, behatted ladies to our left and right shot upright in their seats. 'Four fucking million! Well, you scoundrel, I think you've cracked it at last! The ladies and the fucking gentlemen! Well, well, well. You rascal!'

This is tremendously exciting. Emma Jane shall have a new pair of boots and I'll be up West again in a chalk-stripe suit, striding nicely with my toes turned out and my head held high.

❈ ❈ ❈

To a football match with my publisher, who's called Mike Franklin M.A. His team, Shepherd's Bush, at home to my team, Derby County. Emma Jane, whose aversion to football had hitherto verged on the unnatural, announced at the last minute that she wanted to come too.

'You never take me to the football,' she said.

'I never go to the football. And anyway, you don't like it.'

'That's not the point,' she said. Then she told me to be home in time to cook the dinner. 'And this week I want to see you eat up all your vegetables.' Small wonder I have separatist aspirations.

I've supported the Rams ever since they won the Cup in 1946. Most of that fine team must have joined the grim sweeper in the sky long since. Reassured to find that the present Rams still favour 1946 hair-cuts. No modish decadence here. Short back and sides, two weeks with the wife and kiddies in Majorca, lights out at 10.30 and no monkey-business in the showers.

Watching football in the flesh is most unsatisfactory. It's much harder to figure out what's going on and, on those rare occasions when anything interesting happens, one finds oneself waiting for the action replay. I even missed John Motson's characteristically bizarre observations, such as 'Oh dear, so many promising moves seem to break down with the final pass', and 'This man Masson must have radar in his boots'. Be that as it may, Toddy was majestic (of course), Nishy elegant, Riochy immaculate, Newtony abrasive, Lee-y fat, flash and provocative (not a real Ram), Daviesy out of his head, like a camel on mandies. Shepherd's Bush were rubbish. Riochy scored with his educated left foot while Parkesy was still touching his toes and saying his prayers. As the only Derby supporter within two hundred miles, I kept my excitement on the leash. Three minutes later Lee-y pirouetted himself onto his backside and had to go home to his mummy. Good riddance in my opinion, except that it left Bowlesy as the only contender for the afternoon's flash little prat prize. Bowlesy spent the first half sulking and calling Becky a dozy cunt. Becky, a new bug, became demoralised and quickly lost the use of his legs.

During the interval, Mike Franklin M.A. was very subdued, as befitted a man whose team were, in the words of Joe Mercer, 'getting stuffed one none'. Second half, more of the same. I'm wearing a magnanimous expression, the Rams are doing it on their pricks, then – goats and monkeys! – Toddy has eleven of his majestic lapses and Shepherd's Bush score six goals in ten seconds.

After the football we took tea in the Earl's Court Road. Since Franklin was now in a better mood, I brought up the subject of my book: not something I'd normally do, least of all with Franklin, whose interest in *belles-lettres* verges on the marginal.

'I think we can expect it to be quite a flop,' he said happily, stuffing his face with toast and marmalade.

At least he's consistent. He's been predicting disaster from

6

the word go and I puzzle constantly over why he agreed to publish it. I think his pleasant typist-cum-senior reader, Jane, must have told him (misleadingly) that it had to do with naughty girls and that he consequently allowed himself to become involved. Poor soul. I know only too well how this can happen. When I was of the live theatre I always found it easier to mount some worthless little show than to disappoint its anxious author. People should be told precisely what they want to hear, and the last thing a writer wants to hear, God knows, is that you think his work lacks merit.

'I doubt very much,' continued Franklin, with an air of huge contentment, 'whether any of the more reputable bookshops will care to stock it.'

'Really? Why's that?'

'It's not the sort of book they like.'

This was a poke in the eye and no mistake, but I pressed on gamely, mentioning all the bad publicity we could hope to get if we played our cards right. In the past, I said, the yellow press – *The Daily Mail*, *The Sunday Express* and *The Daily Express* – had always been good for an insolent paragraph or two. And what about *The News of the World*? Was it not the case that its crusading reporters scoured the sewers and back alleys day and night for just such low types as myself? And surely the saintly Larry Lamb went off to sleep at night snuggled up to Mrs Lamb, but fantasising about exactly such headlines as: '"My life in a brothel" by the producer of *Beyond the Fringe*.'

'Beyond the what?' said Franklin.

Perhaps he'd never heard of it, and indeed why should he have? What a dated old fruit I am! Like expecting me to have heard of *Bob's Your Uncle* with Leslie Henson and Vera Pierce, which of course I have. But then I'm of the live theatre. What with the Rams getting turned over by Shepherd's Bush and now this bucket of icy water all over my literary hopes, a depressing afternoon.

I arrived home to discover that Lord Dynevor has moved in. His wife, he complains, now understands him and has consequently thrown him out. She has grown tired, it seems,

7

of his arriving home in the dog-watch as pissed as a parrot. He has brought with him a French loaf, a giant economy size tin of Nescafé, a History of Wales in sixteen volumes and a bunch of bananas. After dinner, Emma Jane got a surprise booking, so Lord Dynevor and I had to be farmed out with Dawn Upstairs. Lord D became very agitated about his bananas, fearing that they might be burglarised in his absence by Emma Jane's client.

'What sort of man is he?' he asked. 'Can he be trusted?'

The old sausage couldn't be convinced as to the probity of a punter in the matter of another man's bananas and he insisted on taking them upstairs with him.

Dawn Upstairs has been a bit cheesed off recently due to the lack of a personal life. 'I have to have a man like socially,' she says. (One-Eyed Charlie has pointed out, with characteristic accuracy, that 'you can only get Dawn Upstairs into bed for love or money, never for the real thing'.) Happily a new young man has recently come into her life and now she's her old self again. He's called Trevor and he used to be a tear-arse for one of the big firms recently put into compulsory liquidation by Bert 'Crime is my Business' Wickstead. He looks a bit naughty and he speaks in a sinister bronchial whisper caused by an old gang-war wound to the wind-pipe, but in fact he's as sweet as pie so long as he's kept away from the sauce. One dry sherry and even the riot police take cover. Apprised of his background, Lord Dynevor quizzed him closely about the Krays. For an hour or so, Trevor answered his questions most patiently, then he pointed out politely that it had been the Richardsons, in fact, not the Krays, for whom he'd performed. Assuming that he was guilty of a colossal social floater (which indeed he was: on a par, in fact, with holding forth admiringly about the Monday Club to a member of the Tribune Group), Lord Dynevor spent the next half hour handing round bananas and saying how sorry he was. After a while, however, he recovered his poise sufficiently to ask Dawn Upstairs which of her clients, on the whole and in the long run, gave her the most trouble.

'Begging your pardon, Lord Dynevor,' she said, 'but upper-class Englishmen. You know, Tories and that.'

'I confess I'm surprised,' said Lord Dynevor. 'Received opinion has always been that the Tories give very little trouble, merely wishing to be lightly whacked from time to time.'

'Oh they like a whacking, do the Tories, don't get me wrong. But they can be very heavy in other ways. No manners you know. Take yesterday, for instance. This upper-class client of mine – you know, he lives in Chester Square and knows Lady Annabel Birley and that – rings up and asks me to go over to his place with another girl. He says we have to be very ladylike and that because his sister will be there. His sister! I ask you! So I rang Pretty Marie, but at first she didn't want to know. She'd had trouble with him before, had Pretty Marie. He'd suddenly bit her and she'd thought, "Golly! *That*'s not healthy." She suggested that I take Fat Lynette. "*She*'s not ladylike," I said. "She's got GCE, has Fat Lynette," said Pretty Marie. "You don't have to have GCE to fuck, you know, Pretty Marie," I said. She can be daft, can Pretty Marie. Well, she's Gemini like me. Still, they're very good in bed, are Geminis. Anyway, I finally persuaded her to come with me. So I got all done up like he said, I wore my white suit from Castel, you know, you've seen it, well I don't want to be flash and that, but it only cost £175, didn't it? I'm looking really good, right?'

'Right.'

'So we arrive at this fucking great house in Chester Square and when the butler opens the front door he looks us up and down as though we should have used the tradesmen's entrance or something, but he shows us into the lounge-room none the less. Well, the first thing I see is this debby, far-back lady sat on the sofa and I'm thinking "oooh bloody hell, the *sister*". So of course I say "pleased to meet you" and "been on your holidays yet?" and ladylike stuff like that. And do you know what? She doesn't even offer us a drink or ask us if we'd like to sit down. So we're stood there, are me and Pretty Marie, trying to look ladylike and that, and suddenly my rich punter rushes in and says: "Okay, you two, upstairs!" *Charming*, and in front of his sister! So he hustles us up to the bedroom where there's this great four-poster bed with drapes and that, you know the sort of thing. Then I realise I've left my handbag downstairs. "I've left my handbag downstairs," I say. "You won't need your handbag," he says. "Well," I think, "how does he know whether I'll need my handbag?" Right?'

'Right.'

'"I want to go to the bathroom," I say. "No time for that," he says. "Ooooh," I think, "that's very nice, I must say." Then he tells Pretty Marie to lie on the bed. "Right," he says to me, "go down on her." "Go *down* on her?" I say. "Fucking hell, whatever next? I thought we were meant to be ladies?" So anyway, after a while I'm lying on the bed and Pretty Marie's plating me and that and I'm moaning and groaning, you know how it is, and I'm thinking "*ladies* indeed!" Then suddenly Pretty Marie pops her head up between my legs and says: "I can't stand rich people, they've got no fucking manners."'

'Have a banana,' said Lord Dynevor.

'Thank you very much. You're different, of course.'

❊ ❊ ❊

Lord Dynevor has moved out. He says that London isn't healthy (by which he means he doesn't want to be asleep on our floor when the Morals Squad arrives) and he has returned to Wales, resolved to embark on a keep-fit course. He recently met a man in a pub who told him that the celebrated bull-fighter Louis Miguel Dominguin kept in shape by running backwards with a heavy weight in each hand. Lord Dynevor thought that this made sense and he went out into the grounds of his castle to put the matter to the test. With a sack of goat fertiliser under each arm, he started to run backwards as fast as his old legs could manage, confident that he had his bearings right. He went head over heels into his own moat and had to be fished out by a passing peasant.

Some people think that my occasional references to Lord Dynevor show a certain lack of respect and that from them a picture emerges of a helpless old coot. In reality, he's a ruthless man, well able to take care of himself not only in the study but in the market place too. I know this to my cost. I was standing outside Magdalene in the summer of '56, when he drove up in a sprauncy great motor car.

'Good morning, Rhys,' I said. (This was before he inherited his title.)

'Good morning, Donaldson. Didn't see you at Trubshaw's party last night.'

'No, I felt a bit dicky to tell the truth. Must have had a bad oyster at the Pitt. Definitely felt rum. I say, that's a jolly fine car you've got there. Any particular make?'

'It's a Riley Pathfinder I believe.'

'Is it for sale?'

'Certainly? How much?'

'A thousand pounds,' I said.

'Righty-ho,' said Lord Dynevor, and he stepped out.

I wrote out the gooses and took his place at the wheel.

'Care to come along?' I said.

'No thanks,' said Lord Dynevor, 'I'm in a bit of a hurry actually. I'm orf to fight in the Hungarian Revolution, don't you know.'

'Good show.'

'Do you suppose I should take my dinner jacket?'

'Best to be on the safe side. I'd take it.'

'That's what I thought. Well, so long.'

'Toodle-pip.'

I pointed the car towards Newmarket, intending to take it on a trial spin, but I'd not gone a hundred yards before I realised something was amiss. The car moved forward more or less, but the racket from under the bonnet was appalling. It sounded like two spoons caught in a waste-disposal unit. I got the swine to the nearest garage and just managed to jump clear before it gave a terminal shudder and disassembled fitfully before my eyes, like the clown's car in a circus. The decomposing process took at least five minutes, but at last my nice new toy lay scattered on the ground in its countless separate parts.

A mechanic, who'd downed tools to watch, rubbed his eyes in disbelief. 'I've never seen that before,' he said.

As was the case with most of the Cambridge Brigade, Lord Dynevor got no nearer Hungary than Victoria Station, but he never came back to Cambridge, and by the next time I saw him, in 1961, I didn't think it would be tasteful to refer to the matter of the car. The only undergraduate actually to reach Hungary, as far as I know, was Alan Williams, the adventurer and thriller writer. Determined to smuggle some-one out, he collared a little old lady at the border, popped her into his kitbag and carried her, fighting like a ferret in a sack, to Paris. Here she kicked up a tremendous row, because she, like Alan, had been trying to get into Hungary, not out.

❊ ❊ ❊

Mike Franklin M.A. has been spraying something called the media with proof copies of my book and today the first com-municator bit. Alan Brien came to tea and I must say I was delighted to see him again. He said it had been a very quiet week and that he was urgently in need of material for his *Sunday Times* diary. He was very civil about the book and said he particularly liked the description of my interviewing technique, which was to do all the talking myself. This, he said, had always been his method precisely. He then opened his reporter's note-book in a most business-like fashion, but before I could open my mouth he began to correct my think-ing about Russia. Their attention to detail would see them through, he said.

'The KGB, for instance, are holed up round the clock in underground bunkers, methodically ploughing their way through the whole shooting match from Aristotle to Sir A. J. Ayer, just in case any of it should ever come in handy.'

I gave him another whisky and then, before I could comment on his previous observation, he brought me swiftly up to date on police corruption, the libel laws, Richard Ingrams, sex, inflation, drugs, drink, P. G. Wodehouse, dreams, Royalty, dreams about Royalty, Mrs Thatcher, paranatural phenomena, Uri Geller, Brian Inglis, bores, Sunderland, people who talk too much and people who don't talk enough. Then he sketched in a theory of history that sounded to me dangerously Hegelian, not to say historicist. Something to do with water running down hill and, on meeting an obstacle, simply flowing around it.

I gave him another whisky and he said that he was surprised that in these permissive times call-girls continued to thrive. He then paused fractionally to take a sip of whisky, which gave me a chance to chip in with my theory that all punters are rebelling against the male role. It was absurd, I said, that *women*'s lib should be the issue when it was manifestly the male role that was the more 'unnatural'. Telling evidence, I said, was provided by the behaviour of Emma Jane's customers (a representative sample, as far as I could gather). It was a plain fact that not one of them showed any inclination to comport himself in the manner traditionally expected of a man in this context. The small minority who didn't want to dress up as parlour-maids or pretend to be Princess Anne were as passive as sponges, wanting only to lie back and be authoritatively attended to, relieved for once of the responsibility of taking the lead, of being persuasive and in command. On the other hand, I argued, it seemed unlikely that a brothel for ladies – a place where they could pretend to be stockbrokers and do-it-yourself enthusiasts, where, dressed as marine commandos, Norman Mailer or members of a riot squad, they could bark orders, climb ropes and drill each other – would be heavily attended. Well interrupted, Magdalene.

Alan squinted at me disbelievingly, but whether this was because he found my argument lacking in cogency or because I'd done all the talking for two minutes, I don't know. Then he said, rather encouragingly, that he thought my book might cause a bit of a stir and that I would have to say whether it was fact or fiction. The trouble is I no longer know the

13

answer to this myself. I asked Alan whether he could some-how blur this particular aspect in whatever he wrote in *The Sunday Times*. He obligingly said he'd try, since he didn't want to be the one to get me into trouble. I said I didn't mind trouble, but I was keen to protect Emma Jane from the wrath of her mother, who was a keen reader of *The Sunday Times*. Alan said he'd do his best, and then he trotted off with one of our pussy cats. What a lovely man he is.

After he'd gone, Emma Jane and I held a quick production meeting to discuss the correct line to take with her mother. Since the jig would be up just as soon as *The Sunday Times* reached East Anglia, we decided to strike first with a breezy display of double bluff. A naughty girl with a guilty con-science, we reasoned, would hardly tip her Ordinary Mother off to the fact that she was about to be exposed in the Sunday press. So Emma Jane took two valiums and got on the phone to her mum.

'Hullo, mummy!' she burbled zestfully. 'How *are* you? And daddy? *Super! Listen*, you mustn't on any account miss Alan Brien's diary in *The Sunday Times* this week! It's going to be all about us and the pussy cats! Isn't that thrilling?'

Pray to heaven Alan doesn't call Emma Jane a whore and me a ponce.

※　※　※

Alan's worst is to say that I look like a bald football boot, or something of the sort, and in fact his kind plug has livened things up no end. Today Mike Franklin M.A. phoned to say that the Literary Editor of *The Sunday Mirror* wished to take luncheon with me in St Martin's Lane. I draw pretty well with literary men, so I went along.

I arrived early and had ten minutes to indulge an agreeable attack of nostalgia. The last time I'd been here was with Donald Albery fifteen years ago. I was meeting him for the first time and was naturally somewhat nervous. I called him 'Mr Albery' until he said that this was absurd and that I must call him 'Sir'. I'll never forget a fabulous anecdote he told

14

me involving Binkie Beaumont, Coral Browne and Henry Sherek. Binkie was pissed and...no, Henry was in drag, that's it, and...well scupper me! I've forgotten the damn thing.

Mark Kahn, the Literary Editor of *The Sunday Mirror*, is very nice and perfectly round. Had I stuck a finger in his ear and bowled him down St Martin's Lane he'd have skittled the tourists in Trafalgar Square. Over lunch he said various encouraging things:

1. *The Sunday Mirror* is – all appearances to the contrary notwithstanding – a family newspaper.

2. The family it has in mind likes a bit of soft-core porn with its cornflakes, but it doesn't wish to be told that its leaders are having jiggy-jiggy when they ought to be attending to Public Matters.

3. This being the case, he certainly couldn't lower the tone of its pages by publicising a squalid little book like mine.

4. I would undoubtedly be arrested within the week.

5. Insolence to High Court Judges had rarely been encouraged and mentioning the Police Commissioner's daughter wasn't cricket. Once detained, I could expect his outraged strappers to use me for truncheon practice.

6. Mike Franklin M.A. would also be arrested for Conspiracy and General Attitude. Mr Kahn had gone to the trouble of looking up the law on General Attitude and there was no doubt that Franklin's clear duty as a citizen had been to hand me over to the authorities, not to publish my sordid confession.

While I had hoped, I must admit, for some close textual criticism from the Literary Editor of *The Sunday Mirror*, rather than all this guff, I went home to Emma Jane in a mood of some elation.

'Good news,' I said, 'we're getting somewhere at last. I'm going to be arrested.'

She didn't seem to think that this was good news at all and she begged me to take security measures, such as wearing a false nose, changing my name and leaving the country. Rubbish, I said. Were I to have my collar felt, I'd come first in the 'Silly Bugger of the Week' competition and my little book would be a sell-out. I'd do a year in the slammer – where I'd meet up with all my old friends from the Drugs Squad – and she'd be set up for life. This prospect did little to relieve her anxiety. She's a brave, loyal little girl.

❊   ❊   ❊

My man at Scotland Yard rings to say that a copy of my book is being read at Police Headquarters.

'Hooray,' I said, 'by Sir Robert?'

'Of *course* not,' he said contemptuously. 'Good heavens, Sir Robert's got better things to do than read your book.'

I doubt that, as it happens, but I let it pass.

'Who by then?'

'I don't know. The department that looks into these things, I suppose.'

I take it that there's an Eng. Lit. Squad up at the Yard and that even now one of their best men is writing the close textual criticism that I had hoped for from the Literary Editor of *The Sunday Mirror*.

'In so far as I have carried out a thorough and painstaking perusal of *Both the Ladies and the Gentlemen* by Charles Donaldson, I am now in a position to offer the following across-the-board conclusions in summation. Donaldson, who infers himself to be a middle-aged Caucasian male of some educational and cultural background, avails himself – not altogether successfully in the final analysis – of what is known (cf. Clive James, *The Metropolitan Critic*, Faber and Faber) as a mixed style. While some elements in the community might find it lightly amusing, others will respond to it hopefully more facetiously. Notwithstanding that some of the escapades to which Donaldson gets up with the youths and lasses he frequents are superficially entertaining, the characterisation and narrative techniques are thin and amateur. On top of which Donaldson negates his credibility as a responsible person by promulgating a series of half-baked, woolly-minded and totally unsubstantiated innuendoes

16

against his duly elected betters and – to be deplored still more – against such of our colleagues as have had the misfortune to be arrested in the course of their duty. Happily, we've had these hearsay generalisations all too often before and all but a few dissentients are growing a little tired of it. Finally I would make the following point in conclusion:

a. The literals are a disgrace to the publisher.

2. The book is of negligible interest and can safely be ignored by the authorities.

Signed: Leslie Member, Sgt, Eng. Lit. Squad.'

❋ ❋ ❋

While Mike Franklin M.A. has in no way modified his gloomy views about my book's prospects in the market place, he's certainly giving it a go as far as the press is concerned. Today I was interviewed by Tom Davies of *The Sunday Telegraph*. I didn't much take to him, and vice versa too if I'm not mistaken. He was quite without the class of the Literary Editor of *The Sunday Mirror*, being a crude caricature, I thought, of one of those gritty provincial reporters to be seen from time to time in television plays. He had a face like a fox, an abrasive manner and he seemed to have arrived on a bicycle. All in all he'd have been happier, I felt, following up fatuous consumer gripes or nosing round N.W.3., checking that each street had its statutory number of wife-bashers. He looked me up and down abrasively, as though I was wearing poncey boots and a velvet jacket (which, as it happens, I was), and said that in his opinion my book was pure fantasy, a pack of untruths from cover to cover. Well I never. What on earth, I asked, had led him to this bizarre conclusion? He had been tipped off, he said, by the information that whores put their money into Building Societies.

'Everyone knows,' he said, with the undeceived air of a man who has exposed this, that and the other piffling malpractice for the Sunday prints, 'that they keep it under the bed.'

My friend One-Eyed Charlie has just been commissioned by the Cambridge University Press to up-date Flaubert's *Dictionary of Received Ideas* and it occurred to me now that all I had to do to give him a flying start on this project was to keep Davies talking while I took notes of what he said. First I'd tap his knee, as it were, with a couple of Flaubert's own, just to make sure his reflexes were in good working order.

'ARCHIMEDES,' I said.

'Eureka! Give me a fulcrum and I will lift the world!'

Not bad, not bad at all.

'NEGROES.'

'It's always such a surprise to hear them speaking French!'

Excellent! But now for some new ones; if, that is, there can be such a thing as a new received idea. This would be the real test.

'GENIUS, Men of,' I said, and I held my breath.

'Men of genius belong to the whole world.'

'NATURE, Human.'

'You can't legislate against human nature.'

Tremendous! At this rate One-Eyed Charlie would be able to deliver his first draft by April Fool's Day, if not sooner. It was up to me now to keep the ball in court: a heavy responsibility and for a moment I nearly faltered.

'Ph.D.'

'The root of all evil.'

'Do what?'

'The root of all evil.'

'No, no. *Pee Aitch Dee.*'

'Oh. For a man with a Ph.D., Steiner, you can be pretty stupid!'

'Terrific! JOURNALISTS.'

'The public have a right to know the truth.'

'Ha! Ha! LIFE, Real.'

'You can't top real life!'

'MUSIC.'

'Some things cry out to be set to music.'

'How true, how true. FOOTBALL.'

'Reflects the unrest beneath the surface of society.'

18

'Delightful! DORS, Diana.'

'Real name Doreen Clunt!'

'MILLIGAN, Spike.'

'A goon!'

'SELLERS, Peter.'

'A goon!'

'SECOMBE, Harry.'

'A goon!'

'CHARLES, Prince.'

'The fourth goon!'

I'd had enough. Davies, I realised, could have kept this up all day, but I was exhausted. Fortunately, he seemed to decide at this point that it was now his turn to serve, as it were, and he asked me challengingly what had motivated me [*sic*] to write my book. I had been driven forward, I said, by a desire to set the record straight. To date, all the literature on the subject had sentimentalised – glamorised, some would say – whores and their connections. This was to be deplored. Presented all too often as having hearts of gold and as purveyors of hill-billy philosophy, tarts, in my experience, were in reality no better than journalists, politicians, policemen, advertising agents or merchant bankers, and frequently worse. Not only were they in the habit of selling themselves to the highest bidder, it was often their custom to go to bed with total strangers.

Shortly after this, Davies excused himself abrasively, attached his bicycle clips to the bottom of his trousers and went about his investigative business.

❋ ❋ ❋

Franklin tells me that Davies didn't like me, didn't like my book (which he still holds to be a pack of untruths from start to finish) and has no intention of writing about it or me in *The Sunday Telegraph*.

'Kindly behave yourself during today's interview,' said Franklin. 'It's with Sally Brompton of *The Daily Mail*.'

I said I'd mind my p's and q's, and this wasn't difficult

because Miss Brompton turned out to be a very pleasant lady indeed. She did look at me a trifle warily, but I don't think this was so much from a fear that I might suddenly leap at her or nick her tape-recorder as from an impression she appeared to have been given that I was some sort of practical joker. The conversation went very nicely, or so it seemed to me, and I'm confident that tomorrow's *Daily Mail* will tell its readers that ponces are just like you or me but more so.

❊ ❊ ❊

No it won't. Franklin reports that Miss Brompton's copy was rejected by a scandalised Features Editor who maintained that there were only two possibilities: either I was a prankster – in which case anything *The Daily Mail* published might constitute a libel – or I was indeed a criminal – in which case, by writing about me, they might seem to be condoning my activities. On the whole, said Franklin, they tended to the view that I was a prankster, it being beyond the comprehension of *The Daily Mail* that a genuine defaulter would blow the whistle on himself.

The absolute refusal of the popular press to expose me fearlessly is fast becoming an intolerable burden and my silly boast to Franklin about all the bad publicity that would attend my book's release is beginning to sound like a tinny peep from an extremely cheap trumpet. Indeed, were it not for the constant support of my friend and literary agent, Ken the Australian Horse Player, I would have fallen by now into a black depression. Having sportingly agreed to sell my film rights to Peckinpah, he has now become closely involved in my latest scheme to arsehole *The News of the World*. This centres round the discovery of a fake Emma Jane, who, at the right moment, will present herself in *The News of the World's* offices, ready and eager to make a full confession. The real Emma Jane thinks this is a highly dangerous move, but I'm blessed if I can see the risk. Even if *The News of the World* discovers that their Emma Jane's a ringer, they can hardly publicise their own gaffe. ('The shocking truth! Vice Girl is really a secretary from Pinner!') Anyway, I'm informed by One-Eyed Charlie that ninety per cent of what appears in *The News of the World* is pure fantasy, no more, no less. Frankly I find this hard to believe, but One-Eyed Charlie – a known troublemaker – insists that one of their crusading reporters stands up at an editorial conference and says: 'Look here everyone, I've discovered a Customs and Excise officer's wife in New Malden who holds black magic supper-dances, involving nudity and unnecessary violence, on alternate Fridays. What's your reaction?'

'Very good indeed,' is the editorial verdict. 'That's worth five hundred pounds to the good lady if she'll make a suitably cringing confession.'

The reporter then trots off to New Malden and hunts down a Customs and Excise officer's wife who happens to want a new three-piece for her lounge-diner.

'Good afternoon, madam,' he says, 'I'm from *The News of the World*.'

'I can see that,' she says.

'Thank you. I'd like to talk to you about the black magic supper-dances you hold on alternate Fridays.'

'But I don't.'

'Two hundred and fifty pounds says you do.'

'Ooooh, thank you very much,' says the Customs and Excise Officer's wife, and the reporter cops the other two hundred and fifty.

The real Emma Jane is still unconvinced. 'What about the police?' she says.

'What about them?'

'What if they arrest you for living off the artistic earnings of the wrong Emma Jane?'

'Would you rather they arrested me for living off the artistic earnings of the right Emma Jane?'

That shuts her up for a while. Meanwhile Ken the Australian Horse Player has appointed himself casting director to the venture. I have explained our requirements most precisely – a nicely-spoken girl of twenty-three, white,

English, wholesome, of impeccable pedigree and with an 'O' level in geography to give her an unfair advantage over anyone on *The News of the World* – and so far he's brought round for serious consideration three members of an all-girl steel band from Jamaica, a bombed Swede with no English, a German auntie who could have been *my* age, poor soul, and someone who had the misfortune to look like Nicholas Parsons. Having sat these confused tourists down in the living-room of our far from impressive little flat, he informs them that this is their lucky day and that thanks to him and his pal Will they are about to be launched as international super-stars.

'Very few people,' he says, '*very few people indeed*, know that my pal Will here, *my pal Will*, is the king! Who do you suppose discovered Faye Dunaway? And Steve McQueen? To say nothing of Dudley fucking Moon?'

The mesmerised tourist on the Habitat has no answer to this.

'My pal Will, that's who! Yes sir, he's the king! And *you* could be the one to put him back on top!'

Happily, this apparently damaging non-sequitur is lost on the bewildered tourist. Then he turns to me.

'Isn't she a darling? Isn't she a perfect fucking darling? And *talented*! What do you suppose she was doing before she came to London? Knocking them dead in Paris, that's what she was doing. This girl can do the lot. She's fucking mustard, this girl! You name it, she can do it. She can act, sing, dance, suck cocks. Peter fucking *Brooks* wants to meet this kid! Now, be honest, Will. Who does she remind you of? Look at those eyes!'

'Maria Schneider?'

'Right! Maria fucking Schneider!'

Suddenly fearful, it seems, that the flat may be being bugged by a rival entrepreneur with international connections, he squeezes his eyes menacingly and drops into his out-of-the-side-of-the-mouth, comic in a spy sketch voice.

'I was on the phone to Peckinpah this morning and what do you suppose? He'd just been reading – no, wait for it –

22

*he'd just been reading* the ladies and the gentlemen! The ladies and the fucking gentlemen! And he loved it! Yes sir, he loved it! And he wants us – he wants *us*, mind – to discover a girl to play Emily fucking Jane!'

Three minutes later the amazed tourist is on her back with her legs in the air, grunting horribly in Dutch, German or Swedish as the case may be, and half an hour after that she's been emptied into the streets, never to be seen again. 'Mad molls,' says Ken dismissively, having shown her to the door, 'they're all the same.'

In the course of these casting sessions, it's occurred to me more than once that notable fantasists like Ken are better off than the rest of us. When playing a role, his eyes bulge with madness like an army chaplain's, leaving no doubt that he believes absolutely in the truth of what he's saying. The rest of us are saddled with our own sad biographies, but in the course of a single day Ken can be twenty different people. To his way of thinking, the only point of being a successful person with a potent name – Peckinpah himself, say – would be the ease with which it enabled one to take down a lady tourist's trousers. Since few lady tourists would know the real Peckinpah from a fake, Ken's as well off in this respect as Peckinpah himself. And, unlike Peckinpah, he, Ken, doesn't have the taxing business of getting up early in the morning and making violent films. He has all the advantages and none of the tedium. It makes a lot of sense.

❊ ❊ ❊

But that was yesterday. This evening I took drinks with Kenneth Tynan and as a consequence such blatant PR strategems now seem frightfully crude. Since it is not to be conceived that Tynan would care to be associated with a person written about in *The News of the World*, I am now compelled to change my tactics. Dignity and discretion shall hence forth be my guides. Step out with the quality, that's been my principle in life and it's done me proud to date.

The front door of Tynan's desirable town house in South

Kensington was opened by a lady of such extraordinary beauty – Mrs Tynan, I presumed – that I may have let myself down a bit by saying 'Oh dear', taking a smart pace back and tumbling myself into the street, splattering with mud the smart grey suit I'd borrowed for the occasion from my friend Scott. To recover a degree of urbanity, I quickly congratulated her on her recently published first novel. She thanked me politely – in Spanish, which struck me as slightly affected, I must admit – but she looked puzzled: a circumstance explained seconds later by the appearance of a lady of still more extraordinary beauty, who I recognised at once to be the real Mrs Tynan. The other had been the au pair. The real Mrs Tynan showed me into the drawing-room, where Tynan was gliding around in silk pyjamas to the accompaniment of Vivaldi or somesuch. I wouldn't have been surprised to discover that Tynan now wears silk pyjamas all day long, but he explained that he'd been a trifle under the weather recently and that his doctors had ordered him to take it easy.

My rare meetings with Tynan are marred, from my point of view, by the fact that he scares me stiff. I bump into the furniture, sit on the cat, spill my drink over no doubt priceless carpets and lose the use of my tongue. I can't get over the fact that when I was an impressionable student back in the serious fifties, Tynan was an arbiter of taste, if not *the* arbiter. One is never at one's most deft with early heroes, and in his company now I clutch my knees in alarm and wait for him to confuse me with stylish constructions and cultural allusions that I'll barely recognise as such.

He said he thought my book was rather well written (there was one for One-Eyed Charlie – WELL WRITTEN: said in a tone of slight surprise about books by vets, chamber maids, ponces and prima ballerinas), and I stared back at him like a dead haddock. Then he asked me whether I had thought of it as source material for an evening in the live theatre. I took a deep breath, got a grip on myself and said:

'No.'

Well, said Tynan, he had. In fact he'd given a copy to his

partner, the distinguished stage director Clifford Williams, with whom he happened to have a production company. If Williams shared his favourable opinion, they would like to have it adapted for the theatre. Tynan would convey William's opinion to me just as soon as he received it himself. I stared back at him silently for a while and then said something so foolish that I have been able to wipe all trace of it from my mind. Judging it to be time to leave, I walked into the broom cupboard, put my foot through a Degas, collided with the real Mrs Tynan, knocked over an ash-tray, scattered the cats and let myself out.

How nice it would be, though, if Clifford Williams were enthusiastic too. To slide back into the live theatre through the artiste's entrance, as it were, would be hilarious. And what distress it would cause those douche-bags up at Equity! Better days ahead.

❄ ❄ ❄

Tea and scones in the King's Road with a gent I took to be a Durex salesman. He had little boot-button eyes and his head came to a point like a rat's. I told him my story and, to my surprise, he took it all down in a notebook. That seemed a trifle strange, so I asked him what his interest in the matter might be.

'I work for *The News of the World*,' he said, 'and I'm particularly interested in your connection with Sir Robert Mark's daughter, Christina.'

Odds fish! I'd walked right into it. I made an excuse and left, but the damage had been done. I ran home and got on the phone to Mike Franklin M.A.

'I've just made a complete confession to *The News of the World*,' I said. 'They very much liked the incident of Sir Robert Mark's daughter dining in a brothel and of my holing up at her house when on the run from the police.'

'Good,' said Franklin.

'Good? It's terrible.'

'I thought you wanted publicity?'

25

'Not that sort of publicity. Not now that Tynan's shown an interest. He won't want to treat with a person written about in *The News of the World*. Good heavens.'

We had a quick conference with our PR man, which isn't something one would normally do, of course, but this was in the nature of an emergency. He's immensely cheerful (which more than makes up for the fact that he couldn't get a plug for a bath) and he advised us that our only chance of nobbling *The News of the World* was to get the story into another paper first. For reasons I didn't clearly understand, *The Evening News* was singled out for this honour and in no time at all I found myself talking to a very pleasant fellow called Mike Perry, who claimed to work on that paper's gossip column.

'What's all this about Sir Robert Mark's daughter?' he said. 'Is she a friend of yours?'

I confirmed that she was and added my usual little joke to the effect that I saw nothing to be ashamed of in that, and Mr Perry said that this was fair enough and precisely what he'd tell *The Evening News*'s readers the following day. We shall see.

❋ ❋ ❋

Alas, my quote about Sir Robert Mark's daughter was too good for *The Evening News*. Perry phoned Franklin to say that the paper's lawyers had advised against printing it. The whole squalid thing must be a set-up, they'd said, since it was not possible that a Police Commissioner's daughter would dine in a brothel.

I reported this sad news to One-Eyed Charlie, who happened to be in our flat at the time, laying some new lino in the kitchen under the stern supervision of Emma Jane.

'Good,' said Emma Jane. 'As you know, I don't like trouble in any shape or form.'

'Good?' said One-Eyed Charlie, putting down his hammer, '*Good?* It's a fucking outrage.'

26

'Language, Charlie!' said Emma Jane sharply.

'Sorry, but it's the worst example of the un-American fallacy I've heard in years.'

'Is it really? That's very nice, I'm sure. Now, will you kindly get on with the work I'm paying you to do?'

'Don't you want to know what the un-American fallacy is?'

'No.'

'It was called that during the McCarthy era to describe arg...'

'I said *no*, Charlie.'

'Oh.'

One-Eyed Charlie looked most crest-fallen and since he's been so decent about the contributions to his Dictionary of Received Ideas which I'd offered him after my meeting with Tom Davies of *The Sunday Telegraph*, I decided to give him some more now.

BEAVERBROOK, Lord: 'Ah yes, but what a character! And as for his much maligned son Max, I'd like to remind you that he was flying Spitfires before some of today's so-called Fleet Street whizz-kids were even born.'

BEHAVIOURISTS: Are thought to behave discreditably towards rats. Mention Skinner, but don't get too involved.

BEST, George: He wasn't crushed by the media, but by the intolerable demands of his own talent.

BREEDING: Non-white couple producing offspring.

FAMILY, Raising a: White couple bringing up children.

One-Eyed Charlie was perfectly civil about these and then had the neck to give me some of his own. As it happens, they didn't strike me as any better than mine.

BESIDES: 'Besides! I'm a working girl! Remember!'

COTTAGE, The: 'Listen carefully, Susan, this is important, so don't argue. Pack a bag, take my car and drive straight to the cottage. Wait for me there.'

PROFESSOR: 'He's not just any two-bit Professor, you know. He's Mandel! The top man in his field!'

SCIENTIST: 'Look, Superintendent, I'm a *scientist*. I deal in *facts*.'

27

SEMANTICS: 'A man's been killed, Major! This is no time for semantics!'

'They're bloody silly,' I said, ' and it's quite obvious that you've been watching too much television.'

'Look here,' said One-Eyed Charlie crossly, 'who's been commissioned to do this dictionary, you or me?'

He has, I suppose, but if I include all his entries here, it'll be SPLUUUUGH to the Cambridge Univeristy Press, as I see it.

DOLPHINS: What a shame they can't talk! They're so much more intelligent than humans!

DOPE: 'Dope? I've tried it, of course, but it did absolutely nothing for me. I don't need it, thank God!'

DRINK: 'My word! This calls for a drink!'

INTERESTING: 'This is all very interesting, Inspector, but I fail to see what it's got to do with me.'

LOVE: Being in love needs practice like everything else.

MARRIAGE: In a broken marriage there are no winners.

PORNOGRAPHY: 'Look, I saw *Deep Throat* over at Roger and Kathy's and that Linda Lovelock woman did absolutely *nothing* for me. Quite honestly, I fell asleep!'

PRO, A real: Turns up sober and doesn't bump into the other mimes.

REALITY: Greatly superior to ideas. 'Like all parlour pinks, he's in love with the idea, not the reality.'

RESPECT: To respect others you must first respect yourself.

STANDARD, The Evening: Makes a vital contribution to the artistic life of London.

THINKING: 'No, you go on ahead. I've got some thinking to do.'

❊　❊　❊

For some days now, Dawn Upstairs has been saying to anyone who'll listen 'I'm going to the opening of Willie's book, me,' and last night was the occasion to which she's been referring. Cheek by jowl with media cads and scoundrels (gossips, lady features editors, paperback publishers, PR people and what have you), my team – Mitzi the Japanese Masseuse, Lord and Lady Dynevor, One-Eyed Charlie, 'arding and the Equally Lovely Sarah, Stella Who Stutters, Ken the Australian Horse Player, Pretty Marie and Dawn Upstairs herself accompanied by her backing group – evinced a massive moral authority which made them stand out as a class above the rest. I've seldom been so proud of them.

Missing, to my great regret, was Emma Jane, whom I had forbidden to attend on the grounds that she'd be truffled out by the fake Durex salesman from *The News of the World* and fearlessly exposed. Standing in for her was a phoney Emma Jane, supplied at the last minute by someone at Franklin's office. She was lovely, and Alan Brien, with the authority of someone known to have met the real Emma Jane, introduced her to the gossip columnists and vouched for her credentials. What a good sport he is. I had supposed that there might be some code under whose rules one journalist wouldn't lead another up the garden path, but if there is, Alan ignored it. Oddly enough, the only journalist not to show the slightest interest in our fake Emma Jane was the Durex salesman. I put this down to the fact that he was as drunk as a skunk and wouldn't have noticed a scoop if he'd fallen underneath one. He was eventually discovered cross-eyed under the cold cuts, so all may yet be well.

It wasn't the kind of function I'd normally attend, but since Mike Franklin M.A. had been decent enough to invite me, I decided to give it a go at the last minute. Once there, I was pleasantly surprised. I hadn't attended a party since the coming-out dance given by the Duchess of Argyll in 1955 for her daughter Frances Sweeney (later, and to this day, for all I know, the Duchess of Rutland) and on that occasion no one spoke to me and I was compelled to walk around with two glasses of champagne, thus giving the impression, I hoped, that I was on my way to meet some titled lady on the terrace. Now I discovered what it's like to be a pretty girl – or a pretty man, for that matter – at a party. No wonder such fortunate people are happy to attend the beastly things. Everyone wanted to talk to me, so all I had to do was prop myself up against a wall and carry out my policy of demurring grace-fully, irrespective of what was being said to me. Due to all the party rhubarb, I couldn't actually hear what was being said, so I demurred anyway on the assumption that people were being cordial about my work. If they were seeking directions to the powder room or asking me to shift over a a bit because I was standing on their foot, all my demurring must have seemed a trifle odd.

Either way, the whole thing became tiring after a while and I decided to go home to Emma Jane, the pussy cats and *The Streets of San Francisco*. Since people were still arriving, I walked out backwards, hoping thus to give the impression that I was coming in. (For reasons that I've never clearly understood, people at parties seem to feel unduly threatened by anyone who manages to extricate himself before they do, and they react angrily, like prisoners watching a gaol-break from which they've been excluded.) On the way to the door I overheard snatches from two conversations which struck me as rather strange. Kenneth Jupp the talented playwright was giving a crash-course in how to seduce ladies to an excep-tionally good-looking young man who certainly didn't look as though he needed any instruction in this important area.

'Never fails, my dear boy,' Jupp was saying, 'never fails. The moment they arrive at my flat I take my clothes off. That makes them look silly.'

Ken's delightful, but that's too subtle for me.

Nearer the door, Dawn Upstairs was marking the card of Phillip Hodson, the urbane Editor of *Forum*, who seemed to be taking an editorial and no doubt responsibly societal inter-est in Mitzi the Japanese Masseuse. Dawn Upstairs was explaining, in her original way, that appearances can be de-ceptive.

'I know she's wearing a long dress and that,' she was saying, 'but she doesn't *do* it, you know, she doesn't do it at all. She never has.'

BOOK, Writing a: We all have one inside us, the problem is finding the time to write it. If you are a comedian or a celebrated high hurdler you will be asked by journalists (see

JOURNALISTS) why you wrote it. Say: 'Well, all my friends urged me to tell my story, but I kept putting it off. Then my *marvellously* kind and *endlessly* patient publisher gave me such a *huge* advance that I absolutely had to do something! Once I got started, I enjoyed the actual writing enormously! I wrote it all myself in long-hand and now I'm going to write another!' (See WELL WRITTEN and FONTEYN, Dame Margot.)

Franklin, who has at last grasped the significance of Tynan's interest in my book, is now as worried as I am about some vulgar intervention from *The News of the World*. Indeed, he spent much of today trying to persuade someone on its editorial staff that every word I'd said to the Durex salesman had been the exhaust of a deluded mind. The fellow on the editorial staff was unimpressed and confirmed that the Durex salesman's article had been much to everyone's liking. Now I'm distraught, since it seems certain that (a) Tynan will now lose interest and (b) I will be arrested. Since in these matters the police prefer *The News of the World*'s advice to that of supposedly more official functionaries such as the Director of Public Prosecutions, the latter consequence now seems inevitable.

In an otherwise tasteful and perceptive article in today's *Guardian*, Stanley Reynolds says that I'm a 'serious man caught up in a ridiculous situation'. What does he mean? I'm a serious man certainly, but I fail to see what's ridiculous about my situation. Still, it's a sympathetic piece and will do something, I think, to take the curse off tomorrow's lewd effluence in *The News of the World*.

31

Nothing in *The News of the World*! The moral lapses of every unfortunate misfit are laid out for our titillation, but sod all about me! I don't know whether to be relieved or offended. What exactly are the rules? 'All human life is here', but not, it seems, if it involves the Police Commissioner's daughter. That's my theory, and how outrageous! I don't want to blow my bags, but if I'm not precisely the kind of corrupting wood-weevil that *The News of the World* should be ruthlessly flushing out of the fixtures and fittings of society, I don't know who is.

※　※　※

Good news! Tynan's agent, Patricia MacNaughton, rang this morning to say that he and Clifford Williams would definitely like to buy my book for the stage. Would I care, she said, to visit her in her office the next day to discuss the arrangements? Certainly I would. Did I have an agent, she then asked, and if so would I like to bring him with me? I thought quickly. Yes, I said (not wishing to seem deprived in this respect) I did, and I would. Excellent, said Miss MacNaughton, who was he? Toby Danvers, I said. Toby *Danvers*! said Miss MacNaughton, and then she said something about her sainted aunt and where on earth was *he* these days? On the Greenwich telephone exchange, I said, but I was certain he'd take time off for something as important as this. Miss MacNaughton seemed quite surprised, but we have made a date for three o'clock tomorrow.

I then rang Danvers at the Greenwich telephone exchange to give him the good news.

'This is your lucky day,' I said, 'you're now my accredited representative. We have a date with Miss MacNaughton at three o'clock tomorrow.'

'Who the hell's Miss MacNaughton?'

'Tynan's agent. He's bought my book for the theatre. You've heard of him, I suppose.'

'Of course. Nice fellow with a red face. Used to be your accountant, I believe. Glad to see he's branching out.'

'That was *Twyman*, you fool. I said Tynan. Kenneth Tynan. Used to be a drama critic and then went to the National Theatre.'

'Of course. Where's the meeting then?'

'At Miss MacNaughton's office.'

'Can't she come here?'

'No, of course she can't go there! Pull yourself together, you silly old fool.'

'Hm. This is a bit inconvenient, you know.'

Inconvenient! I was offering him a passport back into the laughter and heartbreak of the live theatre, and it was a bit inconvenient! It crossed my mind, I must admit, that I might have appointed him as my agent rather too hastily. No, perish the thought. I'd never met Miss MacNaughton, but nothing in her manner on the phone had led me to suppose that she'd just fallen off a turnip truck. While I'd always been pretty good at this sort of thing myself, it would be an undeniable advantage to have someone of Danvers's considerable experience at my side.

'Oh well, never mind,' continued Danvers, 'I'll probably be able to persuade old Commander Hubble to swop his shift with mine. Do you recall him? Naval man yourself, I believe. He got thrown out after some incident involving the Royal Yacht. Out in Gib. I fancy he sank it. Been a bit funny in the head ever since. Gets the devil of a lot of wrong numbers, but he's a nice old sod and most obliging about this sort of thing. I'm sure he'll help out.'

We got the matter settled eventually and I'm confident that Danvers won't let me down tomorrow.

❊ ❊ ❊

The meeting with Miss MacNaughton went very smoothly and Toby Danvers, apart from falling asleep at a crucial moment in the negotiations, was a tower of strength. I tremble to think what an idiot Miss MacNaughton might have taken me to be had I gone without him. Once we were seated comfortably in her smart little office, she came briskly to the point.

'My clients are extremely excited about this project,' she said, 'and they're keen to close the deal as quickly as possible. But you must understand that they're creative people, not wealthy business men.'

'Of course not.'

'And times are very hard.'

'What! You don't have to tell me. Inflation, you know.'

'Precisely. My clients have no money at all. It's all tied up in capital.'

'What a confounded nuisance!'

'Yes. So the advance will have to be very modest.'

'Naturally.'

'At the moment my clients are drawing royalties from a mere eleven shows.'

'Tch tch.'

'So they've *nothing* to lash out on this sort of thing. Or very little.'

'Of course. Money doesn't grow on trees!'

'Nor it does.'

Until this moment, I'd been battling away on my own behalf, but Miss MacNaughton now turned to Danvers with an encouraging smile.

'I was wondering, Mr Danvers,' she said, 'whether you'd like to start the ball rolling, as it were, by naming a figure acceptable to your client?'

'Zzzzzzzzz.'

'Mr Danvers?'

'Zzzzzzzzzz'

'Oh dear. Mr Danvers?'

'Zzzzzzzzzz.'

I became a trifle embarrassed at this point, and fearing that Miss MacNaughton might think we were not serious people, I decided to give her a hand.

'Toby you daft cunt!' I roared. 'Wake up!'

That did the trick.

'Help!' cried Danvers, coming awake with a jerk that

nearly had him off his chair, 'where the hell am I?' He stared round the little office in terror and astonishment, then managed to focus on the kindly face of Miss MacNaughton. 'Oh thank you, Miss,' he said with evident relief, 'a cheese roll and two white coffees, please. And bring the bill at the same time.'

My God, where did he think he was?

'He works the night shift,' I explained, 'and the loss of sleep causes him to hallucinate. In GPO circles they consider it to be the equivalent of jet-lag. He should be all right in a moment.'

'Of course,' said Miss MacNaughton, 'think nothing of it.' How lucky we were to be dealing with such a sympathetic woman.

'Toby dear,' I said, 'Miss MacNaughton here would like you to name a figure acceptable to us.'

'What the hell for?'

'What *for*? Really! My *book*, of course.'

'What book?'

'Christ! The ladies and the fucking gentlemen!' This was terrible. Any minute now Miss MacNaughton would be taking us for a couple of fools.

'Oh, *that* one.'

'*Yes*. Tynan wants to buy the stage rights. I *told* you.'

'He does? Good heavens. Why?'

'Never mind why. Name a figure, for goodness sake.'

I am now accustomed to Toby Danvers's abrupt changes of mood, but I fancy that Miss MacNaughton, experienced agent though she is, was quite surprised by what he did next. Cracking his fist down on her desk so hard that all the scripts, pens, paper-clips, contracts, plane tickets and photographs of Jean Marsh thereon jumped a few inches into the air before settling down again in a slightly altered formation, he bellowed:

'Two hundred pounds, my good woman, and not a penny more! It's an important work.'

'Oh,' said Miss MacNaughton, 'I must admit I was thinking in terms of seven hundred and fifty pounds at least.'

'What!' Danvers leaned across the desk and squinted cunningly into her face. 'Five hundred pounds,' he said, 'and you've got yourself a deal.'

'Four hundred,' said Miss MacNaughton.

'Three hundred!'

'Two hundred and fifty,' said Miss MacNaughton.

'Done!' cried Danvers triumphantly, 'and, if I may say so, madam, it's been a rare pleasure to do business with you. Now I really must be going. I have urgent matters to attend to in the West End.'

'I'll prepare a letter of agreement immediately,' said Miss MacNaughton. 'Where would you like me to send it?'

'The Greenwich telephone exchange, if you'd be so kind. And pray instruct your clerical staff to make the gooses out to me. On no account should it be made payable to the Postmaster General.'

It had been such a satisfactory afternoon's work that when we got outside I was delighted to fall in with Danvers's suggestion that I should accompany him to the West End to celebrate.

'It has invariably been my experience,' he said, 'that after a session of really hard bargaining, a leisurely stroll round Greek Street and Frith Street's better bookshops is exactly what the doctor ordered. Have you visited them recently?'

'Not for a while, no. I gather that The Old Grey Fox has cleaned them up somewhat.'

'On the contrary. They now show blue films at 10p a time.'

'10p a time? That sounds very reasonable.'

'And a trifle misleading too, I must admit. In fact you can't see the *whole* film for 10p. Each film is divided into tastefully edited episodes, and each *episode* costs 10p.'

'I see. I thought there'd be a snag.'

'But that's where you're wrong, my dear fellow. The system works to the punter's advantage, since he can cut out after only one episode if he finds he's made a faulty choice. Imagine the saving if one had been able to get one's money back after only a few minutes of *Star Wars*. Not that mistakes of that sort should occur. The artistic thrust of each film is clearly advertised on the door of the cubicle in which the particular film is being shown, and it's not uncommon for the front of house display, as it were, to contain a still from the attraction within.'

'There's privacy then?'

'Of course. That's the joy of it. Each man has his own little kiosk or booth, as in a public convenience. You can bolt yourself in and, once safely inside, you can remain undisturbed for the rest of the day. It is not unusual for Commander Hubble on his day off to go along with a packed lunch and a Thermos of coffee prepared by his wife. She imagines he's spending the day at the British Museum putting the finishing touches to a book on the Battle of Jutland. On one occasion, the proprietor shut up shop while the Commander was still inside one of the cubicles. The old fool had to spend the night there, which wasn't as jolly as it sounds because he'd run out of 10p pieces and the proprietor had been sensible enough to take the day's takings home with him.'

Blue movies aren't particularly my buzz, as it happens, but a man whose natural instincts are as sternly corsetted as mine needs to unbutton himself from time to time. I was therefore happy to accompany him to an establishment in Greek Street, whose managing director – an elderly ferret with a watery left eye – evidently knew him well.

'Afternoon Mr Albery,' said the ferret. 'How's the new musical coming along? In rehearsal yet, are we?'

'Not yet, but the casting's going most satisfactorily. I have secured the services of Miss Jane Asher for the part of Christine Keeler and Sir John Gielgud has agreed to play Profumo.'

'Two of our finest artistes,' said the ferret approvingly.

'Indeed. I have also engaged Kirby's Flying Ballet and André Previn is to be musical director. Perhaps you'd care to make a modest investment? It's the customary 80/10 split as between management and backers, so a unit of £250 towards an initial capital of £50,000 carries 5% of the profits. What do you say? Delfont's in.'

'Not today Mr Albery, if you don't mind, but thank you very much for the offer. What would we like now then? The usual?'

'If you'd be so kind, my good man.'

The ferret took a large pile of 10p pieces from a drawer and placed them on the counter. Danvers, as I should have foreseen, then went through the time-honoured pantomime of tapping himself about the upper trunk.

'What a confounded nuisance!' he said. 'I appear to have left myself a little short. Could you oblige on this occasion, do you think, old chap?'

As luck would have it, Emma Jane had given me the day's housekeeping allowance before I'd set off to see Miss Mac-Naughton, so I was able to give the ferret a fiver in exchange for the silver. I'd be on defaulters' parade as soon as I got home and the misappropriation of the dinner money would entail forty-eight hours jankers, but there'd be plenty of time to worry about that after the blue movies.

It was with some excitement, I must admit, that I followed Danvers into the back quarters of the shop and down a dark passage, lined on either side with little viewing booths. On the door of each cubicle was pinned, just as Danvers had described, a brief, though no doubt adequate synopsis of the attraction on show within – 'Duo', 'Trio', 'Lesbos', 'Bondage' etc – together with a still from the relevant film. Danvers, whose tastes in this area I have always found depressingly orthodox, dived like a rat up a drain-pipe into a booth showing, if the still outside was to be believed, the Aldershot Amateur Motor Cyclists' Association having their pleasure of the local trull, but I thought that *Lesamour*, on release in the next-door cubicle held out greater promise.

Once inside, I sat myself down on the little bench facing the door. Fixed to the door was a small screen on which disgruntled punters had scrawled – rather discouragingly – graffiti of an uncomplimentary nature. (Among the unimaginative, though no doubt heartfelt, editorial comments, there was one excellent effort, however, which I don't remember having seen before. Next to 'Bollocks!' and 'You should try our Nell – 437 4017' etc, someone had written: 'Rearrange the following words into a well-known phrase or saying – POPE THE FUCK.') To my left was a kind of slot machine, into which I was able, after a lot of fiddling and groping (for, with the door shut, it was as dark as death in here) to introduce my 10p. I was thinking: 'Lesamour! My hat, this will be a bit good,' when – Great Scott! what was this? – on to the screen flickered not the two delightful naughty girls as featured in the still outside, but a hairy Corsican road mender in purple jockey shorts. Lesamour my eye! The Corsican road mender went through various lewd evolutions of a simulated nature with a cross-looking lady of similarly foreign extraction, and then the film cut out. I was cursing the ferret and wondering under which section of the Trade Descriptions Act to drag the fellow through the courts, when it occurred to me that there might have been some mix-up with the reels and that the investment of a further 10p might yet produce *Lesamour*. I fed another 10p piece into the machine – ready to cry out in rage if the Corsican road mender made another unscheduled appearance – but this time nothing happened at all. My 10p piece was swallowed up, but no film, *Lesamour* or otherwise, appeared on the screen. This was really too much, and I strode angrily out of the booth to confront the ferret.

He was behind his desk, chatting to a portly old fruit in a bowler hat and Brigade tie.

'Ahem,' I said.

'Half a bottle of liquid paraffin instead of its drinking water,' the old fruit was saying. 'My word, I've never seen a parrot look so startled.'

'Ahem,' I said.

'Excuse me Major,' said the ferret, turning to me. 'Yes?'

'I have a small complaint,' I said. 'Two in fact.'

'Ho yes? And what might they be?'

'The film showing in the third cubicle on the left is not as advertised. And even if it were, one would be no better off, since the projector appears to be on the blink.'

'Which film was that then?'

39

I was reluctant to go into too much detail in front of the Major, so I rather mumbled my reply.

'Do what?' said the ferret. 'Speak up Squire, we're all friends in here.'

'*Lesamour*,' I said, somewhat more boldly than before.

'Oh, the les one, eh? That's very popular. Rather up your street isn't it Major?'

'It most certainly is,' said the Major enthusiastically. 'Must have seen it countless times. A hundred at least. Never palls.'

Since he was now part of the discussion, I turned round to have a closer look at him. He had marinated eye-balls, a complexion like a Victoria plum and something of the grand manner and impressive *embonpoint* of Toby Danvers. The Brigade tie suggested past exploits rather than present employment, however, since in bearing, voice and gestures he put one in mind of a cheesey old-time actor-manager – Donald Wolfit, say – rather than a serving officer.

'Well, with respect Major,' I said, 'you won't be seeing it today. Not unless our friend here repairs the apparatus.'

'Let's have a look then,' said the ferret.

He made off down the passage, with the Major padding after him, while I brought up the rear. I now noticed that, as is the case with Danvers, most of the Major's excess living seemed to have settled in the jowls and tummy. His extremities, in fact, were, like Danvers's, definitely dainty, and he walked quite trippingly, but with his body canted backwards to redress the huge weight of his stomach, which would otherwise have caused him to tip forward on his face.

'Been a funny sort of day,' he said. 'Neither one thing or the other.'

'Yes, hasn't it? Doesn't seem able to make up its mind.'

The ferret went into my cubicle, while the Major and I stayed outside. From Danvers's next-door booth there came no sound. The old fool had probably fallen asleep.

'Ur huh,' said the ferret, 'just as I thought. The fucking mechanism's jammed. Not to worry, this usually does the trick.'

So saying, he cocked one little leg high in the air and slightly to the rear, like a dog against the wheel of a car, then suddenly struck out backwards as though executing a karate move. The faulty slot machine was driven almost through the wall and – more dramatically – the door of Danvers's cubicle flew open like a starting stall. My God, my literary agent! The big girl's blouse was sat seated on the bench, eyes closed, a look of foolish rapture on his face, his jacket hanging on a hook as when visiting the jakes, his trousers round his ankles, having a J. Arthur.

'Good show,' said the Major. Then he had a closer look. 'My word,' he said, 'it's Tom Danvers's boy, Toby!'

'Good afternoon, Major,' said Danvers, not opening his eyes nor pausing in his rhythmic self-abuse.

''Pon my soul,' said the Major, 'what an agreeable surprise.'

'More for you than me,' said Danvers pleasantly. 'Unless, that is, you'd care to make a small investment in my new musical.'

'Sir Ralph Richardson and Helen Mirren,' said the ferret helpfully, 'and Kirby's performing seals.'

'That's very good of you,' said the Major, 'but I'm a little under capitalised at the moment. For my sins.'

'Delfont's in,' said the ferret.

'Another time perhaps,' said the Major.

'In that case,' said Danvers firmly, 'I'd be obliged if you could see your way to closing the door. This film has two more episodes to run.'

'Of course, my dear boy.' The Major closed the door and shook his head in wonderment. 'What an amazing thing, meeting Tom Danvers's boy like that. Glad to see he's doing well. He a friend of yours?'

'Indeed. He's my literary agent.'

'Good show,' said the Major, but the coincidence of meeting Tom Danvers's boy like this proved too much for him. He suddenly broke wind and pitched forward on his face.

'I say,' I said.

The ferret, who had gone back to fiddling with the faulty mechanism in my cubicle, paid no attention. So I said it again, with a greater degree of emphasis.

'I say,' I said.

'What's up?' asked the ferret, without turning round.

'I think the Major's bought it.'

'Passed out, has he?' said the ferret, still without turning round, and showing none of the concern for a customer that the situation seemed to warrant.

'Cold as mutton. One minute he was conversing quite normally and the next he broke wind and over he went. Rummest thing I've ever seen.'

'Often happens after lunch. Better have a look, I suppose, just to be on the safe side.' He came out of the cubicle, bent down over the Major, loosened his tie and then slapped him back and forth on either cheek. The Major gave a little shudder and opened one eye.

'Hell,' he said, 'I've let my country down.'

'No you haven't Major,' said the ferret soothingly, 'no you haven't.'

'But I *have*,' insisted the Major, 'and I let Niffy Ingrams carry the can. Niven must be told the truth.'

'Plenty of time for that, Major.'

'Got to report back to H.Q.'

'Of course you have.'

'Damn legs don't seem to be working. Passed out on parade.'

'It happens to the best, Major.'

'Never to me.'

'Up on your feet then Major. After a rest and a nice cup of tea we'll get you back to H.Q.'

'Mustn't be late for the debriefing session, do you see?'

'You won't be Major, I'll see to that.'

'I think I'll have an early night.'

'That's right, Major, you have an early night.'

He hauled the Major to his feet and managed to steer him back down the passage and through a door marked 'Private'. For one reason or another, I was no longer in the mood for

42

*Lesamour* or anything else, and I was quite relieved when Danvers emerged at last from his cubicle.

'Okay,' he said briskly, 'let's go.'

Outside the shop, I suddenly remembered that we hadn't mentioned Sam Peckinpah to Miss MacNaughton.

'Drat,' I said, 'we didn't tell Miss MacNaughton about Peckinpah.'

'What about him?'

'Ken the Australian Horse Player was good enough to sell him the film rights.'

'What film rights?'

'Christ! The film rights in my book.'

'Really? Perhaps we'd better check on that.'

'Check on it? What do you mean?'

'Just to be on the safe side. You know how Ken's inclined to exaggerate.'

Danvers is cautious to a fault, but I dare say that's really a virtue in an agent. I asked him to have a word with Ken, but he amazed me by refusing. He said he'd never trusted the fellow and that I could ring him myself! What's the point of having a literary agent who works on the telephone exchange if you have to do your own phoning? The absurdity of the situation made me so cross that I fired Danvers on the spot and resolved to appoint Ken the Australian Horse Player in his place. When I got home, I rang Miss MacNaughton to apprise her of the change. I could tell at once that she thought I'd done the sensible thing.

'I naturally didn't want to say anything at the time,' she said, 'since I didn't take it to be any of my business, but I do think you've made a wise decision. Mr Danvers in some ways didn't seem to be quite up to – er – up to – er . . . well anyway. Will you be appointing another agent? Someone more – er – qualified, perhaps?'

'Indeed I will. I've already done so, in fact. And I think you'll agree he's more qualified in every respect.'

'*Excellent!* I'm really delighted. May I ask who?'

'Ken the Australian Horse Player. He's shit hot, so you'd better watch out for yourself!'

43

'Ken the Australian Horse Player? I don't think I've seen his name in *Contacts*. Is he a member of the Agents' Association?'

'I'd have thought so, judging by his list of clients. He looks after Lew Hoad, Big Newk, Gary Player, Dennis Lilley and Thommo, Shirley Bassey, James Hunt, Clive James and a couple of useful young middle-weights. In fact I was very lucky he agreed to take me on. And there's one thing I forgot to mention. He's already sold the film rights to Peckinpah! How about that? I told you he was shit hot!'

'My goodness! Perhaps he could ring me and tell me precisely what's going on.'

'Ah well, that might not be so easy at the moment. He's temporarily off the phone due to some silly misunderstanding with the Post Office. Perhaps we could come up and see you?'

'Oh dear, do you think that will be necessary?'

What a delightful woman she is, so reluctant to put other people to inconvenience. I think I'll take Ken to see her, even though she obviously doesn't want us to go to all that bother. It does seem as if Danvers didn't make such a good impression after all, but I'm sure I can rely on Ken to repair the damage. I'm certain things will go better from now on.

❉ ❉ ❉

Twice a month, Emma Jane trots off to a hotel in South Kensington to visit a branch manager with Commercial Union; not, as might be supposed, to get the strength of the insurance companies round her, but to give the fellow a hiding. Today she returned from one of these outings looking so uncommonly pleased with herself that I couldn't help remarking on it.

'You look uncommonly pleased with yourself. Did you get paid twice?'

'No. In fact, I didn't get paid at all.'

'What!'

'But it was worth it, as I'm sure you'll be the first to agree.

You know the old fool's scene? I'm the Headmistress of some school and he's the assistant physics master or whatever. He's been up to immorality of some sort and I have to carpet him. That old stuff, right? I call him into my study and he pleads with me. "I'll take any punishment, madam," he says, "no matter how severe, but please don't fire me. Anything but that! I couldn't stand the disgrace!" So normally I draw myself up like Dame Ninette de Valois, tell him he should have considered the disgrace before pinching the geography mistress's undies and then I thrash him.'

'So what happened today?'

'I fired him.'

'You *didn't*!'

'I did! Just like that! "No," I said, "this sort of thing has simply got to be stopped. My mind is made up. Believe me, it's for your own good. In the past I've been far too lenient with you. 'Justice must tame whom mercy fails to train.' George Gale. You're fired!"'

'Terrific! How did he take it?'

'Not at all well, as it happens. He opened his mouth and then closed it again. Then he tried a nervous laugh. "Ha! Ha! Very good!" "It's not very good at all," I said, "and wipe that silly expression off your face. You're fired!" Then he started to protest. "Here, I say, hang on a minute, I mean you're going too far. That's not what we arranged. I mean, you can't *actually* fire me, you know. Stop messing about." "I'm not messing about," I said, "I mean it. You're fired." Then I walked out.'

'How was he when you left?'

'He was in a state of shock. He was sitting on the bed in his boxer shorts mumbling to himself.'

I can see the temptation, but I do hope Emma Jane doesn't take this line with all her clients. Not with the price of pussy cat food having doubled in the last year. I'm all for a laugh, but not during business hours.

❋　❋　❋

Lunch with Clive James. He also sees my book as source material for a drama and he wants someone like Michael White (if there is anyone like Michael White) to buy it, so that he can adapt it for the stage. His plan is to translate it into heroic couplets, since he sees it, he says, as 'low thoughts in high language'. If anyone but Clive planned to do this, I wouldn't necessarily think it was a good idea; but if Clive wanted to do it in rhyming Armenian and re-set it in a pork pie factory, I'd find great merit in the notion. I told him that I was already treating with Tynan and asked him whether there was any chance of their getting together. Clive seemed doubtful. Tynan, he said, would want it to be chocks away and full frontal, but it was a comical piece in his opinion, not an erotic one. I still can't make up my mind whether the two things are mutually exclusive – though I suspect they are – and I tentatively suggested that in certain scenes – e.g. the partouze at the end – a degree of tasteful hands-knees-and-boomps-a-daisy might, in the event, be rather jolly. Clive said he'd think about it.

'At the moment,' he said, 'I have in mind an empty stage, except for a gigantic TV screen and one door through which all the mugs will run: British Intelligence, The Wanker, Sir Robert Mark, Joan Bakewell, Googie Withers, Major Mohn, Steady Eddie, Richard Ingrams, Anna Raeburn and me.'

'You?'

'Oh yes. I will be playing Ken the Australian Horse Player.'

'No one could play it better, of course.'

'But you will have to choose between Tynan and me. If you want money, fame and beautiful women, you must go with Ken; otherwise, I'm your man.'

I asked him to talk with Tynan at least, just in case they could come to an accommodation. Okay, he said, he'd give him a ring. I get the impression that he still has tremendous residual respect for Tynan, but feels his most fruitful days are over.

'His achievement in the fifties and early sixties can never be rated too highly,' he said. 'Had he done nothing else we'd be forever in his debt.'

'So we would, so we would.' I nodded in agreement, one serious person to another.

That I must now choose between Clive and Tynan fills me with dismay. I ought to be delighted, but I'm as cast down as in the bad old days. Decisions decisions. For three years now I've not, to all intents and purposes, existed. I have, as far as I know, failed to turn up on any official roll or register. To arrive at the true figure it would have been necessary for the authorities to add one to every national count and for *Panorama* to draw an extra little cartoon man on its explicatory charts – the unemployment figures, 'don't cares' re Europe, those entitled to supplementary whatever and those not entitled, those who intend to stand up to the left-wing bully boys and those who don't. But at this rate I'll be attending meetings again, comparing viable alternatives, discussing terms of reference, receiving solicitors' letters from my solicitor's solicitor, falling once more, that is to say, within the terms of the general situation and thus finding myself knackered. I might fetch up at the business end of one of those ugly official envelopes, become a payer of water rates, perhaps, a member, even, of a tenants' association complaining about the common parts.

❀ ❀ ❀

I have sometimes thought that Dawn Upstairs is, when wearing her madam's hat, a trifle irresponsible. That she should introduce young girls to the way of life seems fair enough; but she should exercise greater care, it seems to me, before pointing old boilers along the downward path. Young chits, pneumatic with the bounce of youth, can shake off the attendant humiliations (if they even notice them), but the more mature are likely to go downhill like greased pigs.

Such thoughts are now on my mind because she has just put me on the game. Soon after I arrived home yesterday, she rang to ask whether I'd like to do a trick. Taking this to be a joke of some sort, I said: 'Of course, but my price is £100.' Too much, said Dawn Upstairs, £25 was the limit

47

and she'd want her usual £5 agency fee. It occurred to me very gradually that she might not be pulling my leg. Nor was she. A charming Indian from East Africa, a Sikh as it happened, had in the course of a recent visit brought up the subject of his mistress. This lady, a Sikh like himself, had an unfulfilled ambition, he'd said, which was to be pleasured by a European gentleman – preferably, it goes without saying, English. It would be piquant, he'd suggested, if Dawn Upstairs could attend to him, even while his mistress was having her fantasy fulfilled in the room next-door. Dawn Upstairs had said that as chance had it she numbered an English gentleman among her friends and that if the Sikh cared to ring her again on Friday she'd tell him what she'd been able to arrange.

Was I interested? It would be excellent experience, she said. I agreed at once, not so much for the experience (which might well be unfortunate) but for the fee. Times are hard and though this writing dodge is all very well, it doesn't fill up the fridge. On top of which, how, if I turned it down, could I ever again accuse Emma Jane of slackness? I'd take the booking, I said, but to be on the safe side I'd do it as Lord Dynevor. As soon as I'd rung off I began to see the problems. These were two: (a) I might be sent away and (b) I might not be sent away. The first – an occupational hazard that can happen to the best (only last week a City gent who in other respects appeared to be as much in his right mind as can be expected in this quarter dismissed Pretty Marie, of all people, with her taxi money) – would, on my first job, make me the laughing stock of the block. And the consequences of (b) might be even more humiliating. The biological composition of men is, as I explained to an incredulous Emma Jane, somewhat different to that of women, and if my client was of a mind-scrambling appearance – or even if she wasn't – I might not come up to the minimum required standard. This, after all, had happened enough times in the past and in far less demanding situations. Meanwhile I try to cheer myself with the thought that she's unlikely to be too terrible. The Sikh, according to Dawn Upstairs, is a fine man and expert

48

lover, so his mistress, it seems to me, is unlikely to be rough beyond natural justice. It seems like a risk worth taking.

❈ ❈ ❈

Dawn Upstairs rings to say that my trick is on. There was an awkward moment, she says, when she told the Sikh that she'd been able to book Lord Dynevor. He'd been most impressed and had said (always supposing that he talks like Spike Milligan): 'Oh dear me, this is very good indeed. A lord won't wish to be being paid, oh bugger me no.' Fortunately Dawn Upstairs can think on her feet and she'd corrected him very smartly. 'Oooh no,' she'd said, 'they're very hard up, are lords. Didn't you know that? He has to do this sort of thing to keep his estates together, does Lord Dynevor. He'll definitely want paying.' The Sikh got the picture and the date is on Monday morning at 12 o'clock. Pretty Marie was in the flat when Dawn Upstairs phoned with the news. 'Oooh,' said Pretty Marie, 'what a terrible time to have to get busy!' I passed this on to Dawn Upstairs.

'Now then Lord Dynevor,' she said, 'I hope you're not going to let me down.'

There's nothing displeases her more than one of her girls proving unreliable, so I hastily reassured her on this point.

'But what,' I said, 'if I can't – er – you know, if I can't actually – er – '

'Oh, that's no problem,' said Dawn Upstairs breezily, 'just rummage around down there, you know.'

Bloody hell, it's not a very romantic profession I've joined.

I'm doing the trick in our flat, which Dawn Upstairs will say she's borrowed from a girl-friend of hers. Lord Dynevor will just be passing through, so to speak, and I must remember not to know where anything is. Emma Jane wants to hide in the literary room, pointing out that this is a privilege she's many times granted me, but for once I've stooped so low as to trot out the contemptibly feminine 'that's different' argument. This time, *she* can jolly well ponce up and down the Fulham Road.

I rang up Lord Dynevor to tell him the good news. The silly old fool was out, so, being full of it, I told Lady Dynevor instead. She surprised me by sounding rather displeased. When Lord Dynevor rang back this evening, he surprised me by sounding even more displeased. People are really very strange. Why on earth should he mind my using his name to do a trick?

'I take it,' he said, 'that this is one of your feeble jokes.'

'Certainly not,' I said.

'In that case,' he said, 'you've gone too far. It just so happens that I'm extremely well known in the East African community, and if news of this gets out, it will be most embarrassing.'

This, if true, could work to my advantage. Word of Lord Dynevor's prowess will spread like a forest fire through the East African quarter – 'Hullo, hullo, is that you Mohandas? I'm telling you the most exciting news, my friend. That fine English gentleman, Lord Dynevor, will be giving your mistress the most severe seeing-to and he'll be charging only twenty-five pounds' – and I'll be turning business away.

❋　❋　❋

Lord Dynevor does his trick. The preparations take all morning. At such times a man needs all the atmospheric assistance décor and lighting can provide; so, even though it's a beautiful sunny day, I close the curtains, burn incense, fill the flat with black sounds, lower the lights and heat up the sauna bath. Everyone, I reason, looks better bathed in its flattering red glow. As for my wardrobe, I opt finally for the clean-cut English look: blue blazer with RNVR buttons (in fact the top half of a blue City suit, borrowed from my friend Scott and duly modified as though for Cowes week), cavalry twill trousers, plain white shirt and – kept in readiness for just such a caddish occasion as this – an Old Harrovian tie.

Punctually at twelve o'clock, Dawn Upstairs, together with her date and mine (the Sikh had insisted on having a preliminary peep at Lord Dynevor) arrive at the flat. I open the door with thumping heart and Holy Cow! my client is the double of the Literary Editor of *The Sunday Mirror* in black face and sari! Mr Kahn is a fine looking *man*, of course, but oh dear oh dear. How can Dawn Upstairs do this to me? Surely she could have taken one look and said Lord Dynevor was indisposed? My client is 4 ft 6 and broad with it, precisely the shape, in fact, of a beer barrel and she could be *my* age! I try not to show my panic. After all, she may take one look at me and call the cops. Stranger things have happened. No such luck. When Dawn Upstairs and the Sikh excuse themselves to go about their personal business, she seems happy to stay. Well, not happy exactly, but she certainly doesn't budge.

'You have the hour,' says the Sikh, 'and then I will be coming down.'

I look imploringly at Dawn Upstairs, but she gives a gay girlish laugh and says, 'Have fun!'

Now I discover that the Literary Editor of *The Sunday Mirror* doesn't drink, doesn't smoke and doesn't speak English. Perhaps she doesn't do the other thing either. This happy possibility causes my spirits to rise. No doubt the whole enterprise is a colossal miscalculation on the Sikh's part and my client will be only too relieved if offered a dignified escape clause. Better bring the matter to a head.

'Would you like a sauna bath?' I say.

She doesn't understand, so I mime the question, which is not an easy thing to do. After about ten minutes of this idiocy, she suddenly gets the picture and, to my dismay, nods in glum agreement. I steer her into the bedroom and then get hastily out of range. The phone rings. Probably Dawn Upstairs checking on how her new girl's making out. I answer it, planning to give her an earful. No, it's Mrs Mouse, my dear little wife. What a time to ring.

'I'm in deep snooker here,' I say.

I explain the situation. Perhaps her young man, little Mark, would care to hop over to help out. He's young and virile enough, God knows.

'Hang on,' says Mrs Mouse, 'I'll ask him.' Rhubarb

rhubarb rhubarb in the background. 'Yes,' she says, 'he'll be right over.'

'Christ, what a relief! That's marvellous.'

'But only to watch,' says Mrs Mouse.

Only to *watch*! They must be mad. I ring off angrily. Then I force myself to have a peep through the window of the sauna bath. The Literary Editor of *The Sunday Mirror* is piled up in a corner like the European butter mountain. I can't leave her in there to roast on her own, but I wouldn't join her for ten times what I'm earning. I tap on the glass and beckon her to come out. I mean her to get dressed, but she dumps herself on the bed in a defeated heap. I place a tentative reassuring hand on her shoulder and say fatuously:

'What do you want?'

Suddenly she can speak English.

'Everything,' she says, 'I want *everything*,' and she grabs me in a combined head scissors and bear hug, the impact of which rolls the pair of us off the bed. I've seldom been so startled, but I fight her off with a karate chop to the back of the neck and a cruel pressure hold on one massive knee. She backs off, I scramble to my feet and we confront each other gasping. What to do now? Another thirty seconds at this pace and I'll be knackered. Up on the toes and keep dancing, that's the thing. Move about and don't let the other fellow know you're fucked. But I'll have to take her out with one shot. I sway to the right, feint with the left and BANG! I land with a right cross to the jaw which would have loosened a rhino's horn. She blinks, but she doesn't go down. Is it always like this? Why haven't I been warned? Then I have an inspiration. I'll take my clothes off. That often gets a laugh, and laughter, in my experience, usually aborts the passions. I divest myself of my RNVR blazer, cavalry twill trousers, Old Harrovian tie, white shirt, pumps, half-hose and linen and place them neatly on a chair. But she doesn't laugh, she goes into an all-in wrestler's crouch and comes at me snarling. We fall to the floor in an untidy grunting heap. I summon up erotic images and rehearse tried and faithful fantasies that have never let me down at demanding moments in the past. But nothing works. Not even Wade versus Evert in the nude with the Ladies' Plate at stake. Zero. Zilch. I'm an abject failure. I've let down Dawn Upstairs and, worse, I won't get paid. I'm pondering this and wondering whether to force myself to one last heroic effort – after all, I am a professional now – when the door bell rings. I get into my clothes in six seconds flat and rush to answer it. It's the Sikh.

'Am I interrupting the good time?' he asks with what would be a roguish leer if someone as dignified as a Sikh were capable of roguishness. 'I can wait for half an hour.'

'No no,' I say, grabbing him by the arm and hauling him into the flat.

'Where is Shrimati?' he asks.

Who the hell's he? Has the Sikh got a pal coming over? Then I realise he's referring to the Literary Editor of *The Sunday Mirror*. I point to the bedroom.

'I'll be having the words with her,' he says.

From the living-room I can hear them holding an excitable production meeting in – not surprisingly – their own language. I suppose she's telling him what a dud I am. Who knows which of their cultural rules or customs I may have violated? Sikhs are a proud people, or so I've always understood, and the penalty for insulting behaviour towards another man's mistress may be serious. The Sikh comes padding into the living-room.

'You need the more time,' he says, and it sounds alarmingly like an order. 'I can wait.'

'No no!' I protest, a shade too vehemently perhaps.

'It is difficult?' he asks. 'She is attractive, yes?'

'Oh yes, she's absolutely *lovely*. It's not *that*.' I gesture helplessly, a sensitive artiste, his concentration broken beyond repair by some clumsy back-stage interruption.

'Ah,' says the Sikh, 'I am understanding now. I wait outside.'

'No no, I couldn't allow that. Anyway, it's too late now.' I shake my head ruefully, then spread my hands in the time-honoured gesture of long-suffering resignation: a Jewish mother gigolo. But the Sikh is not to be easily put off.

53

'Another time? You like to meet Shrimati one afternoon? I book the hotel room for you?'

'That would be *marvellous*!'

I give him Lord Dynevor's home telephone number and explain that if a woman answers he mustn't be put off; that will be my confidential secretary and it will be perfectly in order to give her all the details. With any luck he'll ring one evening when Lord D's receiving Lady Antonia Fraser to dinner. That would stir things up a touch.

I got paid, thank goodness, due to Dawn Upstair's prudent insistence that the Sikh settle his account in advance, but I've received little sympathy either from her or Emma Jane.

'Now you know what *we* go through,' they say.

❋ ❋ ❋

Lunch with Ken Tynan, Clifford Williams and Clive James. My word, these artistic people get down to cases smartly. Status-conscious business men with nothing to do all day need six meetings at least to hammer out in whose offices the first meeting's to be held; but, within three minutes of our sitting down, these three had agreed to work together and, to my surprise, Tynan had argued Clive out of the heroic couplet notion.

'I'll do it in heroic couplets,' said Clive.

'That's a dreadful idea,' said Tynan.

'You're right,' said Clive.

Further surprises were to follow. At our previous meeting, Clive had insisted that the adaptation would take him a year at least. Now he asked how long he'd got to complete the job.

'Six weeks,' said Clifford Williams.

That's torn it, I thought. But Clive merely frowned slightly, consulted his engagement book, hissed through his nose like a Japanese general and said:

'That's fine.'

Tidying up the actual business details took a little longer.

'I don't want any money up front,' said Clive, 'but I'd like a decent share of the gate when the show opens.'

'Agreed,' said Tynan and Williams.

Extraordinary. Business men would still be fretting over whether they'd lose face by speaking to one another.

After an hour or so, Clifford Williams had to return to the Garrick Theatre, where he was in the middle of lighting a thriller opening that very night. This seemed to be leaving things rather late, though not as late as John Bird left things with my first and best show, *Here is the News*: an uncompromising entertainment (the opening sketch had to do with the destruction of the world by nuclear explosion and thereafter the evening became a shade more downbeat), starring Cleo Laine and the Johnny Dankworth band, supported by a team of skinny satirists recently down from Cambridge. This, through a trifling oversight, opened on August Bank Holiday in Blackpool without any lighting at all. Bird thought Sean Kenny was doing it, Sean thought Bird was, and I, being new to the live theatre, didn't know there was such a thing as lighting. I assumed that the stage-door keeper flicked a switch at an appropriate moment to get the ball rolling, as it were, and then flicked it off after the last turn. In the event it would have been impossible, but for the outraged cries of keen young satirists and modern jazz musicians crashing into the scenery and falling head over heels into the orchestra pit, to have twigged that an entertainment was in progress.

❋ ❋ ❋

Emma Jane and I have a hard-won reputation for entertaining unostentatiously, but badly, and last night we gave one of our small dinner parties. Our guests were Dawn Upstairs, One-Eyed Charlie, Gered Mankowitz (Wolf's boy) and his exquisite wife Julia (one of John and Penelope Mortimer's), Fat Lynette, Stella Who Stutters and Nigel Dempster. As a rule, one wouldn't of course, have a person of Dempster's background in one's home, but he's gone to such touching lengths recently to become friends that we locked away our private papers, counted the spoons and forks and asked him over. He's amazing. He has the appearance of a hairdresser, the manners of a cocktail waitress and the intellectual apparatus of a randy lizard. As Julia Mankowitz said at the time, 'You know where you are with a man like that.' He has, too, a disconcerting habit of burying an interesting conversation under some crushing vulgarity. Indeed, One-Eyed Charlie was so busy taking notes for his Dictionary of Received Ideas that he did less than justice to the filthy meal Emma Jane had prepared. At one point, Julia was talking most stimulatingly about Wollheim's *Art and its Objects*, when Dempster had the gall to interrupt her.

'Art,' he said, delivering this bruising idiocy as if it contained great wisdom, 'is merely life with the boring parts removed.'

'Mr D-d-d-d-d-fuck-*Demp*ster,' said Stella Who Stutters, 'you really are a c-c-c-c-c-c-c-c-c-c- . . .'

'Oh dear,' said One-Eyed Charlie. 'Emma Jane, I'm afraid I feel a little faint. Do you think I could lie down for a minute?'

'*Poor* Charlie,' said Emma Jane. '*Please* be more careful Mr Dempster.'

'C-c-c-c-c-c-c-c . . .'

One-Eyed Charlie stretched himself out on the sofa and closed his eye, but he sat up a moment later when Dempster made some crude observation about the ethical standing of my relationship with Emma Jane.

'You've got it entirely wrong, Mr Dempster,' he said. 'It's not nearly as bad as it looks. At first it was true love, as Willie readily admits, but now he's only interested in the money.'

I thought this was rather good, but Emma Jane looked displeased. Dawn Upstairs, sensing trouble on this course, took it upon herself to change the direction of the conversation. As though feeling that the law of identity needs constant affirmation if it is not to fall into disrepute, she has taken to pointing to page 18 of my book and saying: 'I'm Dawn Upstairs, me.' She did this now, whereupon Dempster took out his snoop's note-book and said:

'It says in the book that you're thirty-three, but you told me before dinner that you're only twenty-eight.'

'Ah,' said Dawn Upstairs, 'you shouldn't believe everything you read, Mr Dempsey. Some of it's a novel, you see, but some of it's fiction.'

'C-c-c-c-c-c-c-c-c . . .'

Dempster's unattractive lounge-lizard snigger hinted that he was about to make some clever-dick observation, but One-Eyed Charlie caused him to shut his trap in a hurry by congratulating Dawn Upstairs on drawing our attention to this interesting distinction.

'As it happens,' he said, 'Dawn Upstairs has – not for the first time, I may say – introduced a topic of some philosophical interest.'

'Hell,' said Emma Jane. 'I love your shoes, Julia. Are they Kurt Geiger?'

'Yes. Do you really like them?'

'They're super.'

'While bookshops and libraries clearly take the two terms to be synonymous,' continued One-Eyed Charlie, 'most people agree that some novels are more fictional than others. Some observations recently made by Bryson of Warwick University might be relevant at this point. He had occasion to reprimand Mr David Lodge . . .'

'Oooh, I think I've met him down Tramp,' said Dawn Upstairs. 'Isn't he with Viviane Ventura now?'

'I don't think so. Anyway, Bryson was reprimanding Lodge for a mistaken attempt to define literature. Literature, Lodge had argued, was a category which could include any kind of discourse having *something* in common with the discourse you cannot take out of literature, namely a structure which either indicates the fictionality of a text or enables a text to be read as if it were fictional.'

'You're absolutely right,' said Dawn Upstairs. 'I was thinking of Lance Percival. They're both Pisces, are Viviane

57

Ventura and Lance Percival. Here, I wonder what will happen to Viviane Ventura when she loses her looks?'

'*You* do all right,' said Fat Lynette. 'I've never been frightened of losing my looks.'

'I'm not surprised,' said Dawn Upstairs.

'But, as Bryson rightly asks,' continued One-Eyed Charlie, 'what types of written material would be excluded by the definition? Why shouldn't we read railway time-tables, Mr Justice Melford's judgements or the evidence of policemen as though they were fictional?'

'Here,' said Dawn Upstairs. 'Do you know a business girl called Oddity?'

'*Oddity?*' said Fat Lynette. 'You mean Odyssey.'

'Oh do I? Well anyway, she's being paid a small fortune to do a soap commercial, is Oddity. She lies in a bath all day and gets a thousand pounds.'

'It will be the first tubbing she's had in a month,' said Fat Lynette sourly.

'C–c–c–c–c–c–c . . .'

'A bloke from New York gave me a thousand pounds once,' said Dawn Upstairs.

'American Express?'

'He was quick, yes.'

'On the other hand,' said One-Eyed Charlie, 'how did the definition cope with something Lodge explicitly wanted to include in literature. Pope's *Essay on Man*? On the definition, reflective or philosophical verse or prose would have to be excluded from literature as it was hard to see what reading them as fictional would amount to.'

'*Bull shit!*' said Nigel Dempster. 'I've got two million readers and I don't have to sit here and listen to this rubbish! I'm going.'

He rose to his feet and strode angrily from the flat.

'C–c–c–c–c– U N T!' roared Stella Who Stutters, collapsing with relief.

'Well I never,' said Fat Lynette. 'The man's utterly uncouth.'

'Actually, I rather fancied him,' said Dawn Upstairs.

'That's because he's so common,' said Fat Lynette. 'You want to lower yourself.'

'*Do* I? Oh dear.'

One-Eyed Charlie then read us a paper which he's to deliver at the next meeting of the Aristotelian Society. He doesn't publish much these days, but he's been stirred to on this occasion by the participation of Reginald Maudling in a televised law and order debate. In the course of this, Maudling had made it clear that he considered law-breaking wrong in itself, irrespective of the specific law being broken. This belief, as One-Eyed Charlie argues persuasively in his paper, makes him teeter on the brink of a novel form of category mistake and logically entails the theory that offenders should be punished twice: once for breaking a particular law, and once again for breaking the law generally. Thus, if you were in the frame for holding up a bank, you'd draw fifteen years for bank robbery and an extra five, say, for breaking the law.

'Law-breaking,' as a Tory MP recently observed in a bizarre outburst, 'should be made illegal.'

In the middle of his paper, One-Eyed Charlie was interrupted by a celebrated investigative reporter from one of those abrasive, no-nonsense TV documentary programmes, ringing to do business with Dawn Upstairs. Notwithstanding this fellow's gritty, hard-nosed image on camera, his personal tastes run to being suspended from the ceiling like a casualty case in traction and told he's a worm. Being totally engrossed in One-Eyed Charlie's subtle argument, Dawn Upstairs naturally couldn't be fished to attend to him herself, so she fixed him up with One-Eyed Charlie's ex-wife, German Helga. Having organised this on the phone, she checked with One-Eyed Charlie that German Helga was properly equipped for this sort of carry-on.

'Oh yes,' said One-Eyed Charlie, 'she's got all the gear and that. She ties them up in the garage and many's the time I've had to move my things.'

I was so distracted by the thought of One-Eyed Charlie coming home after a hard day's work researching at the library and not being able to park his car or get at his Black and Decker drill for all the merchant bankers and Tory politicians strapped to his work-bench that I was quite unable to concentrate on the second half of his paper.

This disappointment apart, it was an outstandingly satisfactory evening, I think, in the course of which One-Eyed Charlie claims he was able to collect no less than a dozen new entries for his Dictionary of Received Ideas. If Emma Jane and I give a few more of our dinner parties, he says, he should be able to deliver his first draft to the Cambridge University Press before September. I suppose I should be offended.

❊ ❊ ❊

My reputation in the block has taken an upward turn, due to my having successfully put the squeeze on the Mafia. A few evenings ago, Dawn Upstairs, Emma Jane and Black Danielle arrived home incoherent with rage, having been ripped off by two young tearaways from the East End who now control a colossal pop music empire. (For the sake of my knee-caps, we will call them the Kite Brothers.) After the funny business, the ladies had been hustled off the premises, unceremoniously and without due recompense, by a uniformed bodyguard built like the Marble Arch.

'Who was there?' I asked.

'Just the Kites,' said Dawn Upstairs, 'and an old fart called Jack something.'

Pressed for further details about Jack something, Dawn Upstairs proceeded to describe my old friend from better days, Jack Daniels the band leader turned pop promoter and, like myself, a member of the MCC.

'Good heavens,' I said, 'that's Jack Daniels. A *great* friend of mine. He wouldn't rip anybody off, he's a member of the MCC.'

I realised at once that I would have done better to remain silent. The consensus seemed to be that if I was half a man I'd get straight on the phone to my friend Jack with the strongly worded suggestion – as one member of the MCC to another – that my girls get paid pronto, if not sooner. I ducked and dived for a bit, but the next morning I found myself caught up in the most embarrassing conversation I've ever had.

'Jack! You old sod! Ha! Ha! Well I never. It's Willie, Jack.'

'Hul*lo* old chap. Well well. Long time no – er – er ...'

'Yes. How *are* you?'

'Fine, just fine. And you?'

'Terrific, terrific! Not as young as I was, of course, but which of us is?'

'That's true, that's true.'

'Still keeping a straight bat, Jack? Ha! Ha!'

'I should say so! Still play every Saturday, you know.'

'Get away! How about the series in Australia, then? Not too good, eh?'

'My God, don't remind me, old boy. You know what? I blame Boycott. Let us down badly. With him we might have had a chance.'

'You wouldn't have had him as skipper, would you Jack?'

'Oh no. If we're talking about the captaincy, I'm for Greggy.'

'Not old Phyllis! I'm surprised to hear you say that, Jack. He's a big girl's blouse in my book, Jack.'

'Well yes, I don't know. Still, what are you up to these days, old chap?'

'Oh, you know, bits and pieces.'

'Still putting on plays?'

'Not much, no. Hardly at all, in fact. I'm still in the leisure business, mind. Ha! Ha! That reminds me, Jack, – er – I ...'

'Yes? Is that right? Well it's certainly good to hear from you again, old chap. You keep in touch now! But I must be getting along, I'm up to my bollocks here and I really must ...'

'Jack, er – I – er – '

'Yes, old chap?'

'Er, nothing Jack.'

'Oh, well so long, old chap. Nice talking to you again.'

'So long Jack. *Zoweee FUCK!*' A sharp kick on the ankle

from Emma Jane had indicated that she considered my task uncompleted.

'What the hell was that, old chap. Are you all right?'

'Yes, right as rain, thanks Jack. I just got stung on the nose by a wasp. Er – Jack, I . . .'

'Yes, old chap?'

'Jack, I really don't know quite how to put this. It's a bit embarrassing really.'

'Embarrassing? What is, old chap?'

'Well – now don't misunderstand me, Jack – but it seems you saw three of my – er – that is, you saw three girls I happen to know.'

'Yes, old chap? When was this?'

'Er – last night, Jack. And the thing is, you see, it seems they didn't get paid. There wasn't any *quid pro quo*, if you get me Jack. Isn't that ridiculous? Ha! Ha! Well, you know how it is, Jack, one of them happens to be my secretary, my *ex*-secretary that is, and when they mentioned the matter to me, I naturally said "Good Lord Jack Daniels wouldn't rip anybody off, I'll have a word with him." So, here I am, Jack. I mean, it wouldn't be cricket, would it Jack? Ha! Ha!'

Jack's brain dropped out with a wet thud I could hear a mile and a half away, and within the hour, the uniformed bodyguard turned up in a yellow Rolls-Royce with the gooses.

Fair enough, but this morning *Private Eye* – a paper you can trust – informs us that the Kite Brothers represent the Carlo Gambino family's interests in London and that their business methods include nailing competitors to the floor boards and hanging them out of the window like the Stars and Stripes on the 4th of July. All in all it's two new pence to speak to me at the moment, and when my girls ask me admiringly how I did it, I say: 'Oh, it was nothing. I simply told them that such behaviour wasn't cricket. They got the picture.'

❊　❊　❊

Once again I'm without accredited representation – an infuriating setback. Discovering that the management of my affairs, together with the affairs of Big Newk, Lew Hoad, James Hunt, Virginia Wade, Dennis Lillee and Thommo, Gary Player, Glenda Jackson and Clive James, was less than a full time job, my new agent, Ken the Australian Horse Player, has recently taken to operating what is known in the trade as the pebble-dashing dodge. He and a pal of his called Ted the Head have been driving round the dormitory suburbs in a tank-like machine which squirts concrete, terrorising middle-class ladies into the belief that their homes are falling down. Parking their horror movie monster in an avenue of newly constructed villas named tastefully after trees, they knock on the front door of 'The Elms' or 'The Willows' and say:

'Good morning, madam, allow us to introduce ourselves. We represent the Friendly Pebble-Dashing Company of Mayfair and we couldn't help noticing that your house is in terrible shape. "Fuck me dead," I said to my colleague Mr Ted the Head, "one good gust of wind and 'The Willows' would be as secure as an Abo's shithouse in an earthquake." What you need, if I may say so, darling, is a strong coating of pebbledashing as a protection against the elements. It's a monkey on the fucking table and two more monkeys spread over eighteen months.'

The terrified housewife parts with the money, whereupon Ken and Ted the Head let fly at her home with a quick-drying mixture of rocks and cement. When the man of the house gets home after a hard day selling life assurance to the unwary, he can't tell 'The Elms' from 'The Willows', since both now resemble those pill-boxes that were erected along the south coast during the war as a defence against Jerry. Only by starting at the end of the road and counting carefully can he arrive at his own front door, or rather at the spot where his own front door would be, had it not been cemented over. An aggrieved ratepayer has now complained to the authorities and Ken's been captured once again.

This is a particularly annoying set-back because only

yesterday he and I attended on Miss MacNaughton in her office, and the meeting went really well. Apart, that is, from a tiny awkward moment when she mentioned the agreement negotiated by Danvers. Ken got a funny look in his eye and I thought 'My God, he's going to tell her where she can put it,' and damn it he did.

'Film rights are the name of the fucking game, baby!' he then informed her, and though she didn't say anything, I could tell from her expression that she was rather impressed.

Then this morning I had the embarrassing task of ringing her yet again about a sudden change in my representation. Fortunately, she seems to be an endlessly patient and sympathetic lady.

'Look,' she said, 'I'm sure you know what you're doing, but why don't you let *me* suggest an agent for you? Why don't you try someone like Hilary Rubinstein?'

Well, no disrespect to Miss MacNaughton, but I wasn't going to put my affairs into the hands of some dizzy lady, so I vetoed Miss Rubinstein very smartly.

'Oh dear,' said Miss MacNaughton. 'What about Michael Sissons, then, or Jonathan Clowes, or Richard Simon, or Peter Janson-Smith or someone at Curtis Brown?'

Who the hell were they? I'm sure she was trying to be helpful, but not having heard of any of these people, how do I know which of them has the kind of track record I'm looking for? The wrong agent can do a lot of damage at the start of a young writer's career and I don't want to make another mistake. I'll box clever for a while and if I run into anything too perplexing I can always ring my friend Tom Parkinson. He's in New Zealand now, but in other respects his credentials are impeccable. He used to sweep the stage for Professor Bruce Lacey and The Alberts, and since then he's done even better, or so he tells me.

❀ ❀ ❀

My book's been out for a month now and judging by my mail it's tickled the public palate with all the zest of unset jelly. Until this morning I had received precisely four letters: three from creditors suddenly alerted to the fact that I was still alive, and one from a Naval architect in Devonport wondering whether I had yet formed an opinion of a play he sent me 1966. To my dismay, however, Emma Jane has, from the moment the book appeared, found herself in correspondence with lunatics from all quarters of the land. They write to her about sex, taking her, for reasons that I don't fully understand, to be some sort of expert on the subject. One man, who lives in Nottingham and claims to have no less than seventy hobbies (*soixante-neuf* and gardening) writes to her every other day. Being the focus of so much attention has quite destroyed her reason and she now sees herself as a literary figure on all fours with Margaret Drabble or even Xaviera Hollander.

'Tell me,' she said yesterday, 'which are the better publishers as between Chatto and Windus and Faber and Faber?'

'All four houses are well thought of in their different ways,' I said, 'but why do you ask?'

'I'm persuaded that I ought to bring out my collected letters in book form,' she said, laying down her quill, 'and naturally I wish to place my manuscript with the most serious firm.'

'Of course.'

'I expect my work to cause quite a furore in the world of letters and no doubt I will become the toast of literary London.'

'What about me?'

'You may remain in my life, if you wish, as an ageing and somewhat hysterical admirer whom I treat with thoughtless cruelty.'

I had been growing accustomed, then, to the idea that I would spend my declining years playing Lady Caroline Lamb to Emma Jane's Lord Byron, but this morning's post suggests that I am not yet entirely out of it. Among the twenty or so letters addressed to her were three for me and each in its way was encouraging. The first was from an ex-Guards officer who shows every sign of being crackers; the second was from Donald Trelford, inviting me to submit any occasional journalism I might do to *The Observer*; and the third, by an odd coincidence, was from the philosopher at Warwick University to whom One-Eyed Charlie was referring the other evening.

Taking these in order of importance, I dealt first with Mr Trelford's. In so far as the tape-recorder does all the work, the in-depth interview has always struck me as an attractive literary *genre*, but if I was to have a series of conversations, I needed a peg on which to hang them. In no time at all I had one. 'Has-beens.' What a poignant theme in our success-orientated world! I quickly drew up a list of likely people – Paul Johnson, Lord Hailsham, Sir Robert Mark, Glenda Jackson, Michael Parkinson and Mrs Thatcher – and rang them each in turn. 'Hullo there,' I said, 'I'm interviewing "has-beens" on behalf of *The Observer* and they particularly want me to include you.' 'Bugger off!' they all said, including Mrs Thatcher. Well I never, what a setback! Never mind, I'll interview them none the less. It would be unprofitable to spend time in the company of such people, so I'll rough out a couple of conversations and if they're any good I'll start without them.

Meanwhile, the certifiable ex-Guards officer's letter reads:

> Brook House,
> Windsor Forest,
> Berkshire.

Dear Mr Donaldson,

I am writing to you on two counts – first to congratulate you on your recent book which occupied me for the whole of a non-working day and which I found most informative. I was extolling its virtues to a couple who live nearby in the evening when I was interrupted by my hostess, who transpired to be your sister Jane. I fear that her husband did not share my enthusiasm for your work!

I am like yourself an Old Wykehamist (F 1943–1947) and the current economic problems have forced me to turn my attention to getting paid employment. Quite understandably there has not been a mad rush for my services in the more conventional fields and it occurred to me that you might be able to put me in touch with someone who might be able to offer me an opportunity in a rather different milieu. I am well aware that one should not be too fastidious in the England of today and with taxation at its present rate I am not attracted by pieces of paper that have to pass through banks. I have approached one or two professional ladies and suggested that if I obtain a furnished flat in my name they could run it for me. This has attracted their interest as it seems unlikely that I would be troubled by the police as I have a veneer of respectability (having served for fifteen years in the Life Guards, being a member of White's etc.). Again, if this did come to anything I would be very grateful for any advice you could give me on the management of such an establishment.

I hope you do not mind my writing to you and will quite understand if you feel unable to help. However, this is a serious letter and, for reasons not totally unlike your own perhaps, I am inclined to turn my back on the Establishment (unless it suits me!) and look for alternatives. If you did feel it would be worthwhile to meet I should be delighted to give you lunch one day at the beginning of April. One of the ideas I had in mind is that there might be a place for a 'guide' agency for overseas visitors concentrating on the less conventional and widely known places of entertainment. The merit of this would seem to be that one could reasonably expect a reward from both the punters and the proprietors.

Yours sincerely<br>Martin Dobson-Smythe.

P.S. Perhaps it would be better not to mention to your sister that I had been in touch with you.

Having perused this carefully for about an hour – holding it up to the light, reading between the lines, carrying out various forensic experiments on it – I'm satisfied that it's not a clever trap sprung by the Special Branch in an effort to get me to divulge which cabinet ministers are trotting up our stairs and which aren't, but is indeed from an authentic looney. I have therefore replied, inviting him to phone at his convenience. We have no well-born pillock on the books at the moment and I'm sure he'll come in handy.

❊ ❊ ❊

The philosopher's letter is delightful, but a source of some embarrassment since he ascribes to me arguments due to One-Eyed Charlie. It reads:

> Department of Philosophy
> The University
> Warwick.

Dear Mr Donaldson,

I've asked Julian Mitchell to send this on to you because he knows where you live and because, if you remember, we talked about philosophy briefly and disjointedly at a party of his last year. Emma Jane was asserting that all philosophers are wankers and I was doing my poor best to persuade her that this wasn't necessarily – least of all in any formal sense (see below) – the case.

Re *Both the Ladies and the Gentlemen*: The treatment of pornography (pp 98–105) I found especially stimulating; the introduction of the point about causality being incompatible with identity devastating. Perhaps I should bring in its application to porn when its bearing on the difference between materialism of the Comtean or epiphenomenalist variety and the mind-brain identity theory type is commanding less than total audience absorption.

Of course Lord Longford's special version of the naturalistic fallacy (p 102) needs underlining even if you feel, like me, that morality is ultimately a matter of aesthetics (or good/bad style). I realise that this is an elitist, not to say fastidious, attitude to take, but as an atheist I can't for the life of me see why I have any responsibilities to anyone else, nor why acting *in the general good* gives me a reason for acting (especially if it is to my inconvenience or disadvantage). And what's the use of a morality like Kant's or Mrs Foot's which doesn't give *me* a reason for acting? I'd better add that I realise that some of my taste is extremely bad, and that I don't feel an inclination to do anything about it, so perhaps my view isn't much better off from the motivation aspect. Cf. Wittgenstein: Ethics is aesthetics (*Tractatus Logico-Philosophicus*).

Your remarks about the logical independence of Goodness and God's decrees (p 103) would certainly be agreed to by theologians of a nominalist cast (Duns Scotus, Ockham), but not necessarily by Aquinas, who would have been a Platonist in this respect. Plato's *Euthyphro Dilemma* is the question of how you would recognise a God as a God if he did or commanded evil things. The assumption is that you would only recognise a being as a God if he was good and could be seen as such – an assumption shared by Kant and most modern philosophers of religion. I think this is a totally fallacious argument and betrays a misunderstanding of the difference between religion and morality, as well as causing philosophers of religion to neglect some most interesting varieties of religion, where the believers worshipped not because of any premonitions of goodness in the objects of their devotion, but because they knew they would be trampled on if they didn't.

The remark on Jan Morris, One-Eyed Charlie and Rylean behaviourism is brilliant. One could turn it round and apply it to Jan Morris by saying that if James Morris had been more Rylean we would have been spared those lugubrious maunderings about femininity and the painful pilgrimage to Casablanca.

A small objection: is the minor premise (p 91) true by definition or by fact? I think only a follower of Saul Kripke would want to hold that William Donaldson is *necessarily* a ponce such that a William Donaldson who was not a ponce would not be William Donaldson. Quine is better here, I think, when he says that properties apply necessarily not to objects in themselves but only under particular descriptions (i.e. necessity is *de dicto*, not *de re*).

Finally a puzzle: you say (p 68) that a pragmatist would

think of a person's roles as the whole story about them. I think this would be an odd half-way sort of pragmatism, as I feel that a full-blooded pragmatism would want to assert that saying that someone has such and such a role (e.g. a cricketer) means only that he wears white flannels, swishes around him with a piece of willow, spends a lot of his time drinking beer, playing cards, telling vulgar stories, etc. I don't think a pragmatist would want to go along with the type of social psychologist talk of roles as a kind of aura or buzz that people carry around with them. Your remarks on Lord Hailsham and the Queen suggest that most God-fearing Englishmen aren't pragmatic enough.

I hope you will forgive this intrusion from my provincial ivory tower, but as yet no one seems to have picked up the philosophical intelligence of your book, and writing to you makes a most refreshing change from the high seriousness and bombast of Professor Popper's Third World.

Yours sincerely<br>Anthony Bryson.

This has thrown me into quite a turmoil. It obviously calls for a serious and lengthy reply, but how am I to answer it without revealing myself as a charlatan? My only solution, as I see it, is to persuade One-Eyed Charlie to compose the reply, but even this stratagem raises its own problems. If One-Eyed Charlie's letter is sensible – which, of course, it will be – Dr Bryson will be even more impressed, and he and One-Eyed Charlie will be in correspondence with each other until one or other of them joins the great philosopher in the sky. And what happens if I have a spat with One-Eyed Charlie, or if one of us becomes nervous and moves to the Balearics? Or, worse, what if Dr Bryson, becoming more and more intrigued by this philosophical ponce, wants to meet me? I can hardly send One-Eyed Charlie in my place. Or perhaps I can. I'm lunching with him on Monday, as it happens, and I'll seek his advice on the matter then.

❀　❀　❀

My interview with Glenda Jackson, the abrasively intelligent actress with a mind of her own:

'Good morning,' I said. 'May I start by asking you about some of the famous directors for whom you have worked?'

'You may.'

'What about Peter Brook?'

'P.B.?'

'No, Peter Brook.'

'Yes, P.B. The Buddha. Ah, the time and effort! The suffering! The *boredoms*! But you will never work with a director as remarkable as him. He doesn't settle for boundaries, you see.'

'Doesn't he?'

'No. With Brook anything is possible. It's said that he's a dictator whereas the reverse is true. He gives you total freedom. But he knows when to say "no" *very firmly*. So you try again. And he says "no". And it goes on like this until you think you couldn't possibly find another way. But perhaps you do. And he says, "Yes, that's a bit more like it." And you say "Like what?" And he replies "I don't know, show me."'

'Excuse me,' I said, 'I've just remembered I forgot to turn the stomach-pump off before leaving the house this morning. Good-bye.'

'That's what they all say.'

It was rude of me, I dare say, but if interviewing celebrities entails listening to this sort of rubbish, I may have to give it up.

❊ ❊ ❊

Catastrophe, and not just for me, but for One-Eyed Charlie too. For some months now he has had some piffling drug conviction hanging over him, and this morning he went along to Great Marlborough Street to be sentenced. (At the previous hearing, the magistrate – thoroughly confused by One-Eyed Charlie's speech in his own defence – remanded him on bail while waiting for a psychiatrist's report. The psychiatrist duly certified him sane, hence his reappearance in court today.) On his being searched backstage, it was discovered that the silly fellow had enough cannabis about his person to wipe out half of Greater London. His explanation was that since they hadn't searched him on his last appearance before the beak, he hadn't expected them to on this occasion. Really, these philosophers are so dozey it breaks your heart. Just when I need him urgently he's put himself back in the boob for a two-year stretch. Now who will write to Dr Bryson on my behalf?

❄ ❄ ❄

It occurred to me yesterday that Julian Mitchell is the very person to correspond with Dr Bryson. I rang him up and wheeled myself in for lunch today.

Julian's always been a bit gruff and breezy, of course, and if you don't watch out he gets you doing all manner of things you weren't expecting: such as standing in his garden in a cloud-burst swinging a lettuce above your head; or, worse, helping him to round up two hundred of buffalo in Gloucestershire. He actually had me doing this some years ago. I was staying with him in Cirencester and one morning he said:

'We've got to round up two hundred head of buffalo before lunch. Look lively now!'

I assumed that this was some sort of country dweller's jest, so I set off after him in my lightweight suit and elastic-sided boots.

'Stand there,' he said, pointing to a gap in the hedge. 'When the herd come this way, don't on any account let them through into the next field. Cut them off. Is that clear?'

'Cut them *off*! Good grief, a man could be tossed!'

'Don't be silly,' he snapped.

He trotted away and fifteen minutes later sixty ton of stampeding buffalo thundered over the horizon towards my position. I took off like the clappers, of course, dancing crazily through mangel-wurzels and buffalo flop towards a hedge on the far side of the field I was supposed to be protecting.

Half way across I was joined by a fucking little dachshund, which, imagining itself to be caught up in some sort of game I suppose, yapped at my heels for the last hundred yards. I reached the hedge with bursting lungs and, though it must have been ten feet high, sailed over it in a creditable western roll, touching down, rather to my surprise, in the middle of a river. I was fished out by a party of baffled picnickers, who had witnessed the whole incident. The buffaloes, it seemed, hadn't followed me through the gap in the hedge at all, so the picnickers, unaware of their looming presence in the other field, had been most surprised to see this little City gentleman hurtling towards them and then leaping, for no good reason other than that he was being chased by a dachshund puppy, over a ten-foot hedge and into a river.

After lunch, I produced Doctor Bryson's letter and also the one from the struck-off Guards Officer. Julian put on his specs and fell to examining the Guards Officer's. He read it six or seven times before finally pronouncing it genuine. The decisive passage, he said, was 'my hostess, who transpired to be your sister'. As a novelist of some standing, he could confirm, he said, that this was too good not to be true. Then he produced the *Old Wykehamist Yearbook* from a cupboard under the stairs and there, sure enough, was Major Martin Dobson-Smythe (F 1943–1947), ex Life Guards and listed as now residing at Brook House, Windsor Forest. There only remained the possibility that he now worked for the Special Branch, but Julian discounted this as a paranoid fantasy. He then turned his attention to Dr Bryson's letter, tut-tutting somewhat over the ethical theory put forward therein. This surprised me since his subjectivist position seemed coherent enough. Julian then insisted that I reply to the letter myself. It had been extremely thoughtful of Dr Bryson to write to me, he argued, and to reply by proxy, as it were, would be both cowardly and discourteous.

In spite of this advice, I'm still inclined to send the relevant papers to One-Eyed Charlie in Wormwood Scrubs. This might get him into trouble, of course, since the authorities there might well take certain passages in Dr Bryson's letter to be unconducive to good prison discipline; but such an outcome would seem to be more One-Eyed Charlie's problem than mine.

❋ ❋ ❋

To Thames Television to meet Anthony Stancomb, the producer of the Epilogue. He has a mind to pop me on the God slot, a notion that strikes me as frankly scandalous. Since my book came out, TV producers have, quite rightly in my opinion, refused to let me near their programmes unless I have the decency to appear – as lesbians do and those with non-specific urethritis – in discreet shadow, or, like a Mafia hitman, with my head in a black bag. Now this cheery Mr Stancomb wants to put me on a religious show, and unhooded too!

The programme he has in mind is *Ideas in Print*, in which the authors of seven current books dealing with urgent social questions are to be interviewed by Michael Nelson. What sort of urgent social question do they take me to be? The other books under discussion are serious contributions to the great debate – Brian Inglis's on drugs, for instance – and to allow a facetious ponce to pop up in the middle of such a series seems to me outrageous. Stancomb and Nelson clearly find the whole thing no end of a lark, but if they manage to get my appearance approved by someone they refer to mysteriously as 'the powers that be', I'll complain immediately to the IBA, Lord Longford, the Festival of Light, Mrs Whatsit and whoever next.

❋ ❋ ❋

Clive James phones to say that he's coming to tea on Thursday to 'get a bit of background'. This has put us into quite a dither. Should we be ourselves, or should we put on a special show, as when the Queen Mother visits a gas works in the north? What if he goes right off the enterprise, appalled

74

to discover what a drab, surburban crew we are? And so many of my team are on the missing list: Ken the Australian Horse Player back in the cooler, and One-Eyed Charlie likewise; Toby Danvers snoozing his life away on the telephone exchange; Black Danielle in Kampala taking part in the Black African Kung Fu championships; Big Elaine now an assistant lecturer in business studies at Eton College; and Pretty Marie won't do teas. I've asked Dawn Upstairs, but I doubt if she'll turn up. She certainly didn't sound impressed.

'You're coming to tea on Thursday to meet Clive James,' I said.

'Oh yes? And who might he be?'

'He's adapting my book for the live theatre. Naturally he wants to meet you more than anyone. I'm surprised you've never heard of him. He's extremely trendy and is to be found most nights down Tramp.'

'Really? Is he a member of the jet-set then?'

'Very much so. He has a home in L.A. and when he gives a dinner party Starsky and Hutch wash up.'

'Ooooh I say! Is it business then, or like social?'

'Business, I suppose, but not so much yours as mine, if you understand me. He won't wish to be charged.'

'I don't know if I want this James Kline person picking my brains if I'm not getting anything out of it. I'm not stupid, me.'

They do let you down sometimes. If it was a separates manufacturer with a cheque book coming, or a rock and roll hooligan wired for sound, she'd be here like a shot. All I can do is keep my fingers crossed till Thursday and pray she turns up.

❅ ❅ ❅

I've had a lovely letter from One-Eyed Charlie in Wormwood Scrubs. For some reason – to ingratiate himself with the prison censors, perhaps – he takes it as an occasion to parody a certain kind of bluff moralist (Brand Blanshard, say), striking attitudes which seem to me to have little to do with his own convictions.

H.M. Prison,
Wormwood Scrubs,
London.

Dear Willie,

It was nice to get your letter, but the enclosure from Dr Bryson caused me some surprise and much distress. Surprise, because Bryson has recently done some good work on Popper and distress because he shows in his letter a totally frivolous attitude to morality. If this is the state into which philosophical reflection has sunk, Miss Anscombe's complaints about the corrupting influence Oxford moral philosophy has on the young seem to be well founded. To those of us who have had to make our way in the real world, the Doctor's remarks read like the narcissistic whinings of a spoiled child. Nevertheless, I will assume they are intended as philosophical argument in order to expose the fallacies they contain.

1. To expect a moral reason for an action to give him a reason for acting of a non-moral sort (e.g. that it should do *him* some good) is not only to commit the naturalistic fallacy, but also, and more seriously, to confuse moral judgements with prudential judgements – a slip that would merely be an undergraduate howler were it not so pernicious in its implications. But then bad logic *is* bad morality.

2. A man who does not understand that goodness involves responsibilities to others does not understand (or *professes* not to understand) moral talk at all. Discussion with such a man is a waste of time because he appears not to share the common humanity that must be the basis of any profitable moral discussion. To bring this out, let me remind you of some remarks of Warnock's (without my books I cannot be certain I have his precise words, of course, but the sense will be correct).

'Just as to hold that snow is not white would be evidence for supposing that one did not know what "white" *means*, to hold that a certain action was not morally wrong (a particularly barbarous killing, say) could only suggest ignorance of the meaning of "morally wrong". Since morality is not, after all, a quite meaningless term, nor a term to which one is at liberty to attach any private sense that one may fancy, some things are, as one may put it, morally wrong *by definition*.'

3. The Doctor implies that acting in the general good is the only sort of reason there might be for morality. This is a utilitarian view which I do not share, since I find utilitarianism a grossly immoral doctrine, often running counter to our intuitions about justice, and sanctioning such abuses as the preventative punishment of those declared to have offended (cf. English moral philosophy from Mill to Hare. Hare's consequentialist theory of morality recently led him to say: 'Torture isn't wrong *universally*, but I wouldn't say that to a policeman.' Indeed, on certain stated principles it is *not* wrong to torture or kill. In my view, and I would have hoped in the view of Professor Hare and that of Dr Bryson, these principles are thereby refuted). Even so, there is a utilitarian answer to the Doctor's argument. A society which encourages altruism is a better society for everyone, including the Doctor. So from his disgracefully selfish point of view he should encourage altruism, rather than pander to the fashionable nihilism of his students – a symptom, obviously, of the recent decline in our society.

Willie, don't be confounded, I beg you, by the unthinking glibness of the Doctor and those like him, but learn from those who take moral philosophy seriously; who expect it to tell them *what to do*, who aspire, in other words, to the Socratic tradition.

Love and kisses and a big hug for Emma Jane,
Charlie.


P.S. The clichés don't fall as thick and fast in here as they do outside (no *Spectator*, no *Sunday Telegraph*, no *Any Questions* with Enoch Powell, Jimmy Saville and Lord Stokes, and – which is the greatest handicap of all – none of your dreadful dinner parties), but in spite of this I've been able to do a little work on my Dictionary. I enclose some new entries, but, since the only paper available in here for literary composition is not of a kind the Cambridge University Press is accustomed to receiving through the post, I would be grateful if, before sending one copy to Jeremy Mynott at the CUP, and putting another in my safe deposit box at Harrods, you could transfer them to a more conventional foolscap. Bless you.

*Encs.*

BLOCKHEAD: 'I may be one of the brutal and licentious military, but I'm not a complete blockhead!'

CIVILISED: To be predicated solely of boulevard comedies running at the Globe, Queen's, Lyric and Apollo Theatres. What it means, nobody knows.

DISGRACE, A national: Due to the rapacious activities of philistine property barons, London has only forty-one theatres left in which to mount the plays of Alan Ayckbourn.

FREEDOM: Doesn't mean the same thing as licence. It's not *carte blanche* to abuse privileges.

GAME, The: No one's bigger than the game, not even Pele.

MODEL, Photographic: Being a model isn't all flying off to exotic locations and swanning around in glamorous clothes. It's damned hard work.

NEWSCASTERS: Thought to be as drunk as skunks most of the time. 'Look, there's more to reading the news than simply reading the news, you know.'

NOT, Like it or: Like it or not, we're still basically a Christian country.

PETER: 'When I saw what you were doing to Peter, I hated you. But now I don't hate you any more. I pity you!'

PHILOSOPHY: 'Look. Cut the philosophy. If you've got something to say, say it.'

PREJUDICE, Colour: 'Look, a person can be white, pink, green, purple, striped with yellow spots, black even, it makes no difference to me! Just so long as the lad sticks the ball in the back of the net on Saturday, I'll be happy.'

RELIGION: Unfashionable if organised. 'I don't go to church or anything like that, but I believe in God and if I was involved in a plane crash I think I'd say a prayer.' Modern version of the best bet argument.

SCHOOL, The Cambridge English: 'What a pity none of them ever learned to write English!'

SIXTIES, The: Always refer to them as 'The "so-called" swinging Sixties'. (This formulation is of particular interest, since it is a cliché within a cliché. This seems to indicate that there is a hierarchy of clichés as there is a hierarchy of jokes. Clichés should therefore be divided into various types, so that a cliché or a class of clichés could only be the subject of a cliché of a higher order. Were we not to do this, clichés, like jokes, would be prone to the vicious-circle fallacies which give rise to so many paradoxes in set theory and logic. See Irving Copi on jokes – *The Theory of Logical Types*, Routledge and Kegan Paul, 1971.)

TRAVEL: Ideally, every journey should be a voyage of self-discovery.

TRUEMAN, F. S.: A legendary wit. Most celebrated *mot*: 'Pass the pickles, Sambo.' (To the Prime Minister of Jamaica.)

UNFORTUNATE, Concern for the: Concern for the unfortunate should not be institutionalised in such a way as to destroy all individual responsibility.

❋   ❋   ❋

Clive James to tea. He was due at 4.30, but at 4 he phoned to say that he'd be an hour late. This was just as well since we were having a hell of a time getting our special guest artiste, Dawn Upstairs, into the starting stalls. She'd thoughtlessly accepted a last-minute booking with my old school friend Swainston, and at 3.30 she phoned to say that owing to unnatural desires he had acquired since his last consultation she was now behind the clock.

'*Here*,' she said, 'the things they taught you at your old school! He suddenly spat at me, did the head of your house, and now I've got to wash my hair. I thought you said he was captain of cricket?'

I told her to fall in as soon as possible, but by five o'clock she'd phoned four more times, seeking advice as to her wardrobe and accessories. We finally decided that her white number from Castel at £175 would be the outfit most likely to blow Mr James Kline's mind, but since he arrived at 5.30 and by 6.30 there was still no sign of her, it began to seem doubtful whether he would ever get to see it. Emma Jane and I did our best to keep him entertained – and she scored valuable bonus points for having heard of Pete Atkins, which was more than I had, I'm ashamed to say – but by ten to seven Clive, who had already announced that he had to be on the other side of London by seven-thirty, was making moving-on noises. At seven o'clock, Dawn Upstairs – looking good, I must admit – made the kind of shattering entrance that went out of fashion, or so I'd always supposed, when Frankie Laine ceased trading. Twenty minutes later, Clive tottered away looking fairly shell-shocked. As soon as he'd gone, Dawn Upstairs asked us how we thought she'd done.

'You did fantastically well,' I said. 'You saw for yourself how impressed he was. It's extremely doubtful whether he's ever met anyone quite like you.'

'Good,' she said, 'because I've been thinking. Why can't *I* play me in this silly stage show thing of yours? I mean I've done extra work and that in films – and not the kind of films *you're* thinking of William Donaldson, thank you very much – though I've done them too, of course.'

'Of course.'

'When I was with Tony from L.A., that was. You've met Tony from L.A.'

'I have?'

'*Yes*. He gave me that four-hundred-pound-watch from Cartiers, did Tony from L.A. I showed it to you, don't you remember? So how about it then?

'How about what?'

'How about *me* playing *me* in this silly stage show thing of yours?'

'No one could play the part better, of course, but I foresee problems with Equity. Are you a member by any chance?'

'No, but I'd be prepared to join.'

'That's not as easy as it used to be I'm afraid. They're cur-

80

rently adopting a very stuffy pigs attitude towards undiscovered super-stars.'

'Ah yes, but there's something you're forgetting, isn't there? I know Kenny Lynch, me.'

Well, that changed things entirely, of course. Had I known of her friendship with Kenny, I naturally wouldn't have said anything so stupid. Before tripping away to give Kenny a ring, she said:

'Hey, I quite forgot to tell you! Last night I played this smashing joke on Pretty Marie and Twigg the Well Known Playwright, didn't I?'

'*Pretty Marie?* Why Pretty Marie?'

'Well, she's been getting a bit flash again lately, has Pretty Marie, putting herself about and that. So listen, you know what a randy old man he is, Twigg the Well Known Playwright, always luring silly young girls over to his flat with the promise of a part in some play of his and then fucking them and that? Disgusting right?'

'Disgusting, I quite agree. But Pretty Marie would never in a month of...'

'*Exactly!* That's the point! I mean, you know how she is, she can't stand nobody over the age of twenty laying a hand on her if it's like social, can't Pretty Marie. She's different if it's like business, of course, but that's her affair.'

'Of course.'

'She'd go bloody *mad*, would Pretty Marie, if an old man like Twigg the Well Known Playwright so much as touched her. I mean he must be forty-five, right?'

'Right.'

'But she wants to be a film star, does Pretty Marie, as we all know, so it was easy enough to get her to go and see him. "Hey, Pretty Marie," I said, "he's writing films now, is Twigg the Well Known Playwright. Why don't you go over to his flat with them nice new photographs of yours? He might give you a part."'

'Terrific.'

'So she's sat there on his sofa thinking she's going to be a film star at last, is Pretty Marie, and Twigg the Well Known

Playwright's looking at himself in the mirror and patting his hair, and he's breathing heavily and hovering over her in a slim-line shirt that's so tight he's purple in the face, is Twigg the Well Known Playwright what with holding his stomach in. And he's got *Songs for Swinging Lovers* on the record player and he's clanking ice-cubes in a vodka and tonic like some finger-clicking old fart from *77 Sunset Strip* or something! Right? Imagine!'

'Priceless! She'll teach him a lesson he'll never forget!'

'Exactly! One false move and she'll *murder* him, will Pretty Marie! Remember what happened to Toby Danvers the Impresario? Six weeks in traction just for putting his hand up her knickers. I mean, she's funny that way, is Pretty Marie.'

'This is tremendous! So what happened?'

'When?'

'*Then.*'

'Oh, he fucked her, did Twigg the Well Known Playwright. Three times. Once on the sofa, then later on the water bed, and then again this morning.'

Hell.

❊　❊　❊

My two correspondents, Dr Bryson and Major Martin Dobson-Smythe have both telephoned me. The Doctor doesn't seem to have been put off by my version of One-Eyed Charlie's letter and we are taking luncheon together on Tuesday week. After the usual deliberations, we decided that the philosophy counter at Hatchards – a particularly poor one, according to the Doctor – would be the best place to meet. I only hope I recognise him. To be arrested for soliciting the wrong philosopher would be most unfortunate. And would such a mishap be an accident or a mistake? I must look up Austin's *A Plea for Excuses*, which contains, I believe, the celebrated passage about shooting the wrong donkey. Austin's point, if I remember it right, was that if you're out donkey shooting and you shoot the wrong donkey, this is a mistake;

but if you're out after partridges and you happen to shoot a donkey, this is an accident. I doubt whether Bryson is of the Oxford ordinary language school, but for all that it's the kind of thing I should be pondering before our meeting.

The struck-off Major sounded rather jolly on the phone (though manifestly crackers) and I've arranged to meet him at the Cavalry Club this Friday.

❊ ❊ ❊

To Thames Television to record *Ideas in Print*. Had lunch first with ·6 of a friend Bassett, who is now working as a director on the Eamon Andrews show. Bill Grundy, he says, is an even bigger ass than he seems on TV. I sought his advice on the line I should take with Mr Nelson and he said: 'Don't worry, they'll tell you exactly what to say.'

After lunch, I was sitting in the make-up chair' being attended to by a sympathetic lady and trying on a selection of wigs, when who should come padding into the room but Mel Brooks. Had it been anyone else I like to think I'd have remained cool, but this particular person caused me to act spontaneously for the first time since I met Len Hutton at the Oval in 1948. Before I had time to correct myself, I leapt out of my chair, knocking over bottles, sprays, lipsticks, hair-pieces and the startled make-up lady, grabbed one of Mr Brooks's paws in both mine and furiously pumped it up and down as though trying to evacuate bilge from the bottom of a boat.

'You,' I said, rather fatuously, 'are the funniest man in the world.'

He seemed to be absolutely delighted.

'Why, that's quite the nicest thing anyone's said to me since I arrived in England. Tell me, who are you?'

Too late. The enormity of what I'd done suddenly over-whelmed me and I hung my head in shame.

'I'm no one,' I muttered, staring at my boots.

'No, come *on*, what's your name?'

'I don't have a name, no name at all. I'm so sorry.' And I retired to the make-up chair in terrible confusion.

I was still pondering the implications of this when I took my place opposite Michael Nelson in the studio. Bassett's reassuring words had led me to expect some kind of gentle knock-up or rehearsal, so I was quite startled when a studio director did a sort of pre-blast off count-down, followed by Michael Nelson sailing straight in with his first question.

'Tell me,' he said, 'what sort of people visit brothels?'

Well, I could hardly say: 'Here, hang about! My ·6 of a friend Bassett led me to believe that you'd give me not only the questions, but the answers too.' So I began to think about it and meanwhile played for time by saying: 'Men mostly.' Ten minutes later I was still rummaging around in the back of my brain for a sensible answer to this very interesting question, when Mr Nelson surprised me by announcing that the interview was over. Then Mr Stancomb came bouncing into the studio to say that we must do it again.

'I wonder,' he said, in a most kindly fashion, 'whether you could try to think just a *little* more quickly. I know it isn't easy.'

I said I'd do my best, and away we went again. This time all was going well, or so it seemed to me, when Mr Nelson asked me – somewhat provocatively, I thought – what opinion I held of Janie Jones. One of the nicest people you could hope to meet, I said. What did I think then, asked Mr Nelson, of her now doing eight years in Holloway even though she'd been acquitted of the main charge of blackmail? Very tough, I said. Five years was a reasonable sentence for something you hadn't done, eight was definitely too stiff.

'Cut!' screamed someone, and once again Mr Stancomb came running into the studio to point out that I couldn't possibly say things like that on television. God knows why not, and *they* brought the subject up. The next time we got it right, but since the questions had hardly changed, I fear my answers may have become a trifle mechanical. It's supposed to go out on May 10th so I'll start kicking up

84

a row with the moral authorities a couple of days before that.

❊　❊　❊

My date with Major Dobson-Smythe at the Cavalry Club. I was about to announce my business to the porter, when who should come trotting towards me across the hall but the game old soldier I met when viewing blue films with Toby Danvers. He seemed to be in better shape than when I'd last seen him.

'My word,' he cried, 'small world!'

'Isn't it? Quite recovered are you?'

He looked thoroughly baffled. 'Quite recovered? I don't get you, old chap. I haven't been poorly.'

'You passed out on the floor,' I said. 'For a moment I thought you'd bought it.'

'Passed out? Got no recollection of that. Probably had one too many. Happens all the time. Can't remember a thing later. Damned embarrassing. Well well well, I think this calls for a drink!'

'That's very good of you, but actually I'm meeting someone.'

'Really? May I ask who?'

'You certainly may. Some old cunt who wants to be a ponce, if you please. Are you a member here by any chance?'

'Of course. Have been for years.'

'Splendid! In that case you probably know him. What a bit of luck. You can point him out to me. Save a lot of time.'

'I'd be delighted to, old chap. What's his name?'

'Major Dobson-Smythe.'

'Dobson-Smythe? *Dobson-Smythe?* Let me think. Hell of a lot of Dobson-Smythes. Any particular christian name?'

'Martin.'

'Martin Dobson-Smythe! By jove, that's me! For my sins. What an extraordinary thing! You'll be William Donaldson. We're meeting here for lunch today, you know. Well I never. Small world. Look, I've booked a table, so why don't we go straight in?'

At the entrance to the dining-room, a crusty little head-waiter, who had the wild look in his eye of a man who'd bayoneted a few fuzzy-wuzzies in his time, arrested me for being out of the rig of the day. This caused me some pain since I'd gone to the trouble of wearing my suit. My offence, apparently, was to be without a tie. After a bit of the usual back and forth, the head-waiter produced a spare one – kept in readiness back-stage, presumably for just such invading scruffs as myself – and I was allowed to join the Major. The incident brought to mind an anecdote of One-Eyed Charlie's, which I was misguided enough to recount now, since it seemed apposite and might make me appear less uncouth. Like so many of One-Eyed Charlie's better stories, it had to do with Wittgenstein and Ryle. Some years ago, Ryle persuaded an extremely reluctant Wittgenstein to catch a train to – of all places – London. As though this wasn't shocking enough in itself, he further insisted that Wittgenstein meet him at his club. Wittgenstein, dressed as usual in beach shoes and an open-neck shirt, presented himself at the appropriate building, only to be denied ingress by an outraged steward who didn't like the cut of his jib at all. Before they could proceed to dinner, Ryle, who was a large man, had to lend Wittgenstein, who was small, one of his suits. The trousers of this were at least a foot too long and in order to walk without tripping himself up, Wittgenstein had to secure them at the knee with a piece of string, like a straw-chewing yokel about to do a barn-dance.

This pleasant example of Ryle's benign insensitivity seemed to leave the Major completely stunned. After staring at me for some time like a fish that's been truncheoned, he pulled himself together and brought up the subject of naughty girls, of whom he appears to know a great many. His plan, he said, was to rent several flats which he would sublet to loose young ladies who hadn't yet discovered how many beans make five.

'What do you think?' he said. 'Make sense to you?'

86

There was no way, as far as I could see, that I could let him down gently. My whole profession was at risk unless well-meaning fools like this were discouraged from entry.

'Quite frankly, Major,' I said, 'I don't think your feet would touch the ground. It would be a mad scramble to see who could collar you first: rival entrepreneurs, smut-hounds from *The News of the World*, or, which would be more expensive, the police. They like their cut, do the police. Look what happened to Bernie Silver.'

'Don't know the fellow. He a Wykehamist too?'

'I don't think so. He had a couple of habits he might have picked up at Harrow though. The point is he took the precaution of employing half Scotland Yard but even with this flying start he's now doing six years down the river.'

The Major looked most crestfallen. 'Oh well,' he said, 'just a *penseé*.'

'On the other hand,' I said, feeling remorseful that I'd been so squashing, 'I could introduce you to my friend S. Z. Corbett. He's much more experienced in this field than I, and the two of you might come to some mutually rewarding arrangement.'

It had suddenly occurred to me that to bring these two together might be quite a laugh. My friend S. Z. Corbett would go through the Major's capital like shit through a goose, and they'd probably be arrested within the week. But it would be a hell of a funny week. The Major and S. Z. Corbett running a bawdy house together would be the most creative piece of casting since Wilson, Keppel and Betty came together, no doubt of that. This was not a particularly responsible attitude on my part, I suppose, but it seemed to me that the Major was old enough to look after himself. Either way, he was touchingly grateful for the suggestion.

'I say, that's fearfully good of you, old chap,' he said. 'I'd like to meet this Corbett fellow very much indeed. I wonder if he could be old Atty Corbett's boy, the race horse trainer. Just a *penséé*.'

'Possibly. He's from Trinidad and Tobago.'

'Black, is he?'

'Pretty black, yes.'

'By jove! What an extraordinary thing. Atty Corbett's boy being black, I mean. Wonder how that happened. Must have got a frightful shock when Mrs Corbett foaled, what? Look here, perhaps I'd better not meet him at the Club. Doubt if they've ever seen a darky in here. Nothing to do with prejudice, but it might cause an incident. Perhaps we could meet at *his* club. Just a *pensée*. Tell you what, get him to give me a ring here or at White's any afternoon. Bound to be at one or the other. We'll fix something up. Okay?'

I agreed to do this, and then the Major brought up the subject of my sister Bobo, with whom I haven't been in touch for ten years now.

'Fine woman, your sister,' he said, 'damn good value. Great friend of Diana's. She's my wife, do you see? For my sins. Why don't you give her a ring? I'm sure she'd be glad to hear from you.'

I might do just that, as it happens, though it will use up a whole week's ration of courage just to get me to the point of picking up the phone. She's got a mind like an X-ray unit, has my sister Bobo, and she can see right through me and out the other side. Still, when last we met I was living in Knightsbridge and putting on plays, so if she's read my book she'll know I've come up in the world since then. Secretly, I want her approval more than anyone's.

'The trouble is her husband,' I said.

'Christopher?'

'That's the fellow, yes. He banned me from his drawing-room several years ago. One day he struck the table and said: "I'm not having that sewer in my house again. Why can't he go and live abroad. Join the drain drain." I thought that was rather funny. The drain drain, I mean.'

'Yes that's not bad for Christopher. I must say your name didn't go down particularly well at his end of the table when I mentioned you over dinner. But I'm sure your sister would be delighted to see you again.'

After lunch the Major stumbled off to the john to pass

however many gin and tonics he'd had before I arrived, together with the half dozen or so double brandies he'd taken on board since then, and I seized the opportunity of stealing a pile of headed writing paper on which I propose to write indignant letters to *The Times*, blowing the whistle on myself and on anyone else who doesn't behave. When the Major reappeared he suggested that we move down the road to White's. I wasn't too struck by this idea and was about to make a suitable excuse, when I realised that some of their writing paper would come in handy too. Outraged members of White's could then write to *The Times*, endorsing the views of Disgusted, The Cavalry Club.

Outside in Piccadilly, the Major, to my dismay, began to wave his umbrella above his head and bellow for a taxi, even though there wasn't one to be seen, for hire or otherwise, within a hundred yards. At Winchester, once you had reached a certain seniority, you could yell 'Boy!' and, no matter where you happened to be, a trembling junior would materialise within seconds at your side, anxious to carry out your most bizarre instruction. Small wonder, perhaps, that public schoolboys of the Major's stripe go through life expecting assistance from an inferior to be as instantly at hand. Much to his surprise, I now made him take a bus: a mode of transport which, judging by his behaviour, he'd never tried before. When the West Indian conductor asked us for our fares, he said:

'Two to White's, Captain, and keep the change.'

White's seems to have a younger, more raffish membership than the Cavalry, which had resembled nothing so much as a run-down embalming parlour. Here, amid the snooker apparatus and little green-topped tables laid out for dreary games of chance, middle-aged cads confused by drink and loss of capital swayed gently on their feet, complaining about 'that bugger Benn'. Benn's the enemy, no doubt of that, and these squalid patricians feel – with justification, I trust – that he's personally out to get them.

I stole some writing paper and a copy of the Club Rules, then hauled myself towards the door and sanity. The Major, who could hardly stand by now, stumbled with me to the exit and called after me down St James's:

'Don't forget to tell the darky to give me a ring!'

S. Z. Corbett is celebrated for his easy-going disposition, but if the Major calls him darky, sooty, Gunga Din, Sambo, coon, jig, moke, dinge, shine, crow, smoke, boogie, ape, jassbo, jigaboo, eightball, seal, jungle bunny, skunk or Zulu to his face, we're going to be short of a valuable new comedy act. This would be regrettable. Really terrific turns don't grow on trees or come out of *Spotlight*, and if you want the best you have to get out and about. If some enterprising talent scout hadn't taken the trouble to go to Bristol years ago, for instance, Peter O'Toole might still be there and the rest of us would have missed a bloody good laugh. This is precisely what Emma Jane fails to understand. She's a marvellous girl, but not being of the live theatre she tends to sneer at the amount of time I waste – as she thinks – talent spotting. No musical evening can be counted a success, in my opinion, without at least one upper-class looney on the bill, and for too long now ours have been lacking in this respect.

❊ ❊ ❊

I received two unpleasant shocks today. Returning some books to the Chelsea library, I happened to spot mine under 'Fiction'. This won't do. Some earnest old Etonian with a tape-recorder talks patronisingly to a few tarts and the results are filed under 'Sociology'! You write the truth and they put it under 'Fiction'. I don't want to make a molehill out of a mountain, but there's something wrong here. I was recovering slowly from this blow to my self-esteem, when I bought *The Evening Standard* and read that no fewer than three hundred and twelve ponces have been arrested in the last year in the Greater London area alone. Why have they left me out? What on earth do you have to do these days to get arrested? It's an intolerable state of affairs, raising serious doubts as to whether the law is being impartially enforced.

Consider the facts. For two years I have been living off the artistic earnings of a courageous little girl, who, while putting up with it, is by no means pleased with the arrangement. I then have the poor taste to write a facetious memoir, in the course of which I confess not only to this offence but to others too: such as conspiring to corrupt the wives of stockbrokers, taking dope, watching too much television and aiding fugitives from justice, not least myself. To ensure absolutely that the authorities take notice, I deliberately cheek Sir Robert Mark, specifically accuse six policemen of serious corruption and at least one Government Minister of immorality, and, just to be on the safe side, call a senior High Court Judge a pig's arse. And what happens? *The Daily Telegraph* says I have a future as a comical writer and Sir Robert Mark, in a letter to a relative, faults my prose style. So what can be the explanation? It certainly isn't that the police cast a benevolent eye on poncing. Unless, it seems, you write your memoirs. My colleagues, who failed in this respect and who now, thanks to this oversight, are in the boob, would no doubt testify to this.

My legal adviser, John Mortimer Q.C., has suggested that I take out a private prosecution against myself, having first detained myself under the correct citizen's arrest procedures. That's fair enough, but with me prosecuting I'd probably lose. Or do I mean win?

❊　❊　❊

Rang my sister Bobo at her country seat in Berkshire. She sounded slightly off (or 'orf', actually) which wasn't so surprising, perhaps, after ten years' silence. After a bit of tentative back and forth, she suddenly shifted her weight the merest fraction of an inch and squashed me as flat as a dab.

'I read the book.' She invested the words with a note of pained forbearance as in 'I did the house-work' and followed them with a terrible pause, cruelly held.

'Yes?' Heart thumping like a road drill.

'Yes. *Quite* amusing, but . . .'

91

Another pause, more terrible even than the first. I'm set up like the last pin in a bowling alley, but I can take it.

'But what?'

'It's just... no, I mustn't say it.'

'You bloody well must.'

'It's just – oh, I don't know – but why did you have to write the beastly thing *now*? I mean, all that cheeky thrashing around and desire to shock would have been all right when you were nineteen, say, but now it's – well – *embarrassing*. Don't be cross now.'

Nice one Bobo. Quite amusing but infantile. Fair do's, I suppose, but I fought back: not something I always do with Bobo.

'Well,' I said, 'at least Tynan liked it.'

I knew this was a mistake as soon as I said it. There was a slight pause, followed by curious explosive noise, hard to define precisely, a cross between a loud raspberry and a squeal of rage, like two pigs under a gate. One way or another, Tynan and I were blown together by this derisive snort into some infantile and despicable limbo.

'I'm not surprised!' she said.

In spite of this, I've agreed to visit her tomorrow at her home near Sunningdale.

❧   ❧   ❧

Delightful day in the country with my sister Bobo. Arrived at Sunningdale station with half an hour to spare. Lived here until I was eighteen. Not at the station, but at a suitable villa near the golf course and then – a move to outshine my parents' friends – at a vast Victorian folly which had recently been a country club with sixteen bedrooms (each with a bath *en suite*) and fourteen acres through which I and Jeremy Pinkney used to prowl with small-bore shot-guns killing things.

Wandered round for half an hour sampling the security I've not known since. Felt vaguely Larkinish and sad. Everything changed for the worse. Beatty's, the coffee-shop where well-born ladies of a certain age had once mourned the death of Leslie Howard, now a Chinese take-away. Saxby's, the honest neighbourhood car dealer from whom, to my father's great dismay, I bought (with two weeks' pocket money) a Triumph sports car even though I couldn't drive, gone completely. And Mr Lee the friendly greengrocer, who during the war had come to an under-the-counter accommodation with my mother whereby her little boy received more than his fair share of citrus fruits, now a heartless supermarket.

Back in the station yard a frightful honking announced the arrival of Bobo. An assertive woman, my sister Bobo, and that she's a honker came as no surprise. In a shooting-brake, of course, and with the youngest of her brood of five, Claudia, aged eleven. Never met Claudia before. A nice little girl with excellent manners. Bobo introduced me to her as 'your wicked Uncle Willie'. I see. At my suggestion, we set off on a nostalgic tour of early haunts. First to the golf course. Parked the car at the second hole and walked. Bobo, swinging a stick, strode ahead barking. Doubt if she'd have much time for light-weights or woolly-minded liberals, my sister Bobo. We came to the house where I was born and peered at the garden through the hedge. Gone, mysteriously, were the verandah steps down which Bobo tipped me in my pram aged one. I hit my head on concrete, which accounts, I've always thought, for my difficulties with mathematics, and much else too. The dug-out in which we hid on noisy nights from Jerry was now a bank of roses. I reminded Bobo of the night Jerry scored a bull's-eye with a doodlebug on the house next door, blowing old Mrs Huggins out of her bath and onto Colonel MacCracker's croquet lawn. Our chauffeur, Saunders, thinking the invasion had come at last, grabbed one of my father's shotguns and stationed himself at the dug-out's entrance.

'The Hun will get at you and the children over my dead body, ma'am,' he said.

And he meant it. An entire panzer division under Von Rundstedt could have emerged from the rhododendron bushes and Saunders would have stood there potting at them. They don't make them like Saunders any more. At the first general election after the war he voted Labour and my mother sacked him on the spot for gross ingratitude to Churchill. Quite right too.

These insistent potent memories caused a dull sense of loss. A sudden desire to be tucked up safely in bed on a fine summer evening, being gently lulled to sleep by reassuring Dornford Yates-like noises floating up from the garden. My mother and father enjoying a late, undemanding set of tennis with their friends Daph and Gee Pinkney. The happy clink of ice in Pimms and ping of ball on Maxply Dunlop. A burst of happy laughter following a cross-court jest by Daph. Daph was a wit, still is for all I know.

'How lucky you are,' I said, 'to be married with children,' thinking that through them she could re-live the innocence of childhood.

'Rubbish!' she barked. 'It's not on. The perspective's different. Not surprisingly. Anyway, you're married and a father too. Pull yourself together.'

This hadn't occurred to me, I must admit. Then she gave me the disturbing news that my son Charles is at Eton, together with the still more disturbing news that he shows special aptitude in the gymnasium and on the running track. He's up a rope, it seems, like a ferret with piles. Fathers shouldn't interfere, God knows, but I may have to look into this.

Back to Shooters Lodge, Bobo's country seat, for lunch. A nice house with suitable improvements since the date of purchase. Heated swimming pool, hard tennis court, field for donkeys. Met two of her sons, Simon and Tom, both currently at Harrow, but poised and charming for all that. Really extremely nice boys. 'This is your wicked Uncle Willie' stuff again. Over lunch, much talk of money and how hard-pressed everyone is. Flat to the boards in fact, thanks to 'that bugger Benn'. Bobo's had to give up *The Sunday Times*. It's enough to break your heart. Suddenly Bobo said:

'Leave the room children, I want to have a word in private with your wicked Uncle Willie.'

Christ, what was this? On the carpet for some old offence,

or something new? The children trooped out obediently and I began to shake.

'I'm most concerned,' said Bobo sternly, 'about your having met Major Dobson-Smythe.'

'You know about it then?'

'Yes, he's admitted everything. And his poor wife Diana can't sleep at nights with worry.'

'Good lord, why's that?'

'Now don't be silly, you know perfectly well why. God knows the terrible things you may get up to. And Diana's a JP.'

'Oh come now, you really mustn't concern yourself. What possible harm can come of it?'

'A very great deal. People can get led astray, you know. Especially the weak-willed. I want you to promise me that you won't see the Major again.'

This made me cross. A certain amount of sisterly concern was to be expected, but I didn't come down in the last shower exactly and the suggestion that I was weak-willed I found offensive.

'Now look here,' I said, 'I agree that the Major's a bit of a rascal but I've remained utterly unviolated by far wickeder men than him. Good heavens, I was once within spitting distance of Lord Hailsham at a cocktail party and he...'

'I'm not worried about *you*, you fool, I'm worried about the *Major*.'

Light dawned. She actually thought that *I* might be a bad influence on *him!* The notion was so far-fetched that I'm afraid I began to laugh. Then I explained carefully that while the Major was certainly not an irredeemably evil man himself, his friends and associates, whom I'd seen at play only the previous Friday, very definitely were. That her younger brother had come into contact with such riff-raff should cause her deep concern, I said. No go, she couldn't see it; indeed she assumed that I was being facetious. What could I do? It had been so long since I had moved in circles where being a pusher of stocks and shares or alcohol or index-linked funeral schemes counted for more than running a brothel – indeed

95

I assumed that such circles no longer existed – that I couldn't be fished to rehearse the old decisive arguments.

There was a last day of the hols outing to London planned, which suited me well since it involved my getting a lift home. Just before it was time to leave, Gerard, Bobo's eldest son, appeared on a motorbike. Like his brothers, absolutely charming. Currently a waiter at a Maidenhead hotel owing to a spot of career confusion. Bobo very worried about this. 'Completely aimless,' she barked, when he was out of the room for a minute. In fact he's one of the sanest people I've met in a long time, and I said as much to Bobo. She let fly with one of her contemptuous snorts and I fear that approval from me will have done his cause no good.

Passing Windsor Castle on the way back to London, I was stirred to mention something that has been puzzling me for some time. Do the Windsors, outside of the formal game they've agreed to play, think of themselves as *naturally* royal? The poet Mary Wilson is in no doubt:

> She notes a crumbling wall, an open gate;
> With countrywoman's eyes she views the scene;
> Yet, walking free upon her own estate –
> Still, in her solitude, she is the Queen.

'I wonder,' I was foolish enough to say to Bobo, 'whether the Royal family think of themselves as essentially worthy of respect, that it's their natural due on account of unique, separating qualities of birth? Or do they break up behind the backs of fawning courtiers? Sane people, after all, couldn't be sir'd and madam'd for more than a few minutes except in very ritualised circumstances, such as when acting in a play.'

'Hold your tongue!' roared Bobo. 'How dare you! Of course they think respect's their natural due, as indeed it is. My goodness me, I expect a certain recognition of my status, so how much stronger this feeling will be with them.'

'Great heavens, do you mean that you expect – both in the descriptive and prescriptive sense – some acknowledgement by the lower orders of your superior station?'

'Indeed I do.'

'And familiarity from a worker would embarrass you?'

'Most certainly.'

I hadn't heard such talk in years, and coming from my sister Bobo! She's a smashing person, mind, just as my mother was, and that's the paradox.

❧ ❧ ❧

Lunch with Dr Bryson. I got to Hatchards early and wondered whether to call on Lord Dynevor, who is working as a salesman in the children's department. He plans to open a bookshop himself and he's here for a couple of months to discover how it's done. It was a bit close when he arrived for work last Monday, so he threw open a window and half a hundredweight of books newly delivered by Collins fell two storeys onto the passers-by in Piccadilly. He got blown up by Mr Giddy and was docked a week's wages. Since he is not being paid anyway, this is not so serious, but I didn't call on him now, lest the shock of seeing me startle him into another mishap.

Dr Bryson is perfectly correct about the Philosophy Department not being up to scratch. Indeed, I'd go so far as to say that it doesn't have to do with philosophy at all, being devoted, it seems, to the reflections of Indian gentlemen who spend their days (if the dust-jackets are to be believed) balanced on their heads in their underwear playing the banjo. When he arrived, Dr Bryson agreed with this assessment.

'It's as if John Lennon were the buyer,' he said.

Except that he's got a beard like W. G. Grace, the Doctor looks like the cleverest boy in the sixth form, blinking with hurt surprise at the unthinking rowdiness of those around him. He has a charming, diffident, bird-like manner and a careful way of expressing himself, which entails many fastidious qualifying clauses and stinging parentheses. When I described Malcolm Muggeridge – rather loosely – as seemingly determined to spend his declining years playing the village idiot, he picked me up rather sharply.

'Paradoxically – though not in any formal sense, of course – from the fact that you're playing the village idiot it doesn't follow that you're not the village idiot. Or does it? I'll have to think about this. In fact, if "playing" in this context is synonymous with "pretending to be" then I think it does follow. Unless you were suffering from amnesia, you could hardly pretend to be what you already are. I mean, what sense would one make of my saying "I'm pretending to be Dr Bryson"? I withdraw what I said originally. From the fact that you're playing the village idiot, it follows necessarily – unless you've received a crack on the head – that you're not the village idiot.'

Thank goodness we got that cleared up, even though it seemed to let Malcolm Muggeridge off the hook.

Over lunch, he was most interesting, *à propos* his book on Popper, about the pressure put on teachers to publish. Just as promotion in the police force is geared to the successful arrests criterion, so academics who seek advancement *have* to publish. The Doctor described this as a kind of reverse censorship. I then asked him whether he ever fancied his students, and when he said he did, I told him, as a cautionary tale, of the untidy end to my own teaching career.

Soon after I married Mrs Mouse, the bottom unexpectedly fell out of my business as a visiting masseur and I was forced to seek other employment. After a bit of this and that, I took a job at an establishment in Maida Vale cramming the over-privileged offspring of Golders Green merchants in 'A' level English, History and British Constitution. I found myself at a certain disadvantage in that History wasn't really my thing and I'd never even heard of British Constitution. Indeed, if challenged in the street I'd have said there wasn't one. Stumped for much to say, I used to while away the long school hours trying to pull Miss Osband, a charming young lady of sixteen. 'Right,' I'd say, 'today we're going to have a general knowledge quiz. First prize will be lunch with Sir at the Caprice.' I'd then go round the room asking swinishly difficult questions until I got to Miss Osband. She wasn't a particularly bright girl, but the posers I set her were so

98

simple – 'What's your name?', 'Where do you live?', 'What's the capital of England?', 'What's your telephone number?', that sort of thing – that she usually managed to get about ninety per cent, which was eighty-nine more than she needed to be declared the winner. Alas, she had an admirer in the class, a disagreeable young thug who became pissed off at the number of lunches Sir had swung with his beloved. In an attempt to tip the balance in his favour, he first tried threats, taking out his flick-knife and using it in a most ominous way to manicure his finger nails before stabbing it suddenly into the top of his desk. When this failed to warn me off, the young blighter stooped so low as to sneak on me to the Head.

'I'm not learning anything, sir,' he said, 'because Mr Donaldson is too busy getting busy with Miss Osband, sir.'

I denied the allegation, of course, but the Head, a silly old goat if ever I saw one, took it upon himself to believe the young criminal and he fired me on the spot. Dr Bryson was duly impressed by this sad tale and he promised to keep to philosophy.

❋   ❋   ❋

After lunch I took him back to the flat, where to my pleasure he hit it off nicely with Emma Jane, despite her reservations about the intelligentsia in general and philosophers in particular.

'Now look here, Emma Jane,' he said, 'I may be educated, but I'm not stupid,' and he immediately proved the fact by teaching her the rudiments of symbolic logic in five minutes flat. Having caught her attention by saying that the propositions he intended to encode schematically for greater elegance were 'All philosophers are wankers' and 'All pussy cats are perfect', he took a large student note-pad out of his brief-case and said:

'Ignoring the propositional calculus for the moment...'

'That's a blessing.'

99

'Please don't interrupt, Emma Jane, or we'll get nowhere. As I was saying, we'll ignore the propositional calculus for the moment and concentrate on quantification theory. First taking a universal statement such as "All men are mortal"...'

'Oh *really*,' said Emma Jane, 'you academics and your sweeping generalisations!'

I thought this was rather nice, but the doctor looked displeased.

'Oh dear,' he said. 'All right, moving onto less controversial ground, we can supply a formal proof of a proposition asserting the perfection of your magnificent Siamese cat, Bernard Blue, as follows:

$$(x) \ (Px \supset Ax)$$
$$Pb$$
$$\therefore Ab$$

where $P$ is a pussy cat, $A$ is perfect and $b$ is Bernard Blue.'

'I see,' said Emma Jane. 'Now, could we have that in plain English?'

'Certainly. The symbols stand for: For all $x$ if $x$ is a pussy cat $x$ is perfect. Bernard Blue is a pussy cat. Therefore Bernard Blue is perfect.'

'Oh I *do* like that,' said Emma Jane, quite enthralled now. She pondered the matter for a while and then said: 'Do you mean that the formal proof of "Dr Bryson is a wanker" – no offence intended – would be:

$$(x) \ (Px \supset Wx)$$
$$Pd$$
$$\therefore Wd$$

where $P$ is a philosopher, $W$ is a wanker and $d$ is Dr Bryson?'

'You've *got* it!' said the Doctor. 'That's really very good.'

＊ ＊ ＊

Later that night I got very blocked and had an agreeable summing-up session in the bath. Where am I at? I've achieved one important stage in my development, it seems to me, in that I no longer do anything I don't want to do. This is progress. The trouble is I don't do anything I do want to do either. It's the case that I've cut out lunch with film producers, dinner parties with married couples, keeping gin in a cupboard for visiting advertising agents, talking to dogs, drunks and children, visiting the theatre and worrying about what's to be done with Bill Grundy and Jean Rook. But what sane man didn't cut out all these things, and a lot else too, long since? And what do I do instead? Nothing. I'm too old to settle down yet and my present dream is to live with another mature party in a style suitable for single gentlemen. We'd share a colour supplement penthouse in the S.W.3 postal district, in which my quarters (bedroom and study) and his (the same) would be far enough apart for privacy (mine, not his: he'd be instantly at hand if needed). He'd be of a vaguely artistic cast of mind, a writer perhaps, or some sort of painter fellow, but not doing too well, since I wouldn't want to feel insecure. After a communal breakfast on one of the balconies (fresh orange juice, croissants and coffee) we'd each retire to our own quarters to work on some serious and important undertaking. At one o'clock I'd trot off to have lunch with Sir Hermann Bondi, say, or, on frivolous, lighthearted days, Jonathan Miller, and at 2.30 I'd be back at my desk for a further session of serious, important work. At five o'clock I'd take tea and toast with the other old fruit, followed by a gradual wind-down and civilised conversation (Harold Nicholson and Vita come to mind, as do the Woolfs) about the day's work. After a light but pleasant dinner which would appear as if by magic at eight o'clock, the lights would fade of their own accord to an erotic amber, the soft drugs would come out of their hiding place, the other old fruit would be shut away in his quarters, and through the door would float a *corps de ballet* of certifiably vacuous sex objects, who, speechless and unprompted (a religious silence is so important at such times), would proceed to divert me with every lewd practice in the book. At 2 a.m. they'd float away as mysteriously as they'd arrived, and I'd retire alone to bed for eight hours guiltless sleep.

What could be nicer than that? There's a snag, however.

I have worked out that it would cost not less than £50,000 a year after tax to finance this extremely sensible life-style. In the past three years I have grossed (apart from what I call invisible earnings, e.g. rent-free accommodation, a small dress allowance and mad money from Emma Jane) exactly £770, made up as to:

| | |
|---|---|
| Advance from Talmy Franklin against royalties | £500 |
| Advance from Ken Tynan re sale of stage rights | . £250 |
| Fee from Sikh for immorality with mistress . . | £20 |

This amounts, as I see it, to a gross annual income of £257, which falls a trifle short of the required figure. Either I must give up all thoughts of achieving the only life-style I'd find acceptable, or I must get my skates on.

My entire output for the last eighteen months consists of one television play, which took me a whole day to write and which I judge to be excellent. It deals amusingly, or so it seems to me, with a daring escape from a P.O.W. camp in which all the guards are women. (The assumption is that the sex war suddenly boiled over and that the men lost.) The prison Commandant is pure marshmallow, a romantic Barbara Cartlandish old tart, ruling with a rod of love; her second-in-command is a somewhat brisker lady of Mrs Thatcher's stripe; and each unfortunate prisoner has a loving personal guard called Fiona, Hilary or Pamela. Attempts to escape from this hell have always been foiled in the past by such ruses as bursting into tears and statements of the order of: 'But I thought you said you loved me! Boo Hoo!' Suddenly the prisoners can stand it no longer and the SBM (*Senior British Male*) forms a new escape committee. Plans are drawn up for a daring break-out, but alas there's a fifth columnist in the prisoners' midst and he rats on the others to his personal guard. She goes straight to the Commandant, who, clever old girl that she is, resolves to teach her ungrateful charges a lesson they'll never forget. She allows them to escape, but so fixes things that they tunnel their way into a nearby fantasy pleasure palace, where a team of disorderly sirens offer them all the loveless delights ever dreamed up in the over-heated minds of thwarted men. Such unaccustomed, stark eroticism shocks them into petrified impotency. They turn away in terror and, like whipped dogs, slink back to the unconfusing familiarity of their personal guards, whimpering 'I love you!' and 'I'll never leave you again!' I made the mistake of showing this to Emma Jane. She read it as though she had a kipper under her nose and then ruled it 'childish'. So I tore it up.

What then can I expect by way of income from *Both the Ladies and the Gentlemen*? Eff all if Mike Franklin M.A. is to be believed, which I don't suppose he is. Its sales bear little relation to those of hot cakes and no one wants the paperback rights. (The serious houses, oddly enough, judge it to be insufficiently salacious, and the salacious houses find it lacking in seriousness.) So it's all up to Clive James, as I see it, and he's doubtless got problems of his own. I'll ring him tomorrow none the less. 'My future's in your hands, dear,' I'll say. I hope he doesn't buckle under the strain. Emma Jane's earned a rest, God knows, and anyway she's far too busy with her own literary career to subsidise mine by entertaining men. Last week I caught her leaving the flat at 12.30 wearing her best hat.

'Off to see John from the North?' I asked hopefully.

'Certainly not,' she said. 'It so happens that I'm being lunched by Secker and Warburg.'

'Rosenthal?'

'Gesundheit.'

Now I'm getting nervous.

❈  ❈  ❈

Lunch with Major Dobson-Smythe. It seems he had a most fruitful production meeting yesterday with my friend S. Z. Corbett, in the course of which he shrewdly appointed Corbett as his business manager. The Major turns out to be a member of Lloyds and he has just received gooses from that source to the tune of £4000. Not wishing to see this handy sum vanish into a deep overdraft, he has resolved, following a sensible suggestion by S. Z. Corbett, to start a fun portfolio of high yield investments, controlled by Corbett and spread as to: £1000 in the management of naughty girls, £1000 in the distribution of soft drugs, £1000 in scrap metal and £1000 in bent transistor radios. Who knows from transistor radios and scrap metal? But naughty girls and soft drugs are more my thing and their plans under these two headings sound interesting.

It so happens that the Major's on the organising committee of a Regimental dinner to be held next month at the Savoy. At S. Z. Corbett's suggestion, he now proposes to book a large suite upstairs on the same night, whither, after a hortatory speech by Earl Mountbatten of Burma no less, the sozzled Lancers will repair for more informal fun. Here, S. Z. Corbett, in a monkey jacket and at his most obsequious, will be waiting with further refreshments and a dozen or so of naughty girls. What with all the wallets, gold cigarette cases, credit cards and regimental cuff-links lying around the room, this should be a profitable night for S. Z. Corbett and his team of naughty girls, but the soft drugs scheme sounds even jollier. S. Z. Corbett is to purchase, at wholesale prices, two monkeys worth of grass, which will be stored, pending distribution at street level, either in the Major's garden or in his private locker at the Cavalry Club. The temptation to have the Cavalry Club turned over by the law will be considerable, but I shall resist it. Probably.

'What's your reaction?' asked the Major. 'Sound sensible to you? One has to be a bit unorthodox these days, thanks to that bugger Benn. Damned if I'll give up my standard of living to please him. As far as I'm concerned, anything goes.'

'It certainly does. My philosophy precisely.'

'You can't spot any loose ends, then? Must get the admin right. Diana, that's my wife, is a JP, do you see? Damn awkward for her if I got arrested with a darky. Nothing to do with prejudice, but damn awkward.'

'Of course.'

'You think we'll make money, then?'

'A fortune. No doubt about it.'

'Good show.'

❊ ❊ ❊

A row, as Malcolm Muggeridge once observed (though there may be some truth in it for all that) is never about what it's about. Emma Jane and I were waiting for our dinner guests, Shirley the Perfect Secretary and Gregg in Computers, to arrive last night, when we suddenly had a tremendous misunderstanding about her trading under my name. We were chatting of this and that, when she let slip the information that she occasionally calls herself Mrs Donaldson when doing business. I said that this was a bloody silly thing to do, or words to that effect, whereupon her lower lip started to tremble dangerously. Deliberately mistaking the grounds for my objection, she leapt to the assumption that I didn't like her trying to pass as my wife. Which – since I'm happily married to Mrs Mouse – is perfectly true, but that wasn't the point now.

'Why *shouldn't* I call myself Mrs Donaldson?' she said. 'You call yourself Mr Crampton.'

'What! Never!'

'You *do*.'

'When?'

'The other day, in the newsagent. You were ordering the papers and when they said "What name?" you said "Crampton".'

'I didn't say *my* name was Crampton. I told them to put the order in that name so that you'd get the bill.'

'Oh yes, you make bloody certain that I get all the bills. You're happy to use my name to ensure *that*.'

Now what on earth did this have to do with what we were talking about? I pointed out that while I had no objection to her using my name at any other time, it was absolutely the wrong name under which to do business. Names were as important in real life as they were in novels, I explained,

105

and 'Mrs Donaldson' simply didn't have a promising ring to it in this context. What hope would there be for an artiste who put up a card in a tobacconist's window saying: 'Lovely young model. Full theatrical wardrobe and large chest for sale. Ring 354 9689 and ask for Mrs Donaldson'? And would it be sensible for Dawn Upstairs to ring a client with the exciting news that she was coming over with 'Four delightful girls: Pretty Marie, Mitzi the Japanese Masseuse, French Simone and Mrs Donaldson'?

It simply wasn't on. Names had to conjure up the right image. For the Commissioner of Police, say, to trade as 'Gorgeous George' or 'The Masked Strangler' would be as self-defeating as for an all-in wrestler to call himself 'Sir Robert Mark'. And a naughty girl trading as Mrs Donaldson could expect to do about as well as a firm of solicitors foolish enough to set up shop as 'Miss Whiplash & Co'.

'You're ashamed of me and that's all there is to it,' said Emma Jane, and she allowed the tears that had been threatening for the last ten minutes to well up out of her eyes and down her cheeks.

I gathered her into my manly arms, of course, and had gone some way towards comforting her, when Shirley the Perfect Secretary and her young man Gregg in Computers arrived at our front door, accompanied – to my incredulity, but as though it was the most natural thing in the world – by their son Horace, aged two and a half. What's the world coming to?

Shirley – about whom Dawn Upstairs once observed that since becoming pregnant she'd had to give up work and had gone back to being a secretary – is now on the game once more, but Gregg in Computers, who's got short hair and smiles all the time and is presumed, therefore, to be straight, isn't supposed to know. In my opinion he's been in full possession of the facts all along, but has wisely feigned ignorance. Were he to admit knowledge of what's going on, Shirley, with the characteristic contrariness of her sex, would become hysterical and demand to be told why, if he loved her, he hadn't stopped her. Meanwhile she operates behind an

106

elaborate net-work of alibis, aliases and code-words, none of which would fool anyone who hadn't chosen to be fooled.

The most far-fetched of these alternative identities, but one which has provided us with a useful new euphemism for immorality, is that of flat-racing buff. Having genuine occasion early on in their relationship to visit her ailing granny, Shirley said to Gregg in Computers 'I'm off to Newmarket', offering, as is the way when acting innocently, no additional explanatory details. Gregg in Computers accepted this story without question, and the next time she left the house at an unusual hour, dressed as though to take part in the cabaret at a Berlin brothel, he looked up from *The Journal of Computer Analysts* and said:

'Off to Newmarket?'

Shirley the Perfect Secretary, who was teetering towards the door in a black plastic skirt slit to the suspender belt, fish-net stockings and shoes with eight inch heels, was so surprised that she said:

'Yes I am, as it happens.'

'Put a couple of bob on something for me, would you?' said Gregg, and then he went back to reading *The Journal of Computer Analysts*.

At ten o'clock in the evening? If further proof were needed that Gregg in Computers knows exactly what's going on under his nose, this incident, as far as I'm concerned, would have provided it. We are now so accustomed to referring to tricks as 'going to Newmarket' that when Emma Jane's mum rang last week to speak to her, I said, without thinking, 'I'm afraid she's gone to Newmarket' and then had to spend the next twenty minutes discussing the runners and riders.

The shock of my evening going for six thanks to the un-welcome presence of young Horace, coming on top of my upsetting quarrel with Emma Jane, put me in such a gloomy mood that I sulked throughout dinner. When we had finished, I switched on *That's Life*, hoping that Esther's leery puns would terrify Horace out of his wits. In fact it sent him to sleep, whereupon Shirley the Perfect Secretary said:

'Oh dear, Horace seems to be quite done in. Do you think I could pop him into your bed?'

Why couldn't they take the little bugger home? I was about to suggest as much, when Emma Jane said, 'Of course,' and led Shirley and Horace through to the master-bedroom. When they returned to the living room, Shirley said with a gay laugh:

'I hope he doesn't wet the bed! He sometimes does, I'm afraid. Ha! Ha!'

Emma Jane looked rather faint, but I assumed that this was some sort of joke. It was not possible, I decided, even in these liberated times, that an Ordinary Mother would encourage her child to piss in a gentleman's bed. So I put the matter from my mind. Half an hour later Shirley went to have a look at him.

'Oh my!' she called out cheerfully, 'he *has* wet the bed! I said he might! *Poor* little fellow.'

Scarcely credible! Still less credible, however, was the total lack of embarrassment forthcoming from Shirley the Perfect Secretary or Gregg in Computers. While Emma Jane struggled to turn the mattress and make up the bed with clean sheets, they beamed with fatuous parental pride and, for all the world as though *Horace* might have had a nasty shock, comforted the little swine. And, when Emma Jane had finished making up the bed, Shirley said 'that's better' and *popped him back between the sheets*. That did it. Remembering a trick of old Lord Home's, I switched out all the lights by cutting the supply at the mains and locked myself in the literary room. It was some comfort to me, at least, to hear our guests' feeble cries for help as they staggered around in the dark and fell over the furniture in their painful search for the front door.

Two extraordinary telephone conversations with Michael Winner. He's just read my book and now he says he wants to film it. Michael is sweet, but too unassertive for his own good. In the past he's allowed people – including me, to my eternal shame – to walk all over him. The feeling in the business has always been that if he'd had the drive to match his great artistry, goodness knows where he might have ended up. Aware at last, however, of the muffled nature of his personality, he's now taken the sensible step of fixing an amplification device to his telephone, which has the distressing effect of reproducing his voice in booming stereo in your apartment. Furthermore, he has perfected the disconcerting tactic of repeating, in a voice of outraged incredulity, the last thing you said. This gives him time to think up an answer and also makes your remark – duly amplified and left echoing in the air – sound exceptionally foolish. I thanked him for his interest and then explained mildly that Mr Tynan had the rights, whereupon he started to bellow at me.

'Tynan got the rights?' he roared. '*Tynan* got the rights? Nonsense! I've never heard anything so silly. How can Tynan have the rights? What's going on here?'

'He bought them.'

'*Bought* them? What do you mean bought them? How much for?'

'Mmmmmand fifty pounds.'

'What? Speak up, my dear, I can't hear a word you're saying.'

'Two hundred and fifty pounds.'

'What! *Two* hundred and fifty pounds? For two hundred and fifty pounds you shouldn't have lunch with him. You've been done, my dear. Have you got a contract?'

'Um.'

'Um? *Um?* No good umming, my dear. Where is it?'

'Somewhere.'

'Somewhere? *Somewhere?* Do me a favour! Where?'

'Here.'

'Right. That's something, I suppose. I'll have a look at it. See how we can break it.'

'But Michael, I ...'

'Never mind that. I'll send my driver straight over for it. What's your address?'

'But Michael, I don't think I can ...'

'Look, stop messing me around, my dear, I'm a very busy man. In an hour I'm lunching with Lew and Leslie Grade. Both personal friends of mine. What's your address?'

I gave him my address and quarter of an hour later his chauffeur was at our front door. Within half an hour, Winner was back on the phone.

'Well, you've been done, my dear, just as I said. Tynan hasn't got the film rights.'

'What? But he ...'

'Never mind the but he. He hasn't got the film rights and that's all there is to it. The contract refers only to dramatic rights and under the Copyright Act 1956 a cinematograph film is specifically excluded from the definition of "dramatic work". So he hasn't got the film rights and there's an end to the matter.'

'But he *thinks* he's got the film rights and ...'

There was a curiously ear-splitting noise at the other end of the line: something between a gasp of pain and an insistent hiss like a saucepan of milk boiling over.

'*Thinks* he's got them? *Thinks* he's got them? Since when did thinking you've got the rights in something give you those rights? *Thinks* he's got them! Do me a favour, my dear! Hullo! *Hullo!* Where the hell have you gone?'

I recovered the receiver with some reluctance. 'But Michael, I still think that ...'

'Don't think, my dear. Have you got an agent?'

'No. Sorry.'

'Right, you need an agent. I'll fix you up with Jonathan Clowes. He's got a lot of good writers. I'm always using them. I can't think of their names right now, but I'm sure I'm always using them.'

'Perhaps he won't wish to take me on.'

'*What! Won't wish to take you on?* My dear, I'll *instruct* him to take you on.'

110

'Of course. Sorry.'

'Have you got a lawyer?'

'Not at the moment. I have had, of course.'

'Well, you're going to need one again, that's for sure! Oh dear me, this is very good. Do you know Michael Rabin?'

'Alas, no.'

'Right, he'll do. I'll instruct him to take you on. Knows a certain amount of law. My dear, this is going to be a *lot* of fun!'

'But Michael, Tynan's been very helpful. When I needed encouragement he...'

'Encouragement? *Encouragement?* Does encouragement give him the rights? Can you bank encouragement? Look my dear, if you want encouragement, I'll give you encouragement! Well done! Good work! Keep it up! There, is that better? Will you be eating better tonight? Will encouragement pay the rent? *Encouragement!*'

'But Clive James and...'

'Who?'

'Clive James.'

'Who the hell's Clive James? Television critic isn't he?'

'Yes and he's...'

'What's he got to do with it? Has he been encouraging you too?'

'He's adapting it for the stage and...'

'What! A television critic? What does he know from writing plays?'

'He's a poet too and...'

'A poet! My life! So I'm sure he writes lovely poetry. Full marks to him. A poet! Look, if it was Alan Ayckbourn encouraging you I'd be impressed. A poet!'

'But I need Tynan and...'

'Need them? *Need* them? What are you talking about? My dear, *they* need *you*, believe me! They haven't got a brothel behind them!'

Oh dear, what a pickle. Winner phoned three more times, instructing me that I have a meeting with Mr Rabin next

111

Tuesday, and one with Mr Clowes a week later. He further instructed me that I am lunching with him this Sunday. I'm delighted by his interest, of course, and that the film rights in the book might be worth something is as pleasing as it is surprising. But how can I possibly pull the rug out from under Tynan and James? Whatever the contract may say, it was certainly their intention to acquire the film rights along with the stage rights, and I can hardly take advantage of what appears to be a slip by their agent. It's not that I'm more honourable than Winner – alas, the reverse is probably the case – merely that I'm a coward. Whereas he could get on the phone to Tynan and say, roughly, 'I've got bad news for you, my dear! Your agent's made a blunder!', I prefer to weasel around behind a person's back. It's important to me that people think I'm nice and for reasons of my own I feel that they are more likely to do so if I trip them up when they're least expecting it. Eyeball to eyeball confrontations bring on my ulcer pains. Apart from which, there seems to me a strong likelihood that Tynan won't go ahead with a stage production unless he's got the film rights. And on the whole I'd rather it was staged than filmed. This is precisely the sort of situation I prefer to avoid. Perhaps my Mr Clowes (not that he is yet) will be able to sort it out.

❊ ❊ ❊

Lunch with Michael Winner. I had assumed that this would be an occasion for grown-ups only, so when he arrived to pick me up, Emma Jane was still tucked away in bed. He had brought with him, however – as a kind of film director's obligatory accessory, I suppose – a very pretty blonde model girl.

'Now then, my dear,' he said as he strode through the front door, 'what's going on here?' He was wearing riding boots, and carried a megaphone. 'Where's Emma June?'

'Jane.'

'And her.'

'In bed.'

'What! In *bed*? Where's the bedroom? Never mind, I'll find it.'

After banging about for a bit, opening and closing doors, offering criticism here and there ('Nice to see someone isn't bothering to keep up with the Jones's,' was one of his observations), he found the room he was looking for and strode in.

'I'm Michael Winner,' he announced. 'What's going on here? Look lively, we're off to lunch in a minute.'

While Emma Jane cowered in bed, he walked round the room opening and closing all the drawers, examining their contents and looking for Arabs in the wardrobe. Not everyone could get away with such behaviour but Winner's confidence is so disarming that his most outlandish procedures seem quite harmless. Satisfied at last that nothing was being concealed from him that shouldn't have been, he returned to the living-room. At that moment the phone rang.

'I'll take that,' he said. 'Hullo. This is Michael Winner speaking. What? No, I'm afraid you can't talk to her now, we're just going out to lunch. Good-bye.'

'Who was that?'

'How the hell do I know? It wasn't for me.'

That made sense.

'Tell me something,' said Winner. 'You remember that car I sold you? How much did you get for it? Come on now, I want the truth?'

Twelve years ago he instructed me to purchase his smart white sports car, and I obliged, of course, even though I naturally had a smart white sports car of my own. I gave him the eight hundred pounds he demanded, drove the car round the corner and sold it for five hundred pounds to a dealer. He must have been in a turmoil of worry ever since, wondering whether I might have made a profit on the transaction.

'Seven hundred and fifty pounds,' I said.

'You should have got more, my dear,' he said, but he was beaming with relief.

Once Emma Jane was up and dressed, he took us to that

113

nasty Italian place in Romilly Street, where film producers and account executives snap rusks and tell each other lies. I begged him to check his megaphone at the door, but he refused.

Winner has always fascinated me. I've never been able to discover whether he's really a monster or merely camping it up, playing the part for publicity purposes. Since he's always let me get away with a degree of insolence (perhaps because he knows I'm fond of him), I now decided to clear the matter up once and for all by obtaining a ruling from him.

'Tell me Michael,' I said, 'something's always bothered me. Are you really a cunt, or are you just pretending?'

He looked amazed and for a moment I thought I'd over-stepped the mark.

'What the hell are you talking about?'

'I'm referring to your reputation as a fearful bastard. Take your rages, for instance. Are they simulated or for real?'

'Oh, they're genuine, my dear, believe me they're genuine. I scale them from one to three. A number one even frightens me. I tell you, someone gets a number one, they're never the same again.'

Within minutes, as it happened, we received a practical demonstration. He asked for fresh lemon juice as starter, whereupon some misguided waiter pointed out that there wasn't such an item listed on the menu.

Winner blinked in amazement. 'I've never heard of such a thing! No fresh lemon juice indeed! Fetch me the manager!'

A trembling *maître d'hotel* approached, bowing and scraping and jerking off generally, to receive the mother and father of all rollockings from a now steaming Winner. Having elicited the information that there were lemons on the premises, he demanded to be told whether it was beyond the wit and competence of the assembled staff to squeeze some three of these into an appropriately positioned glass. If it was, perhaps the head waiter would care to bring to our table the necessary ingredients and squeezing apparatus, since he, Winner, would be only too happy to perform this complicated operation

114

for himself. The head waiter correctly identified a certain ironic undertow, and Winner's lemon juice shortly appeared. Further difficulties arose, however, when the waiter was taking our orders for the second course.

'I'll have the duck,' said Winner.

'Excuse?' said the trembling waiter, 'Sir would like what?'

'Good grief,' said Winner, 'is everyone deaf in here?' He picked up his megaphone and put it to his mouth. 'DUCK!' he bellowed, and across the room Lord Braborne – the producer of *Sink the Bismarck* and Lord Mountbatten's son-in-law no less – dived for cover underneath his table.

'Golly,' said a shaking Emma Jane, 'what number was that?'

'My dear,' beamed Winner, 'that was nothing.' He was now in a tremendously good humour

I wouldn't want to be in the same town, let alone in the same restaurant, when a number one blew up, but I think I now understand the problem that confronts him as he goes about his business. He's one of those luckless people who become enraged by life's trivial irritations. Most men, after all, wouldn't give a stuff whether they got squeezed lemons or not; *they're* driven to the brink of madness by the larger issues: why their wives won't live somewhere else, say, and what's to be done about Mrs Thatcher. Winner, on the other hand, gibbers if he's thwarted by some minor idiocy or petty example of incompetence. Hence his undeserved reputation as a bully, forever rucking with trembling carpenters and sad old extras, but able to keep his equilibrium with celebrated stars. I imagine that Marlon Brando, say, or even Oliver Reed, would only be difficult on a truly Byzantine scale and wouldn't, therefore, get his goat in the same way as some obtuse minor functionary. If Her Majesty herself said: 'I'm sorry, squire, you can't film here, you know. Not on a Tuesday afternoon, and not without form B7639XT,' she'd rightly cop a number one.

He's off to America tomorrow and in his absence I'm instructed to behave exactly in accordance with the wishes of Mr Clowes.

'I don't want to come back and discover that you've fucked everything up,' he said.

❊ ❊ ❊

A most interesting day working as a casual labourer for Toby Danvers the Impresario. He was fired from the telephone exchange for making obscene calls and reversing the charges to boot. He is now working part-time in the contract plant business, while raising the capital for *The Christine Keeler Story*. He decks out offices with climbing green arrangements and then puts in a bill for maintenance. Some of his customers have asked for this improvement in their premises, he tells me, and some of them haven't. I'd guess that today's punters – an oil shipping company in Grosvenor Place – on the whole, and judging by the fact that not a soul in the place knew what the hell we were doing there, hadn't. Their bewildered attitude to our coming and going didn't bother Danvers in the least. He trotted from room to room, bellowing at dozing executives, moving furniture, throwing open windows, spilling fertiliser over newly fitted carpets and installing monstrous tubs of horror movie vegetation. No one told us to take the stuff away, each assuming, I suppose, that someone else had ordered it.

I hadn't been inside a large organisation since my two days' experience of advertising (actually one day twice) with Ogilvy and Mather back in '58. Nothing's changed. Still ten men doing the job of one and none of them knowing what the job is anyway. On my second and last day with Ogilvy and Mather I was privileged to sit in on a conference to do with BP's new advertising plans. Present round an enormous table were at least thirty people: an Account Executive with two Assistant Account Executives, the Creative Director, the Deputy Creative Director, the Deputy Creative Director's Personal Assistant, the Chief Visualiser, the Storyboard Editor with two strappers to hold up the storyboards, a Film Producer, a Film Director, the Chief Layout Artist, two Illustrators, three Animators, the Senior Copywriter with six assistants (to compose a hundred words between them), the Assistant Comma Inserter, two Market Research Operatives and fifteen sleepy people who seemed to have wandered in off the street but who put forward their suggestions none the less. Various 'concepts' in ascending order of insanity and bad taste were tossed around, until – and I swear to the truth of this, though I don't expect to be believed – someone actually said: 'Well, my wife thinks . . .' and British Petroleum's advertising for the coming year was instantly, and by common consent, built round that good lady's thinking. It was most reassuring to discover that here in the oil shipping company's offices the same situation obtained. Dazed, stuffed organisation men wandered from room to room, manifestly without the faintest notion of what they were meant to be doing, while female potted plants of every shape and age attended to their finger nails and gazed in catatonic stupor at their nice new IBM typewriters.

I became particularly concerned for the welfare of one six foot six zombie with shoulders like a rugger blue's, who sat slumped at his desk staring in disbelief at one of those obligatory colour snaps – blown up by Boots – of himself, his little wife and his two unpleasant children making the most of some horrific ski-ing holiday. Every now and again, lonely and desperate for the warmth of human contact, I suppose, he'd pick up a file and stroll with it into the typing-pool.

'Er – um – ah . . .' he'd say to no one in particular, 'Um – er – has anyone seen old – er – um – ah – haw! haw! haw!'

The secretaries, busy adjusting their eye-lashes and dreaming of their personal lives, rightly ignored him, so he wandered back to his own little cage.

There was a bit of a stir at 12 o'clock, caused by a buzz going round the building that the Chairman himself was about to make an appearance. At the time, Danvers and I were carrying out certain alterations to his office, which, owing to an unforeseen mishap with a sack of fertiliser and an upturned bucket of water, presently resembled a poorly managed market garden after a cloud-burst. Some executive underling got in a bit of a stew about this and begged us to

117

suspend our improvements, at least for the time being. Danvers was outraged, of course, and angrily waved the fellow away. We went on working and the Chairman, an inoffensive little man, shortly made his entrance. We wished him the time of day and indicated by our friendly manner that if he had anything useful to do he should go right ahead and do it, since he wouldn't be disturbing us. He had nothing to do at all, of course, and having declined Danvers's invitation to take up two units in *The Christine Keeler Story*, he wandered away, not to be seen again.

One distressing aspect of the day was that I found myself more than once compelled to inform totally uninterested secretaries that this wasn't how I normally earned my living, that I had been temporarily reduced to this level to help a friend and that I was in fact a ponce. I mentioned this shameful desire of mine to be well thought of to Danvers, and pointed out how surprised our fathers would be to see us employed as humpers of fertiliser. Danvers was unimpressed, but it seems to me that something's gone badly wrong.

It's all very puzzling, and what will my son make of it? Suppose another young blighter at Eton is of a mind to check out my credentials.

'I say, Donaldson, what does your pater do for a living?'

My son can't say: 'Well, normally he lives off the artistic earnings of my Auntie Emma Jane, but sometimes he shifts fertiliser for his friend Toby Danvers the Impresario.'

Or perhaps he can. Danvers certainly thinks so, and he insists that there's no cause for concern.

On the way home, he admitted that he's romantically infatuated with a girl called Jasmine. He's very bothered about this because in his delirium he has even considered the possibilities of straight sex. What, he asked, was it like? I said that in my recollection it was extremely boring, but I couldn't be certain because it was so long since I'd tried it. Yes, but was it *possible*, asked Danvers. I said I thought it probably wasn't, though once it might have been. Was it corrupting, he then asked, likely to ensnare one in its healthy grip? Was one straight experience, apparently harmless in isolation, likely to lead on to experiences ever straighter and less bizarre? I agreed that there seemed to be a danger here, but pointed out that in these enlightened times we were encouraged to try anything, however distasteful, if either party to a voluntary association desired it. No healthy man could hope to enjoy straight sex, of course, but *Forum* and other socially aware journals were now advertising the provocative point of view that women have certain rights in this department. This being so, I said, it seemed reasonable that once a month, say, a man should grit his teeth, inform some whining little lady that he loved her and – to indulge her whims – be a party to a natural practice. If this proved impossible, no doubt there existed men who did this sort of thing for money. Saying something like: 'I don't mind what you do so long as I don't know about it,' one could encourage one's woman to visit one of these professional gentlemen.

Toby Danvers the Impresario looked most troubled, so I told him not to take me as a very reliable guide in these matters. Indeed, it has recently been brought to my attention – by Professor Bernard Crick, to be specific – that I'm mentally ill. He says as much in a book called *Crime, Rape and Gin*. He doesn't exactly name me, of course, he doesn't say on page whatever 'William Donaldson of etc etc is mentally ill'. He merely gives a list of erotic preferences, which taken together seem to me to offer an exhaustive description of sexual desire, and then says that anyone driven by such tastes is round the bend. I have become rather concerned about this. The Professor is no fool, or so it seems to me, and to be told by such an authority that you're wrong in the head is no laughing matter.

❅ ❅ ❅

Meeting with my new solicitor, Mr Rabin. Alert-looking fellow who's had a few unwary people by the balls in his time, I'd say. I wouldn't want to be on the business end of a writ from him. Lightweight suit and out-of-season L.A. suntan. He perused my various contracts, tut-tutted in a pained way and then confirmed Michael Winner's ruling that the film rights are free. There now seems to be little doubt that the other side's accredited representatives (not that I think of them as the other side, of course) have made a blunder. Mr Rabin talked to me as though I was a fairly harmless imbecile, which is just as it should be. Then he asked me for a hundred pounds.

❃   ❃   ❃

My friend S. Z. Corbett has played an excellent joke on Major Dobson-Smythe. Having been given £1000 with which to acquire some dope at wholesale prices, Corbett disappeared for a fortnight (he was using this unexpected windfall to impress a titled lady in the South of France, we've now discovered) and then turned up, without the dope, of course, and without the Major's capital, but with a little black bag which contained, he assured us, enough seeds to produce a cannabis harvest worth £10,000. It would take a year of devoted husbandry, he said, but for such a return on capital the delay was well worthwhile. The Major's eyes lit up like the jackpot window in a pin-ball machine and he immediately took Corbett, together with his little black bag of seeds, down to his house in Berkshire.

Here, Corbett was introduced to the Major's wife Diana as a leading authority on all matters horticultural.

'How do you do, Mr Corbett?' said Diana.

'Right on, baby,' said Corbett. 'Yeah. Wow. You got soul.'

The Major took him into the garden, where he looked around him with a professional eye and ruled that Diana's prize tomatoes must yield their position, since they were hogging the most advantageous site for marijuana farming. The Major put up a bit of a fight – protesting that the tomatoes were Diana's pride and joy – but the strength of Corbett's case was overwhelming. After dinner (plain but good, was Corbett's verdict) and two rubbers of cut-throat bridge at a penny a point, Corbett rolled a joint and handed it to Diana.

'If that don't turn you on, Diana baby, you aint got no switches.'

Diana duly passed out, allowing Corbett and the Major, armed with two shovels and a torch, to creep out into the garden, dig up her prize tomatoes and in their place plant Corbett's seed.

The Major's immensely excited now, but I fear he's in for a shock at harvest time. When he got back to London, I asked Corbett what he'd planted in the garden and he said:

'Hey man, would I swindle the dude? Tomatoes of course.'

He really is a scallywag. A year's a long time off, however, and we'll all have passed a lot of water over the bridge before the Major learns the truth. It will be a miracle, what's more, if he's still around to be offended. Not content, it seems, with the wide-scale distribution of soft drugs, he's just come up with a new get-rich-quick scheme that sets the mind reeling. His latest plan is to have the homes of all his friends burglarised. He has suddenly realised that, being welcome still in Berkshire's better drawing-rooms, he's in a uniquely good position to tip off thieves as to the valuables therein, together with up-to-date intelligence about their owners' immediate movements and security precautions. He wants me to introduce him to one of London's top firms, with a view to his becoming their man in Berkshire.

'What do you think?' he said. 'Just a *pensée*.'

The question is, should I mark my sister Bobo's card? I wouldn't want her gaff to take a spin along with all the others. As I see it, it's all down to that bugger Benn.

❀ ❀ ❀

Meeting with my Mr Clowes, who runs his affairs from a neat little house in an almost inaccessible corner of N.W.1: a precaution, I imagine, against deluded writers running through his door at all hours, wishing to discuss the course of their careers. When I was of the live theatre, his was a name to conjure with and drop, so I was expecting a high-voltage wheeler-dealer with a jolting line of patter. He's not like that

121

at all, I'm glad to say. He's studious and frail, like an antiquarian book collector, and he talks calmly and most precisely, placing the tips of his fingers together after the manner of the school chaplain taking confirmation class. He has the reputation of being able to take care of himself out on the literary cobbles, so his appearance and manner must be deceptive, feinting many a shyster on to a bloody nose. He says he likes my book, but hopes that my next one may have a stronger story line. I didn't tell him I can't do stories, lest he ask me to leave. He says that Winner is serious about the film rights but that it may be difficult to untangle ourselves from Tynan. I'm not sure I want to. I'd like the money a film deal would bring, but, even more, I want to step out with a good class of person. All very confusing. I feel more secure, however, now that Mr Clowes and the alert Mr Rabin are in charge of my affairs. I am resolved to do exactly as they say, and, to let him know he wasn't dealing with a literary backwoodsman, I said as much to Mr Clowes:

'I shall in all my best obey you, madam,' I said.

'I'm not a madam,' said my Mr Clowes.

❉ ❉ ❉

My appearance on this Saturday's epilogue is now advertised in the *TV Times*, so today I rang Mrs Whitehouse to protest. I got her home number (Rock 266260) from the London office of NVALA and she answered the phone herself. She really sounds a most genial old tart and we hit it off immediately.

'Now look here, Mrs Whitehouse,' I said, 'my name's Major Dobson-Smythe and I don't normally do this sort of thing but...'

'What's the trouble, Major?' said Mrs Whitehouse most soothingly.

'Well, now don't get me wrong, I've knocked around the world, you know, I'm no prude, live and let live I say, but this is damn bad. Damn bad.'

'What is, Major?'

'Having a ponce fellow on the Epilogue. That's it, I said to my wife Diana, that's the final straw, I'm going to ring up Mrs Whitehouse and...'

'A ponce on the Epilogue! Great heavens! When's this, Major?'

'On Saturday night! In fact, it will go out early on Sunday morning. On the Sabbath! What can we do? Can we take steps? Can we visit a judge in chambers?'

'No doubt we can, Major, no doubt we can. But give me some more details, if you would.'

'Well, this fellow wrote a book about – er, excuse the expression – prostitutes. *The Ladies and the Gentlemen*, or some such thing. Boasts about living with 'em! *Boasts* about it! Now the blighter's on the Epilogue! That's the limit. I said to Diana...'

'Have you read this book, Major?'

'Read it? *Read* the filthy thing? No, of course I haven't read it. It's not the sort of book I read.'

'Of course not.'

'I don't have to read the thing. I know what it's about. But putting the fellow on the Epilogue! What can we do?'

'We can do a lot, Major. You'd be surprised. We can...'

'Now don't get me wrong. As far as I'm concerned, people can write what they like. Within reason. I'm no fuddy-duddy. Don't know why they can't write decent stuff, but that's their business. *The Moon's a Balloon*, that was a good book. Had me in fits of laughter, so no one can call me a prude. Quite near the knuckle, some of it, but Niven knows when to stop, do you see? Never goes too far. But television is a different matter altogether. Someone on television is a guest in my home, that's the way I look at it. And I don't want a guest in my home boasting that he lives with prostitutes. Do you?'

'No, I...'

'And on a religious show, what's more. Do you see?'

'I do, Major, I most certainly do. They think they can get away with anything, but they can't. Now, just as soon as

123

you've rung off, I'm going to get straight on the phone to Robin Young at the IBA, and you must do the same. The more people who ring the better. Then I'll ring the head of religious programmes at Thames. We've got to put a stop to this sort of thing.'

I gave the old girl my address and she's going to send me some of her Association's literature. I'm confident that I can now leave the whole matter in her hands. What a lark if she manages to get me censored! Emma Jane thinks it would be better to kick up a fuss *after* the programme has gone out, but to get it stopped altogether would cause a greater commotion, in my opinion. It will be interesting to see whether she carries as much clout as the liberals fear.

&#x274b; &#x274b; &#x274b;

Clive James to tea again. The purpose of his visit was to get some more inside information from Emma Jane. He said he couldn't talk intimately in front of me, so I was sent out to take tea in the Fulham Road. How long, I wondered, should I give them? When Emma Jane is doing a trick, I stay out for about an hour, but what should one decently allow for intimate talk? How ironic it was, I thought as I sipped my lonely cup of tea, that Emma Jane would now be apprising Clive of all the saucy details that she'd so consistently refused to divulge to me. Small wonder that so many competent judges have found my book tame and unexplicit to a fault. In an otherwise kind review in *The Times Literary Supplement*, the fine art critic William Feaver complains that, true to my subject, I offer more than I reveal. But how, if sexy snippets are denied me, could it be otherwise?

With this in mind, I insisted, later in the evening, that Emma Jane give me a full account of her conversation with Clive. At first she refused, but after much relentless probing, she at last apprised me of one indecent detail she'd drawn to Clive's attention, and which I can now reveal for the benefit of Mr Feaver and anyone else who wants the lowdown. When call-girls make love to one another for the pleasure of a customer, they are most careful to caress not the intimate parts of their opposite number, but their own thumbs. To do otherwise would be considered over-familiar and a breach of professional etiquette. Interestingly enough, it is with girls who are in fact engaged in a small romance that this rule is most strictly observed. They, not unnaturally, are particularly averse to allowing a gonk to share their secrets. Anyone hoping for further revealing details will have to wait for Clive's play or Emma Jane's book, whichever is the sooner.

My money – not that I have any – says that the latter work will reach the public first. Letters pour in by every post and last week Emma Jane took a sample of these along to Geoffrey Strachan at Eyre Methuen. (She fell out with Secker and Warburg, it seems, when she discovered they were the British publishers of the wretched American porno writer Erica Jong.) If I'm not mistaken, I had the honour many years ago of publishing Mr Strachan's early verses, so I know him to be a man of discerning taste. In the circumstances, it's hardly likely that he'll be impressed by Emma Jane's odd and, to my mind, rather vulgar little book, and I said as much to her.

'Mind your own beeswax,' she said. 'I know what I'm doing.'

Not in this case, I'll wager; though other, less fastidious publishers than Mr Strachan might be deceived into seeing merit in her work. I'm not a mean-minded man, but this would sink me.

✳ ✳ ✳

Mrs Whitehouse turns out to be a paper dragon after all. At 12.30 last night I switched to Thames Television, expecting to see one of those 'We regret that owing to circumstances etc. etc.' cards, as when rain stops play in a Test Match. But no, there I was twitching and talking balls, so I switched off in a hurry. Emma Jane turned it on again, so I locked myself in the bathroom and ran the taps full blast. I'll know better next time than to leave matters of consequence to Mrs White-house.

❀ ❀ ❀

I'm not done yet though. This morning Mike Franklin M.A. sent me along to the Savoy Hotel, there to treat with a Mr Packer, who also wants to buy the film rights to my book. (This recurring desire to be-mime it, either on stage or screen, while gratifying of course, surprises me. I had taken it to be a fact-packed documentary, a mine of useful information, but no more suitable for filming than Lady Arabella Boxer's *Garden Cookbook*.) Mr Packer is not a film producer, as it happens, but since he owns Australia we don't hold this against him. He sat me down in his suite, ordered coffee, apprised me of his heart condition and said he wasn't a man to beat about the bush.

'I'm a straightforward man,' he said, 'and I like to meet a situation head on.'

Since he must weigh upwards of thirty stone, I wouldn't want to be the situation. Should I accept at once, I wondered, or should I hear the details of the offer first? I didn't have long to ponder the question. Speaking very fast and, as is the way with Australians in my experience, with a fair degree of emphasis, he brought certain matters to my attention. My book had caused him to laugh, he said, but it wouldn't make a stage play. Bad luck Clive James. Clive was a clever fellow, but the task would defeat him. The book would make a 'viable' film, however, and on his pay-roll he had the very person to adapt it and play me. Dame Edna Everage! Dame Edna had read it, he said, and was in accord with the idea. My book was in fact a poignant love story (my own feelings precisely) and this aspect, though Mike Franklin, he said, had scoffed at the idea the night before (well sod Mike Franklin), would be brought out in the film. How much did I want for the rights? I was working on this – £100, £200, even, with time to pay? – when Packer suddenly put me on the phone to Dame Edna herself. She was most

126

cordial but sounded as if she had a gun in her ribs. Then I left.

I'm not taking any of this too seriously. I have learned over the years not to go to pieces when an Australian tells me he is a straightforward man and then threatens me with pound notes. On the other hand, Packer, who seems to be travelling under his own name and with authentic papers, is not the kind of Australian I usually meet.

✳  ✳  ✳

Packer is offering £7500 against ten per cent of the profits for an outright purchase. This is seductive talk to a man who at no time in the last two years has had more than £3 in his pocket. I retired to my study (the bathroom, now that Emma Jane has requisitioned the literary room) and did some sums. Being more than usually provident and not forgetting my many responsibilities, how could I best spend £7500? I jotted down, in descending order of merit, the following sensible possibilities.

1. Give it all to Miss Picano.

2. Book a suite at the Hilton and invite Pretty Marie and French Simone to go the other way one hundred and fifty times.

3. Give half to Miss Picano and book Pretty Marie and French Simone a mere seventy times.

4. Donate the lot to Sir James Goldsmith's 'Sink *Private Eye* Fund'.

5. Open up another model agency with Ken the Australian Horse Player.

6. Go back into the *partouze* business with Toby Danvers, but properly capitalised this time.

7. Pop it all in the bank and hope for the best.

I then rang up my Mr Clowes, who wasn't at all impressed. The offer was derisory, he said, and who was this Mr Packer anyway, to say nothing of Miss Picano? Michael Winner was a serious man and his offer – just as soon as he got round to making it – would be very much better.

Better? Using one naughty girl as a basic unit of currency, exactly how much better did he mean? Fifty naughty girls three hundred times? Three hundred naughty girls fifty times?

'Winner's offer,' said Mr Clowes, 'will certainly be in the region of £500.'

Five hundred pounds! God help us, *that* wouldn't impress Miss Picano and it would book Pretty Marie and French Simone a mere ten times! Since there was no point in his supposing that he represented an idiot, I said as much to Mr Clowes.

'Ah yes,' he said, 'but the sum of £500 would only be an option. If Winner made the film you'd get at least £15,000.'

Option schmoption. Pretty Marie and French Simone don't do teas on options. A man needs pound notes in his claw these days to impress young ladies, not options. I begin to wonder whether Mr Clowes is a suitable person to handle my affairs. He says he will ring Winner in Los Angeles and that in the meantime I must on no account traffic with Mr Packer. Speaking for myself (which I do realise I have no right to do), I will be sorely tempted to traffic with the first person who writes out a gooses in my favour for a sharp sum.

❈　❈　❈

Packer is becoming impatient and I'm still day-dreaming in private of the secret and awful uses to which I can put his money. Emma Jane, who has a couple of dreadful ideas of her own about how best to spend it (putting the paper work right, she calls it), Dawn Upstairs, Mitzi the Japanese Masseuse, Lord Dynevor, 'arding and The Equally Lovely Sarah and Daft Des the local newsagent all counsel me to sign with Packer. Standing firmly against them is my Mr Clowes, and I, not for the first time, find myself a floating 'don't know'. Mr Clowes is against Packer because he favours Winner, but my hesitation is caused by a fear that by selling the film rights – whether to Winner, Packer, or anyone else –

we'll upset Tynan and spoil the chance of it being done on stage.

Today, however, a dozen or so increasingly persuasive, not to say hysterical, phone calls from Mike Franklin M.A. caused me to capitulate. Having at last convinced myself that if Clive's script for the play is good Tynan will put it on whether he has the film rights or not, I gave Franklin the go-ahead to do a deal with Packer.

Representing Packer is Lord Goodman, no less, and an appropriate document, which we are supposed to sign before Packer returns to Australia on Saturday, is now being drawn up. The familiar insistent feeling that I'm about to do something criminal has returned and I've not mentioned a word of this to Mr Clowes. Soon enough to come clean with him when I'm fortified by having seven thousand five hundred balloons in my kick, that's my thinking. He'll call me an ass, and worse, but at least I'll be an ass in a new suit and with the price of a cup of coffee. What Tynan and Winner will call me scarcely bears contemplation.

❅ ❅ ❅

An unusually busy day. A letter agreement duly arrived from Lord Goodman and I, resolved to be as business-like as the circumstances still allowed, sent it along to my Mr Rabin for his perusal. He, predictably enough, said it wouldn't do and that I must on no account sign it. And what was my game anyway? he asked. As he'd understood the situation from Mr Clowes, we were waiting until Winner had come back from Los Angeles. That was all very well, I said, but I needed money. Fair enough, said Mr Rabin sportingly, didn't we all? But that was no reason why we should deliver ourselves bound, plucked and ready for stuffing into the hands of this Mr Packer, whoever he might be.

'He owns Australia,' I explained.

'Well he can keep it,' said Mr Rabin testily. Then he said that he himself would now draw up an agreement that made

129

at least glancing reference to our interests in the matter. Lord Goodman's, he suggested, failed notably in this respect.

He worked on it all day and at 5.30 I went round to his office to pick it up. He'd expanded Lord Goodman's thin page and a half into six pages of tightly packed conditions, the more relevant details of which he now brought to my attention. Speaking very slowly, as though to someone of severely diminished responsibility, he said:

'I'm compelled to say that I'm not at all happy about this, but you're my client, after all, and if your mind is made up, what can I do? The important thing to remember is that you must sign absolutely *nothing* except this document, drawn up by me, which I now have in my left hand.' He waved it to and fro under my nose in the way that you might educate a gun dog. 'This one here. On no account must you sign this other one, which I'm now holding in my right hand and which has been drawn up by Lord Goodman. Do you understand? This one here *good*, this one here *bad*.'

'I think I've got the general picture,' I said.

Mr Rabin still didn't seem convinced. If anyone at all, he said, of any age, shape, sex or ethnic background approached me between now and midnight with a piece of paper which I didn't instantly recognise as the document drawn up by him I must wave such a person angrily out of my path. He didn't at all like the idea of my going to the Savoy unchaperoned, he said, and but for a prior dinner engagement he would have come with me himself. Was there a responsible person, he then asked, into whose custody he could place me until the morrow? What about Emma Jane? he said. He'd gained the impression from my book that she had her head screwed on.

Well really! There is a limit and at this point I was prepared to become nettled. I quickly filled Mr Rabin in with a few details from my past – off-break bowler and cautious opening bat (coached in the hols by the great George Geary), officer in the Royal Navy, member of the MCC, visiting masseur, teacher of History and British Constitution, marinero on a glass-bottom boat, bouncer in a bawdy house and now a man of letters – and implied that these qualifications made me more than a match for one overweight Australian from Wagga Wagga. What, I demanded to be told, had Emma Jane – sweet girl though she was – to place against these attainments?

Mr Rabin looked to be on the point of telling me, then changed his mind. Okay, he said, I could go to the Savoy on my own, but I must promise I'd speak to no one. I must do no more than deliver Rabin's agreement to someone at reception and then scarper. I must on no account come into contact with Packer unless, and until, he'd signed Rabin's contract. Then, and only then, could I re-present myself at the Savoy. It was an important condition of the contract that the gooses was handed over on signature and I must on no account sign my half or leave Packer's suite without the money in my pocket. Then he said – rather shatteringly – that the whole thing was a waste of time. Why? I asked. Because, he said, demanding money on signature was unheard of and Packer would be most insulted. That was ridiculous, I said. Why should Packer fly back to Wagga Wagga with my film rights while I walked away with nothing? Mr Rabin said he was blessed if he knew, but that was the custom. An unreasonable custom, I said spiritedly, and one that would have to be changed if Packer wanted to do business. That was the right attitude, said Mr Rabin, but he for one was prepared to put his money where his mouth was. If I left the Savoy with the gooses, he'd take me to lunch at any restaurant I cared to nominate. Fair enough, I said. However, if I failed to come away with the gooses, he said, I'd have to take him to lunch. Well, as an officer and a gentleman I could hardly refuse to take the wager, but if I failed to collect the gooses Mr Rabin would have to settle for a salt beef on rye at the Nosh Bar in Great Windmill Street.

We parted on this sporty note and I took a taxi to the Savoy. As instructed, I handed in Mr Rabin's contract at the reception desk and then got out of range as quickly as possible. All was quiet until:

6.30. Mike Franklin M.A. phones to say that Packer is furious and that the deal's off. He uses a bit of bad language and

131

then hangs up on me. Well I never. Silly sod, but he'll ring back.

6.35. Franklin rings back. 'Let's be reasonable about this,' he says. 'Packer is prepared to negotiate.' 'Well,' I say, feeling very smug that I'm carrying out Mr Rabin's instructions so precisely, 'I'm not.' So Franklin hangs up on me again.

6.45. Dr Bryson arrives for the week-end. Thank goodness for him. I already have a feeling that we'll need a philosopher before the evening's over.

6.50. Franklin phones again and tries to persuade me to meet with Packer at least. 'I have been advised,' I say, drawing my voice up to its full five foot ten, 'not to meet Packer again, unless to sign Mr Rabin's document and to pick up the gooses.' 'You're being very badly advised,' says Franklin. 'Allow me to be the judge of . . .' but the bugger's put the receiver down on me yet again.

6.55. Dr Bryson, who has now unpacked, gives me the proof of the final chapter of his book on Popper to read. I'm about to give this the close attention it deserves when:

7.00. Phillip Hodson, the urbane editor of *Forum*, phones. What's this? Has he some new wrinkle to pass on about how to get the most out of a real human relationship? No, he merely wishes to say that while this is none of his business, of course, he just *happens* to be having a drink with Packer at the Savoy, and while he naturally doesn't want to interfere, he would just like to say that in his opinion Packer is one of the few Australians who can be trusted. Thank you very much, I say, I'd never doubted that for a moment.

7.05. A Pakistani gentleman phones. What the hell's this got to do with him? I angrily tell him to mind his own effing business and slam the phone down on him. Then I realise that he was merely trying to arrange immorality with Emma Jane. Never mind. A cold shower will be better for him in the long run, and Emma Jane's too caught up in the slowly developing drama to be cross with me.

7.06. Phone rings again. It's a man's voice, so I, taking it to be the Pakistani gentleman coming back for more, apologise for telling him to eff off, but go on to explain that Emma

Jane's too knackered to work tonight. If he cared to ring the next day, she'd probably be able to accommodate him. It's Emma Jane's father. Hell.

7.07. Lock myself in kitchen to cook kedgeree.

7.15. Franklin phones to ask me what I intend to do. Finish cooking the kedgeree, I say. 'You're always cooking fucking kedgeree,' he says. This strikes me as unreasonable. I'm hardly ever cooking kedgeree, as it happens, and certainly not with any greater frequency than the next man.

7.50. Kedgeree cooked, served and eaten, and nobody looking much the worse for it.

8.00. Packer phones. He doesn't sound at all cross. An Australian, but a smoother operator than Franklin for all that. Let's have dinner, he says. That would have been nice, I say, but I've just had kedgeree and anyway I've got a house-guest for the week-end. In that case, says Packer, why don't I hop down to the Savoy for an after-dinner drink? He was leaving in the morning and even if the deal was off, we could still meet for a laugh and a chat, couldn't we? Put like that, how could I refuse? Okay, I say, I'll be along at about 9.30. What a bloody nuisance, though, what with Friday being such a cracking good night on the telly.

8.10. Conference with Emma Jane and Dr Bryson. Emma Jane doesn't trust me to go to the Savoy on my own, and the Doctor, reluctant though he is to miss *Hawaii Five-O* (one of his favourites, he says), agrees with her. They insist, in fact, on coming too. 'I'll be of considerable assistance,' says the Doctor. 'If Packer gets naughty I'll clap him in a paradox.' To be able to announce that I've brought my philosopher with me is tempting, but the implication that I can't be trusted on my own annoys me. I've not the slightest intention of signing *anything*, I say, and while I'm grateful to them for their kindly meant offer, I can handle the situation on my own. Emma Jane and the Doctor snort and exchange know-ing glances. On the other hand, I say, if the Doctor would care to drive me and Emma Jane to the Savoy in his little car, they could discuss Strawson and related matters in the bar, while I polished off Packer upstairs in his suite. Then

133

we could all return home together. Emma Jane and the Doctor don't look too pleased, but they finally agree to this suggestion.

9.00. The Doctor, Emma Jane and I set off for the Savoy. The Doctor drives like a philosopher so I tell him a story of One-Eyed Charlie's involving the late Master of Wadham and Dr Brabant. Brabant kept a car and drove it badly even by academic standards. Once he drove straight into a cow and knocked it down. When the man in charge of the cow said, quite mildly, 'Look out where you're going,' Brabant said fiercely, 'Mind your own business!' and drove on. The Doctor is so diverted by this tale that he drives up a street clearly marked off as for the sole use of buses. An insolent young constable waves us down officiously, pokes his silly head through the car window and asks the Doctor whether he's a bus. The Doctor blinks at him in amazement and says: 'A bus? A *bus*? No, of course I don't suppose myself to be a bus. Why on earth should I take myself to be a bus? I've seldom heard anything so absurd! Do I have a bus-like appearance? The extension of the term bus-like, which is, as you should know, the class of all the objects of which the term bus-like is true – in this case the class of all large machines painted, at least in London, a characteristic red colour and used to transport members of the public from A to B – does not, I assure you, stretch to include me. I, on the other hand, am a member of the class of all...' 'All right! All right!' says the constable, withdrawing his head and making a mental note that he must re-enrol at the Hendon Police Academy, there to bone up on the 'Elephantine Irony' course. 'On your way, but don't do it again.'

9.30. Arrive at the Savoy. Emma Jane and the Doctor retire to the bar and I go up to Packer's suite. Present are Packer, Mike Franklin M.A. and Packer's fiancée. Dinner still in progress. Lots of booze, pink perspiring faces, *doubles entendres* and inexplicable laughter. Fancy my Mr Rabin not trusting me with this lot! I can handle them with one hand tied behind my back. I'm playing a vague artist type, pained at being dragged into the market place. They try to get me soused.

No go. I give the impression that they're wasting my time. I don't go so far as to yawn and look at my watch, but I'm doing well. Hullo, what's all this money lying about the room? Little stacks of £5 notes everywhere. Do they suppose I can be bought? I ignore it. I don't know though, I might palm a wad or two if they all go to the bathroom at the same time: not such an unlikely possibility, as it happens, bearing in mind all the booze being taken on board. No one wants to open the bowling, as it were, but at last Franklin measures out his run, takes two little hops and a short run-up and says: 'I really think you ought to consider blah blah blah...' I switch off, examine my finger nails, sigh, look bored to death. If only Mr Rabin could see me now, how pleased with me he'd be! Imagine his thinking an English gentleman couldn't handle one overweight Australian! I wonder how much money there is lying about the room? I can count half a dozen little piles without turning my head, and there may be more hidden under furniture. It could total as much as £500, I calculate, and possibly nearer £1000. My goodness. That's Pretty Mar...no, perish the thought.

10.00. Emma Jane phones from the bar. I recognise her voice, but she's talking gibberish. '$(\exists x)$ $(Hx . Ax)$ $x(Ax \supset Gx)$ $(\exists x)$ $(Hx . Gx)$' she says. 'What the hell are you talking about?' I say. 'I encoded the message, with the Doctor's help,' she says, 'in case anyone's listening in. As you can see, he's taught me how to use the existential quantifier.' 'I'm delighted,' I say, 'but could you now decode the message, do you think?' 'Certainly. Its thrust is "For some $x$, $x$ is human and $x$ is Australian. For all $x$ if $x$ is an Australian $x$ is a gangster. For some $x$, $x$ is human and $x$ is a gangster." We thought we should remind you. I hope you haven't signed anything.' 'Of course I haven't signed anything. What do you take me for?' Then I ask her whether she and the Doctor are all right. Not really, she says. The Savoy bar's not really their speed and they're thinking of moving on to the Shagarama. Would that be in order? Yes, I say, it would be a considerable relief. Okay, she says, they'll catch me later. I notice that there are two more piles of fivers by the phone.

135

The amount scattered around the room must be nearly £1000. That's Pretty Marie forty times. Goodness. Just as well I'm not a punter.

10.30. 'Make a terrific film, your book,' says Packer. 'Barry Humphries rhubarb rhubarb ...' I'm thinking about Emma Jane and the Doctor waltzing at the Shagarama. Wish I was with them. £1000? Pretty Marie and French Simone twenty times. It might not be £1000, of course. Might only be £750. That would make sense, ten per cent of £7500. Pretty Marie and French Simone a mere fifteen times. Still, not to be sneezed at.

11.00. 'I really think blah blah ...' says Mike Franklin M.A. Why can't they get the message? I'm a rock. It would be nice to have a suit, though. What would a suit cost these days? About £50? Let's say one suit and Pretty Marie and French Simone fourteen times.

11.30. Packer is purple in the face and his shirt is soaked in sweat across the bosom and shoulder blades: an effect I've only seen in Westerns and in war films set in the jungle, and which I've always taken to be bogus. I begin to worry about his heart condition. 'Why have you gone cold on the deal?' he says. 'I haven't,' I say wearily, 'it's a grand deal, but my Mr Rabin says I must sign nothing but *his* contract, and you'll only sign Lord Goodman's. Why can't we wait till Monday?' 'It's got to be settled tonight,' says Packer, 'because I'm flying back to Australia tomorrow morning.' Impasse. A Polaroid camera would be a nice toy. £25 say! A new suit, a Polaroid camera, Pretty Marie and French Simone thirteen times and Pretty Marie once on her own. Good thing I'm no punter. Have been, of course, but never again.

12.00. 'Blah blah blah ...' says Franklin. I've been here three hours. Why don't I get up and leave? What could be easier than that?

12.30. 'Rhubarb rhubarb rhubarb ...' says Packer. What's holding me? It isn't the money, God knows. That's of no interest to me. Besides, if I snatched it and signed Mr Packer's laundry list no one would ever speak to me again. Not Tynan, nor Clive James nor my Mr Clowes nor Mr Rabin nor Emma Jane nor the Doctor nor Daft Des nor Sir Robert Mark. Pretty Marie might, but I'm no gonk.

12.45. 'Look,' says Packer, 'there's £750 here in cash and...' Fuck it, I sign Mr Packer's laundry list, grab the money and scram.

01.00. Arrive home. Will Emma Jane be in, and if so, will she be asleep? Peep through letter box. Hell. The light is on in the bedroom, which means she's at home and awake. How do I smuggle the money in? Suddenly realise that I haven't counted it. Better do that now. I'll never sleep wondering whether I've been cattled. Tip money onto the doormat. Bad time to be mugged. I have just established that it's the right amount when Dawn Upstairs, returning late from a trip to Newmarket, creeps up behind me.

'Ooooh,' she says, 'you've been going through Emma Jane's handbag, you have! You naughty thing!'

'I have not! And keep your voice down, for goodness sake.'

'What's all that money then?'

'As it happens,' I hiss, 'as it *happens*, I've just sold the film rights to my book.'

'At *this* time of night? Whatever next? And why's it all over the doormat?'

'I'm counting it.'

'*Counting* it? I don't know. Here, who's playing me then?'

'Esther Rantzen if you breathe a word of this to Emma Jane.'

'I can keep my mouth shut,' she says, and she trips off upstairs.

Now, where the hell can I conceal it? Under the mat? Not safe. Under my hat? I'm not wearing a hat. Decide to stick it up the back of my shirt. Okay so long as I show Emma Jane my frontal elevation only, since from the rear or side I now look like a hunchback. Enter flat and walk carefully, in order not to rustle, into bedroom. I move forward in a straight line, but queerly, as if this is not my accustomed manner of progression: like a tipsy crab, in fact.

'My *God*,' I say, lowering myself gingerly onto the bed, 'what a terrible time I've had.'

137

'You poor love,' says Emma Jane. 'You didn't sign anything, did you?'

She's got a one-track mind, has Emma Jane.

'No, of *course* I didn't sign anything.'

I realise with alarm that my sitting down has caused the
money to shift its position dangerously, so that it is now
fighting to break out through a gap between my shirt and
the top of my trousers. I clutch at my back as though suddenly stabbed by kidney pains.

'Why are you holding your back like that?' asks Emma
Jane.

'I've been stabbed by sudden kidney pains,' I say. 'Please
excuse me a minute.'

I reverse out of the room as though away from royalty,
with one hand up my back holding the money in place. Now
I've got to move like lightning. Emma Jane's paranatural
powers may have alerted her already to untidy goings-on and
any minute now she may come looking for me. Where to
hide the loot? In a cornflakes packet in the kitchen, as Big
Elaine used to do with her ill-gotten gains? (Once she saw
an Arab on a Friday night and the next morning, still half
asleep, ate her fee for breakfast.) No, Emma Jane tends to
eat cereals in the middle of the night. Behind a copy of *Spotlight* on the top book-shelf in the living-room? That's
the answer. Anyone wanting to consult *Spotlight* in the
middle of the night's an idiot, and Emma Jane's no idiot. In
the morning, before Emma Jane gets up, I can recover the
money and hide it in my black brief-case, which I always
keep locked. I can't do this at the moment because the brief-
case is in the literary room, which is presently the Doctor's
bedroom.

I steal into the living-room and, without switching on the
light, manage to grope my way towards the book-shelves.
I take down *Spotlight* push the envelope towards the back
of the shelf and am just returning *Spotlight* to its place when –
Fuck me dead! – the lights are suddenly switched on.

'What on earth are you doing?' asks Emma Jane.

'Checking something in *Spotlight*,' I say.

138

'In the *dark*?'

'I was going to take it into the bathroom.'

'The *bathroom*! Why?'

'I didn't want to wake you up.'

'But I'm awake.'

'So you are.'

'What's your game? You're up to something, aren't you? Come on now, what's going on?'

'Of course I'm not up to something. I just want to check on someone in *Spotlight*.'

This is ridiculous. I'm a man of forty and I have to account for my every move! Why shouldn't I look someone up in *Spotlight* if I want to? Why, if it comes to that, shouldn't I dispose of the film rights in my book to whomsoever I wish and then stash the proceeds where I like? I'm tempted to say: 'Look, I'm a man of forty, I wrote the fucking book, I'm entitled to do what I like with it and what I've done is sell the film rights to a charming and tasteful Australian gentleman in return for a down-payment of seven hundred and fifty balloons, every one of which I intend to spend just as soon as possible on unnatural practices with naughty girls. Play your cards right and you might be one of them. Ha! Ha!' I say nothing.

'What are you looking up?'

'I've forgotten the name of that mime who plays the lead in that thing.'

'*What* thing?'

'Er – *Warship*.'

'Vanessa Redgrave.'

'That's the fellow. Thank you very much.'

'Now can we go back to bed?'

I get away with this for the moment, but Emma Jane is now on full alert and I can't leave the money where it is. I'll have to wait till she's gone to sleep, sneak back into the living-room, take the money from behind *Spotlight*, creep with it into the Doctor's room and, without waking him, lock it away in the black bag. If Emma Jane has one of her nights when she can't sleep, I'm in deep snooker.

139

2.00. Emma Jane is still sitting up reading. I'm pretending I'm trying to sleep, but in fact I'm fighting to stay awake.

'Am I preventing you from sleeping?' asks Emma Jane. 'If I am, say so and I'll go and read in the other room.'

'No, no, I'm fine. Don't do that. What are you reading?'

'*Christian Morals* by Thomas Browne.'

'My word, why that?'

'My publisher wishes me to tighten up my prose a notch. He is anxious that I should avoid what he calls 'the coy emotionalism of so many women writers' and has set me a course of reading in the seventeenth century. Listen to this: "Generations pass while some trees stand, and old families last not three oaks." Good? Or this: "The long habit of living indisposeth us for dying."'

This is murder. Emma Jane is quite capable of reading all night and I can't afford to take my eye off her. The absurd idea crosses my mind that she's waiting for me to go to sleep so that she can burglarise my money. I feel like the hero in a Western who can't afford to go to sleep in case the bad man nicks his water bottle. And what if she decides, in a fit of thoughtfulness, to go and read in the sitting-room anyway? I can hardly insist on sitting in there with her. Well, I could, I suppose, but it would look odd to say the least.

3.00. Emma Jane switches out her light.

3.05. Emma Jane breathing deeply. Too deeply? It may be a trap, an attempt to gull me into a false move. I'm almost delirious now from lack of sleep, like a political prisoner, but I decide to wait for another ten minutes.

3.12. Emma Jane still breathing deeply. I get out of bed very carefully, move like a mouse into the living-room and take down *Spotlight*. If I'm caught again, whom shall I say I'm looking up this time? Or should that be 'up whom shall I say I'm looking'? I really am delirious. I don't think I'll bother. I'll hand myself over and plead 'undue stress'. It worked for Stonehouse. No it didn't. I take the envelope with the money, return *Spotlight* to the shelf, creep with cat-like stealth towards the room where the Doctor is sleeping (I hope) and open the door with extraordinary care. A faint zzzzzzing comes from the Doctor's bed. So far so good. I take the black bag from its place under what used to be my desk (now it's Emma Jane's) and – sod it – I haven't got my keys. Where the hell are they? In my trousers in the bedroom. Can't go back in there. I'll hide the envelope under the Doctor's bed until the morning. I'm bent double with my arm reaching as far as possible under the bed so that the envelope will be well hidden, this manœuvre causing my face almost to brush the Doctor's, when – goats and monkeys! – the zzzzing suddenly stops, the Doctor opens one eye and gives a little yelp of alarm. He switches on the bedside light and there I am, crouched over him either to commit murder or worse.

'Great heavens, what are you doing?' he says. Whatever explanation I come up with will be inadequate because I can see he's already thinking: 'The man's not a philosopher at all, he's a weirdo. He pretended to be a philosopher in order to get me under his roof. Emma Jane's no more than a smoke-screen behind which he can hide his foul proclivities. She's probably an accomplice, in fact. God knows how many philosophers have, in this very bed, met a fate worse than having the collected works of Ronald Butt read aloud to one when wearing wet socks.' He clutches the bed-clothes and looks at me in horror.

'I couldn't sleep,' I say, 'and I was suddenly overtaken by a need to check on something in *Spotlight* – I mean *The Tractatus*. For reasons that I won't go into now, I thought I'd left my copy under your bed. But it seems I was mistaken. I'm terribly sorry to have woken you.'

Threadbare stuff, but unlikely to be challenged by the Doctor, whose one thought will be to get me out of the room as quickly as possible.

'I know how it is when one can't sleep,' he says. 'I'd lend you my copy, of course, but I'm afraid I forgot to bring it with me.'

'Well, goodnight,' I say, 'and I'm terribly sorry to have woken you.'

I return to my own bed, more concerned now about my

141

reputation with the Doctor than about the possible discovery of the hidden money. That should be safe enough under the Doctor's bed, but I'll have to offer him a more plausible explanation for my behaviour in the morning. I might make a clean breast of the whole thing. Not to Emma Jane, of course, but to the Doctor. Like all criminals, I already have a desperate need to spill the beans to someone.

❄ ❄ ❄

The Doctor, who normally sits down to breakfast in a pair of the most unphilosophical silk pyjamas, appeared this morning fully dressed. I can't say I blame him; a deviant can strike at any time. During the night I'd cobbled together some sort of story, which I now ran up the flag-pole, as we used to say in advertising, to see whether anyone saluted.

'You must be wondering,' I said, 'why I thought my copy of *The Tractatus* was under your bed.'

'Not really,' said the Doctor.

'Nevertheless, I feel I must explain.'

'If you so wish.'

'Since there was nothing more immediately to hand, I had occasion a day or two ago, to jot down on its fly-leaf some information which, if it had fallen into the wrong hands, might have proved incriminating: Pretty Marie's new phone number, to be precise. No sooner had I done so than Emma Jane, who was trained as you know by Colonel Ioanndis, came upon me by surprise. I just had time to toss the book under the bed, and there I supposed it still to be. In fact I must have retrieved it at a later date.'

'I see,' said the Doctor. 'I was a trifle concerned, in fact, that I hadn't been of greater assistance. When they buzz around in one's head in the middle of the night these problems can be the very devil. They swarm in the brain until one is forced to go to one's shelves for consultation with the original texts. You will recall that Wittgenstein himself kept Russell up all one night by threatening to commit suicide if Russell retired before the problem they were working on was solved. I was alarmed that intellectual despair might cause you to take your life, and I confess I nearly came looking for you. What, in fact, was the nature of your problem?'

Fortunately, I'd been anticipating this question and I had my answer ready. I'd been lying awake, I said, thinking about the fuss caused in learned circles by the Vienna town council's recent order that the house built by Wittgenstein for his sister must be demolished. As the Doctor was no doubt aware, thinkers the world over were up in arms over this crass piece of bureaucratic philistinism, with the exception, naturally, of Emma Jane's friend Auberon Waugh, who, enraged that there should be such a to-do over a house of no apparent historical or architectural interest, constructed by a jumbo pseud for his equally pseudish sister, was launching a counter-campaign, offering the local council its support. No one was taking Bron's campaign seriously, of course, and so far only Kingsley Amis, Arthur Askey, Malcolm Muggeridge, Richard Ingrams, Billy Bremner and Captain Mark Phillips had signed his petition. But wasn't Bron mistaken – not for the first time, of course – in holding that the house was of no interest? For in its severely functional design – plumbing, joints, wiring etc. all showing – was it not a practical illustration of Wittgenstein's argument (following Russell's Theory of Descriptions) at some point in *The Tractatus* (and it was this that had been keeping me awake) that just as clothes conceal the body underneath (or a house's decorative scheme its inner workings) so language disguises thought, that a proposition's surface grammar and its logical grammar are different?

The Doctor took this up with greater enthusiasm than I had anticipated. My contributions to this sort of discussion are nothing much at the best of times, and this morning I had important matters on my mind. My one concern, in fact, was that the Doctor should go and trim his beard in the bathroom so that I could nip into his room, take the money from under the bed and lock it away in the black bag. It took an age, but at last the Doctor completed his impromptu lecture on Wittgenstein's picture theory of meaning, excused himself

143

and went to the bathroom. Quick as a flash, I was into his room and down on my hands and knees. The envelope was still there, thank God, and I was about to pop it into the black bag when I was consumed with curiosity as to what exactly I'd signed. I separated Mr Packer's laundry list from the sticky bundle of fivers, put the former into my pocket for study later, locked the money safely away in the black bag and returned as cool as a cucumber, to the living-room.

When the Doctor vacated the bathroom, I took his place therein, locked the door and fell to perusing Mr Packer's laundry list. It's thin stuff, certainly, and I'm not surprised that my Mr Rabin was so determined that I shouldn't sign it. Still, no good crying over spilt milk, and there seems little doubt that for the payment of £7500 (payable – and this came as rather a blow – as to half on the signing of a formal contract and the balance three months thereafter) Packer now owns the film rights to my book. Lord Goodman is obliged to produce a proper document within two weeks, and Franklin and I then have a further week in which to sign it. If Lord Goodman fails to produce a contract within the agreed period the deal's off. It occurs to me that this condition may serve to rescue me. Once back among the bright lights and sheep-shearing carnivals of Wagga Wagga, Packer may find the production of silly films in London a most remote and unattractive prospect, and perhaps he'll instruct Lord Goodman to pursue the matter no further. In which case I'd be seven hundred and fifty balloons to the good (there being nothing in the laundry list about the return of same) and, more importantly, I wouldn't, after all, have done anything to upset Tynan. We shall see.

Meanwhile, I'll be in the tantalising position of a bank robber who can't spend his share of the loot without drawing attention to his suspiciously altered circumstances. Not only are toys and treats of all sorts out of the question, I can't even, however surreptitiously, subsidise the weekly budget. Were our standard of living suddenly to rise, due to my having added a fiver, say, to my weekly house-keeping allowance,

Emma Jane would be on to it at once and she'd quiz me relentlessly as to the source of our new affluence. Since I can't possibly tell her of my windfall, I'll either have to burn the lot in an immorality explosion like a North Sea blow-out or leave it in the black bag until I get the balance of £6750 into my claw. And if by then I've spent the £750, how do I account to Emma Jane (who can do long division in her head) for the short-fall?

Plenty of time to worry about that sort of thing, however, and the great thing about the Doctor is that he gets us up to all manner of capers we wouldn't normally contemplate. He likes an outing, does the Doctor, and today he helped me forget my problems by bundling us into his car and driving us to the Safari Park at Windsor. Once there, he queued for hours to see the killer whale perform its tricks, but I preferred, as always, the hippopotami. Not that there were any. Who ever heard of a Safari Park without a hippopotamus? Still, there was a nice little baby elephant which I wanted to take home with us, but Emma Jane, who can be unimaginative, flatly refused to buy it for me. When I sell my film rights (not that I haven't) if I want a baby elephant, I'll have a baby elephant.

We drove back to London through Eton, where, to our great surprise we found ourselves caught up in the Fourth of June celebrations. Emma Jane, ever a warden of the bourgeois values, wanted to stop the car and search out my son Charles, but the Doctor and I, being unshaven and dressed as for a nature ramble, didn't take this to be an appropriate occasion for him to be confronted by his long lost father. I kept my eyes open, though, and couldn't help wondering which little upper-class egg – each more mortified than the next, it seemed, that *his* dumpy sister, braying elder brother back for the day, deranged mother and wheezing red-face father were manifestly so much more unsuitable than the attachments of all the other little boys – was him. What an environment for the young shaver to grow up in! Emma Jane thinks I'm unfeeling, but I'm seriously concerned, as it happens, and I have every intention of making contact with

145

him through his mother, so that I can introduce him to some nice people before it's too late.

❅ ❅ ❅

Realising that I can't forever hide my guilty secret from Mr Clowes and Mr Rabin, I have made appointments to visit them both this week. I'm calling on Mr Clowes on Thursday morning and, in satisfaction of my gambling debt, I'm taking Mr Rabin out to lunch on Friday. Meanwhile, I've made Mike Franklin M.A. promise not to breathe a word to anyone about the £750 *doucement*, least of all to Emma Jane. I think he finds all this secrecy a trifle mystifying, but he's not yet accustomed to my business methods.

I'm in a state of some confusion. The balloons in the black bag are bringing me no joy at all, yet I'd scream like Dawn Upstairs's five-year-old daughter if anyone suggested I hand them back. And I'm dreading my meetings with Mr Clowes and Mr Rabin.

At least I've taken the first step in my plan to set my son Charles along the right path before it's too late. Today I wrote to his mother, suggesting that I make contact with him at Eton. I only hope she replies.

❅ ❅ ❅

Visited my Mr Clowes this morning and he wasn't disagreeable at all. Thanks to my midnight act of sabotage, his plans to treat with Michael Winner now lay in ruins at his feet, but he mustered a thin smile and said something about making the best of a bad job. What a delightful man he is. He then read Mr Packer's laundry list with an expression of mounting concern, however, and by the time he'd reached the end he looked a little faint.

'I think we'd better send this over to Mr Rabin,' he said, laying it to one side with careful distaste, like an official at a clap clinic ruling that a slide containing the offending discharge must be sent elsewhere for more rigorous analysis.

'The circumstances under which you signed it seem so peculiar that it may not be enforceable.'

This was precisely what I'd hoped to hear. If the laundry list wasn't a binding document, I'd keep the contents of the black bag and, which was even more important, I wouldn't have thrown a spanner into the works of Mr Tynan and Mr James. It would be the last time that Packer did business with an English gentleman, but worse things happened no doubt, on Bondi Beach.

At that very moment Emma Jane rang to say that Tynan had just been on the phone, wishing to speak to me urgently. Hell. Mr Clowes suggested that I ring him back at once, and this I did, somewhat nervously.

'Ken!' I said, far too brightly, 'how *are* you?'

'I *was* all right, darling,' he said, 'until I got back from Spain this morning to be told that you've sold the film rights in the book to Michael Winner.'

'I've done *what*?' I said, with the relieved indignation of a man accused of stealing his neighbour's milk when he's merely had it away with his morning papers. 'What on earth gave you that extraordinary idea?'

'Then you haven't?'

'What! Of *course* I haven't.' Well, that was true at least. 'Why would I do a crazy thing like that?'

'I was surprised, I must say. It's perfectly clear that *we* own the film rights.'

'Nothing clearer.'

'And to dispose of them before the production of the play, not that you could, would be madness.'

'Utter folly.'

'So you haven't?'

'Of *course* not. How could I have? Even if I'd wanted to, which of course I don't. As you yourself say, *you've* got the rights.'

'Quite. Well, that's all right then.'

'Terrific!'

'Okay.'

'Ha! Ha!'

Bollocks. At least Mr Clowes agrees with my analysis of the present situation, if not with my having signed with Packer. He feels, as I do, that Tynan, once in possession of the truth will let out a scream of rage audible in Wagga Wagga, but that once the dust has settled he'll put the play on *if* it's any good. Plays *are* produced, after all, even when the film rights have been sold to someone else. But what a shame I lied to him. Why couldn't I have said: 'Hard cheese Ken! Your agent's made a blunder of which I'm taking full advantage. It's a hard life, but that's the way it goes. Ho! Ho!' I don't say he'd have been delighted, but it would have been better than being shifty. Fatalism can be shown to be fallacious, as One-Eyed Charlie has demonstrated to me many times, but that Tynan will discover the truth is, to say the least, inevitable. Sociologists tell us that the middle classes plan their lives in accordance with something they have termed, in their peculiar jargon, the Delayed Gratification Principle: a 'pay now, live later' programme suitable for prudent squirrels and exemplified, I suppose, by Mrs Thatcher's advice to housewives on the best hoarding techniques. Middle-class males on their death-beds obtain a gloomy gratification, it seems, from the knowledge that adequate provision has been taken for the wives and children. I, on the other hand, manage my affairs in accordance with the Delayed Balls-up Principle, so organising things that the longer the balls-up is delayed the more shattering will be its impact.

❋ ❋ ❋

Having plundered the black bag to the tune of £20, I took my Mr Rabin out to lunch today at Cunningham's. I tried to get him drunk, but he was on to this in no time.

'Why are you trying to get me drunk?' he said. 'What have you done? Come on, you'd better tell me.'

'I signed Mr Packer's laundry list,' I said.

'You signed *what*?'

Rather literal minded, these lawyers, not accustomed to

the figurative or metaphorical use of language. I explained what I'd done, and while he was certainly more obviously shocked than Mr Clowes had been, he didn't sever all connection with me on the spot. After a while, indeed, he became ominously elated, like a surgeon about to perform an operation that will certainly kill the patient, but which will make medical history none the less.

'My word,' he said, gleefully rubbing his hands together in anticipation of all the fun and writs to come, 'this has all the makings of a *major* legal confusion.'

Then he asked me for the £100 he mentioned at our last meeting. At this rate the black bag will be empty by the end of the week.

❄ ❄ ❄

Lunch with ·6 of a friend John Bassett up at Thames Television.

After lunch, who should we bump into but the cheery Mr Stancomb, the producer of *Ideas in Print*. In fact he seemed distinctly less cheerful than when I'd last seen him. I put this down to wind or a chance meeting with Bill Grundy in the canteen, until I realised his bad mood had been caused by my alerting Mrs Whitehouse to my appearance on his show. From his point of view, I suppose, my action must have seemed akin to someone pulling the bung out of their own boat. I asked him about audience reaction and he said they'd had an angry letter from a retired naval man now living in Dorset. What's the world coming to? You put a ponce on *The Epilogue* and *one* person complains! According to Mr Stancomb it's only a primitive terror of noises with no reference – i.e. bad language – which causes the middle-classes to protest in their thousands.

❄ ❄ ❄

A formal document has arrived from Lord Goodman, so there goes my only chance of getting out of this muddle with an ounce of dignity (to say nothing of seven hundred and fifty balloons). I'm disappointed to discover that it's not from Lord Goodman at all, in fact, but from a junior in his firm called Leighton James. Leighton plays on the left wing for Derby County and Wales, if I'm not mistaken, and is justly celebrated for his general elusiveness and speed out of the tackle. My Mr Rabin will have to be on his toes, or he'll finish on his backside. On the theory that what you don't know about can't bring on the ulcer pains, I sent the document on to Mr Clowes without reading it.

❉ ❉ ❉

The Major's careful preparations for tomorrow night's Regimental dinner and immoral cabaret have received a set-back. His partner in the venture, my friend S. Z. Corbett, was arrested today for fraud and grievous bodily harm. The fraud, which has to do with moody credit cards, was to be expected, but – since Corbett is totally non-violent – the GBH charge comes as a surprise. Both offences were committed in Harrods, where Corbett, armed with an Access Card in the name of the Marchioness of Northamptonshire or some such innocent party, was trying to knock off a fur coat. The sales-lady looked at the card, then into Corbett's beaming black face, then at the card once more. Something fishy here, she thought, and she called the manager. Corbett, sensing that his goose was cooked, decided to make a dash for freedom. Sprinting round a corner at full speed, he had the misfortune to collide with a large auntie from the home counties, who was in full sail in the opposite direction with six parcels and a peke. Hit amidships, the old tart went down like an ox in an abattoir. She didn't stir for ten minutes, but the collision didn't do Corbett much good either. He made it to the exit, at which point delayed shock caused him to drop like a stone, allowing a posse of security men to catch up with him. Now he faces this ridiculous GBH charge on top of the other thing.

We were told of this mishap by the Major, who turned

up this evening in a state of great agitation, having spent the previous three hours at Great Marlborough Street, trying to fix Corbett's bail.

'Really damned embarrassing, do you see?' he said. 'Couldn't have happened at a worse time. Slap in the middle of one of Diana's do's. You know the sort of thing: tea and cucumber sandwiches for the committee of some local law and order organisation. To do with young offenders and the spread of hooliganism, I think it was. Old Admiral Hatchett was in the chair and scheduled to make a speech. Silly old fool. Do you know him by any chance? Naval man yourself, I believe. Just a *pensée*. Anyway, I'm expected to attend such functions for my sins – Rules and Regulations, do you see? – and I was chatting away to the Admiral about the decline of moral standards, when Jane – she's our au pair – called me to the phone. It was this character at Great Marlborough Street saying they'd captured S. Z. Corbett and could I come at once.'

'My word, Major, that *was* awkward. What did you do?'

'What could I do? I had to say I'd go. Can't abandon a member of the platoon who happens to fall into enemy hands. When I went back into the drawing-room, the Admiral had started his speech.

'"Thirty years ago we'd have known what to do with the young baskets," he was saying. "Let 'em cool their heels in the brig for fourteen days, that's what we'd have done."

'The assembled ladies nodded and clucked approvingly, but I had to interrupt. I stuck my hand up.

'"Excuse me, ladies," said the Admiral. "Yes, Major, what is it?"

'"Afraid I'll have to be pushing off, Admiral," I said. "My partner's just been arrested for fraud and grievous bodily harm, don't you know. Needs my help, do you see?"

'"Good show," said the Admiral. He's not a bad old duck, I suppose, but it was a tricky moment, I can tell you.'

'Damn tricky. Was my sister Bobo there, by any chance?'

151

'She certainly was.'

'Hell.'

'Yes, she chairs several sub-committees. Diana looks on her as her right-hand man. Anyway, I drove to London and went straight to Great Marlborough Street. Too late to get bail today but I fixed him up with a visit from Diana's family solicitor. Bit outside his normal practice but that couldn't be helped. Old ladies' wills and a bit of simple conveyancing are about his limit. Couldn't use my fellow because he's one of my trustees and I didn't want him to think I was mixing with undesirables. He's up in front of the beak tomorrow – S. Z. Corbett, that is, not Diana's solicitor – so we'll try to get bail for him then. Looks as though my plans for tomorrow night are up the spout though.'

'Oh dear,' I said, 'we can't have that.'

'Yes we can,' said Emma Jane, sensing trouble and therefore exercising her right to veto.

I ignored her. 'What have you arranged so far? You've booked the suite at the Savoy, have you?'

'No, we abandoned that idea as being too expensive. Corbett was going to secure a suitable apartment and wait for us there with the girls. The Regiment were to be pointed in that direction by myself after Mountbatten's speech. Operation naughty cabaret.'

'Operation bullshit!' said Emma Jane with a snort of derision that would have done my sister Bobo credit.

'*Please*, Emma Jane. This is serious. How many? Potential mugs, I mean.'

'Hard to say at the moment. I've chatted round the Regiment, of course, and had a very good response. Damn gratifying. Could be as many as twelve.'

'What are you charging?'

'£50 a head. That would have been a profit of £360 if we'd booked six girls at £40 a girl. Not to be sneezed at, what? For my first attempt, that is? No?'

'£40 to go with *two* men!' said Emma Jane. 'That's ridiculous!'

'Oh dear. S. Z. Corbett said that was the going rate.'

'S. Z. Corbett's a wanker. He'd have arranged one girl to do the work and another to go through your friends' pockets while they were otherwise engaged.'

'Emma Jane's had little faith in S. Z. Corbett ever since he burglarised the flat of her friend Lucy,' I explained. 'Never mind. Perhaps *we* can be of some assistance. We'd be delighted to help.'

'No we wouldn't,' said Emma Jane.

'Excuse me,' I said, '*excuse* me, but I had the impression that this is precisely the business we're in. Correct me if I'm wrong.'

'You're wrong.'

'Oh.'

'You were never in it. I was once, but not any more. I am now a writer, as I keep telling you. Imagine what my publishers Eyre Methuen would say if I was up on a charge of corrupting the Brigade. It's not to be contemplated. They publish Winnie the Pooh. Good heavens.'

'You're absolutely right. It would be best if you left all the arrangements to me. That's settled then, Major. You can use this flat and Dawn Upstairs's too, perhaps, and I'll book as many naughty girls as look like being necessary. Tomorrow you must give me the exact numbers. Don't worry about a thing.'

'I say, that's most awfully good of you, old chap.' The Major seemed immensely grateful. 'I certainly didn't want my first venture to be a cock-up. And naturally I'll cut you in for half the profits. That could amount to as much as £180 each. Not bad, eh?'

Emma Jane let fly with another contemptuous snort, but, to my great surprise, she offered no further objections. The Major knocked back a bottle of brandy and then drove home to Berkshire. After he'd gone, I asked Emma Jane why she hadn't continued to put her foot down.

'No point,' she said. 'It's all a wank.'

'How can you be so sure?'

'Stag parties,' she said with an air of papal infallibility which was highly irritating, 'always are.'

153

We'll see. Emma Jane was last wrong about something at 3.42 p.m. on Thursday March 24th 1963, but there can always be a second time. Meanwhile, it's good to be back in show-business.

❋ ❋ ❋

A most agitating day, with the Major – obeying his instructions most conscientiously – phoning in a dozen progress reports between noon and six p.m. The first guest-list contained the names of seven Majors, three Captains and a Lieutenant-Colonel (rtd.), but new and increasingly bizarre names were added with each phone call. I begged Emma Jane to do something.

'Like what?' she said.

'Christ! Like booking some naughty girls! What's the matter with you? Do you want to pleasure the whole Regiment on your own?'

'*Me?* It's nothing to do with me. I told you, I've retired.'

'*Exactly.* That's why you ought to do something.'

'It's all a wank,' she said, but at last she agreed to put Dawn Upstairs on a vague stand-by call.

I had a lunch appointment, but as soon as I got back to the flat I checked on the evening's arrangements.

'Who's coming?' I asked.

'Who's coming to what?'

'Bloody hell! Who's coming to the Major's party?'

'Oh *that!* Hang on a minute, I've got a list somewhere. I wrote the names down because I thought they might make you laugh. Ah yes, here we are. Majors Hawke, Gibbens, Tupper, Buchanan-Swine (I think I've met him), Dunlop-Hardy, Marjoriebanks...'

'Here, I knew a Majoriebanks. He was in the Navy. Got among Jerry in the North Sea and caused frightful havoc. Sank three frigates and rammed an aircraft carrier. He was court-martialled of course.'

'Court-*martialled*? He should have got a medal.'

'This was in 1965.'

'Do you want to know the rest of the guest-list?'

'No.'

'Captains Rocksavage, Dipwick, Grim...'

'Okay, okay, just give me the grand total.'

'Twenty-four.'

'Twenty-four! My hat, our troubles are over. We'll make a fortune. Which girls have you fixed to come?'

'None.'

'*None?* Why ever not?'

'It's all a wank. You'll see.'

She wouldn't budge an inch, and by the evening I was up the wall with worry. When Dawn Upstairs rang to say that she was going to accept another booking, I ran out of patience.

'You're both fucking mad! By eleven o'clock tonight you could have half the British army in your front hall.'

'Don't *worry*,' said Emma Jane. 'She'll be back in plenty of time to help out if anything happens. Not that it will.'

At that moment, the Major – already as drunk as a judge, by the sound of it – checked in for the fifteenth time.

'Is that H.Q.? Bravo Charlie here.'

Bravo Charlie? What was the fool talking about?

'Hullo Major. How's it going?'

'Everything's under control here. I'm at the Savoy and dinner's about to be served. All well your end?'

'Of course. How many customers can we expect now?'

'Could be eighteen. Poor old Dunlop-Hardy had a stroke in Boodles this afternoon so he may be a bit late. And a couple of others have fallen by the wayside. I'll report in again after Mountbatten's speech. Better synchronise our watches, don't you think? I have exactly nine pip emma.'

'Near enough.'

'Right. Out and roger!'

'It looks like eighteen,' I said to Emma Jane. 'You're quite happy to see them on your own, are you?'

'Huh!'

'Huh won't help you when eighteen pie-eyed Lancers

155

come dancing through that door looking for naughty girls and only you sat seated on the sofa.'

'I bet you no one turns up.'

'How much?'

'10p.'

'Okay.'

'You haven't got 10p.'

Little does she know.

There followed two hours of nerve-stretching calm, broken only by Dawn Upstairs phoning in to say that she had returned from her early evening booking and was now ready for more work if needed. That was something, though it still seemed doubtful whether she and little Emma Jane would each be able to handle nine angry Lancers. Then, at eleven o'clock, the Major rang again. Pissed as a pudding now and kicking off once more with the H.Q. and Bravo Charlie nonsense.

'Hullo Major, how's it going?'

'Very well indeed, old boy. Mountbatten's just sat down. Not before time, I may say.'

'How about the numbers?'

'What numbers, old boy?'

'Christ! The *punters*, dear. How many punters?'

'Oh yes, so sorry. Not thinking. Had a bit to drink, do you see? Not a bad champagne they do on these occasions, not bad at all. Only reason I come.'

'Yes yes, but how many?'

'Haven't been counting, old boy. Probably about six glasses.'

'No *no*. How many *customers*? You know: johns, mugs, *gonks*, for Christ's sake. I'm trying to run a business here and I'm surrounded by wankers.'

'Ah yes, so sorry, old chap. Could be as many as ten.'

'Ten? It was eighteen an hour ago. Some dropped off, have they?'

'Yes. Frankly I blame Mountbatten's speech. Said it wasn't bloody good enough. Went on for an hour. Still, ten's a creditable start, don't you think? Should represent a profit

156

of a hundred pounds to you and me. Not bad, eh? Everything lined up your end? Got the girls organised, have you?'

'Of course. Perhaps you'd better ring once more, however, just before you leave.'

'Will do. Out and over.'

'I told you it would be a wank,' said Emma Jane.

'What do you mean wank? You can consider yourself lucky there's only ten coming.'

'Ten my eye!'

'Well I'm off. I've heard what the soldiery are like on these occasions. They'll be coming through that door any minute now cursing and swearing and spitting on the floor and waving their sabres, and it won't be "Excuse me Madam" and "After you Cecil". They don't take prisoners, you know, the British army. Not after a pep-talk from Earl Mountbatten of Burma. Manchester United's supporters aren't in it. I'm off.'

'Where are you going?'

'I think I'll be safer with Dawn Upstairs.'

'Please yourself.'

I went upstairs and knocked on Dawn's front door.

'Hullo,' she said, 'what's happening?'

She was wearing a rather unbecoming nightdress and her hair was in curlers. How these girls make money I really don't know. It wasn't a couple of Arabs or rag-trade merchants coming round, but the quality: Sandhurst men accustomed to being thrown out of the best brothels from Cairo to Cuba, including Mrs Feather's. And what had we arranged for their delight? One angry little girl curled up on the sofa watching television with her pussy cats and a somewhat larger, more mature lady who presently resembled a north country mime resting between episodes of *Coronation Street*. To a perfectionist like myself, it was heartbreaking.

'Emma Jane's downstairs on her own,' I said, 'and half the Brigade's about to arrive on her doorstep.'

'Ooooh I say! Is there a fire?'

'Not the bloody *fire* brigade. The Brigade of Guards, for goodness sake.'

'What, the Major and his pals?'

'*Yes*. Ten of them on their way over hoping for immorality and *look* at you both!'

'Probably a wank.'

'Don't you start.'

I tried to persuade her to dress a trifle more alluringly, or at least to take her hair out of curlers, but she was having none of it.

'Plenty of time for that,' she said. 'Here, do you know Lady Snipe-Bullock?'

'No.'

'You *must* do. She's one of the jet set, is Lady Snipe-Bullock. She's to do with *Vogue* and that, *you* know.'

'No I don't.'

'Well anyway, she owns this trendy hairdressing salon in the King's Road, doesn't she? And she's going to rent me a chair.'

'Good, it's nice to have somewhere to sit.'

'Don't be *silly*. I'm going to be a free-lance stylist, me, working from the salon.'

'Why?'

'I'm sick of all this. Anyway, that Pulley's putting himself about again.'

'What's Pulley?'

'Frank Pulley, Vice Squad. He called on Linda last week and asked a lot of questions about me. Was I a madam and that? All that stuff again. I don't need it, me. I'm going back to hair-dressing. I'm having some cards printed and I thought you might help me.'

'I don't do hair.'

'*No*, with the words and that. On my business card. I thought I could have one or two of those words of yours.'

'What words?'

'*You* know. Those *words* you use.'

'They're expensive. I'm not stupid, me.'

'That's true. How much have you got left in the black bag, then?'

'Never mind the black bag.'

'I'd watch out if I was you. What with Pulley putting himself about. How would you explain all that cash? Wouldn't look good, you know. Here, who's that on television? *There*. Now.'

'Bing Crosby.'

'Ooooh, Bing Crosby, is it?' She reflected on this for a while and then said, most thoughtfully: 'He's been a good entertainer over the years, has Bing Crosby.'

Well, that was undeniable, but before I had time to say as much a shattering din outside the front door suggested the arrival either of Pulley and the Dirty Squad or, it was to be hoped, the Major and the Regiment.

'Ooooh fucking hell!' said Dawn Upstairs, 'whatever's that?'

'*Domum domum dulce domum!*' sang a deep male voice on the other side of the front door.

'That's my old school song,' I said. 'Well I never. I doubt if it's Pulley. Must be the Major and his pals. What the hell are we going to do now?'

Sod these girls. I'd been warning them of this for twenty-four hours. There could be as many as a dozen guardsmen sitting on the stairs bent on rape and pillage.

'Better let them in before they wake the whole block up,' said Dawn Upstairs. 'You do that while I get myself together in the bedroom. Oh golly, where the hell's Emma Jane?'

I opened the front door rather cautiously, not wishing to be bowled over in the rush, to find the Major squatting outside with his head sagging between his knees. He was on his own.

'Hullo old chap,' he said, raising his head with a considerable effort. 'By jove, it's a fair haul up those stairs. But here I am. Couldn't let you down. Matter of honour, do you see? Emma Jane didn't seem too pleased to see me. Don't know why. Sent me up here with a flea in my ear.'

He was in a terrible state. His medals were askew, his bow-tie had come loose from his collar and was floating above it like a lady's choker and his head was iced on top like a

159

wedding cake. This unusual effect had been caused, I came to see on closer examination, by the boisterous application – not self-administered – of soda-water from a syphon mixed with granulated sugar. I had almost forgotten how much it pleases the upper-classes when celebrating to throw things at one another.

'Where are the others?' I asked.

'Where are the other whats, old boy?'

'The rest of the Regiment?'

'Oh them. Seem to have mislaid them on the way. I set off with old Jorrocks but he fell out of the car going round Belgrave Square. Awkward moment because he was driving. The car had gone another hundred yards and was heading for Sloane Street before I realised he wasn't still at the controls. Damn near entered the Carlton Tower Hotel by the revolving door. Been a bit of a surprise to them to find a Daimler in their lobby, what? By the time I got the thing under control it was too late to go back for him. He'll be all right. Fell from a chopper once during exercises on Salisbury Plain. Landed on his head but got up and walked away. Been a bit slow on the uptake ever since, mind you. But I'm here, just as I promised. Honour of the Regiment involved, do you see?'

I helped him to his feet and guided him into the living-room, where Dawn Upstairs immediately fined him two hundred pounds for time-wasting and bringing the game into disrepute.

'You are *naughty*, Major,' she said. 'Emma Jane and I had six lovely girls waiting for you here. When you didn't show up, we had to pay them and send them away.'

'That's very fair,' said the Major. 'Not quite what I had in mind at the start of the evening, of course, but we'll get it right next time. In any new business you've got to get your knees brown. May I take my clothes off?'

'Of course you can, Major.'

'Thank you very much.'

He undressed with great care down to his black silk stockings and Old Wykehamist rupture belt, and then sank back

160

with a sigh of relief into the depths of Dawn Upstairs's luxurious new sofa.

'Now then Major,' she said sharply, 'I don't want you falling asleep on me.'

'Wouldn't dream of it, my dear. Never pass out on parade. Not done. Do you take cheques?'

'Of course.'

The Major just managed to get his name to the gooses before breaking wind – just as he had when I first met him at the blue movie shop – and sliding slowly off the sofa, feet first, with the smooth, massive dignity of an ocean liner being launched.

'Well I never,' said Dawn Upstairs.

He lay on the floor, plucked, pale and meaty, like a vast mottled turkey ready for roasting: a pitiable victim of the fact that in this particular game the mugs can't win, least of all when they try to change the rules. Later I discovered that Emma Jane, before sending him upstairs, had also fined him two hundred pounds for time-wasting.

'I still say you'd have looked bloody silly if the whole Regiment had turned up,' I said.

'Ah,' she said, 'but they didn't. And you owe me 10p.'

❊  ❊  ❊

Received a letter from my first wife about my son Charles. She agrees to my visiting him at Eton and she says that his ambition is to be an Army officer. Now I'm distraught. I've written to him, suggesting an immediate meeting.

❊  ❊  ❊

Attended a conference with Mr Clowes and Mr Rabin at Mr Rabin's smart office in Curzon Street. The Packer/Tynan/Winner muddle has been further complicated by arrival on the scene of Warner Brothers, no less, with the best offer for the film rights so far. This has made Mr Clowes and Mr Rabin even more determined than hitherto to upset Mr Packer's laundry list. Mr Rabin wants to get the deal ruled unconscionable – whatever that may mean – on the grounds that I'm not a fully responsible person. He and Mr Clowes, sustained by the unbreachable moral authority that lawyers and literary agents share with tailors, hairdressers, wine waiters and public health inspectors, spoke about me and my arrangements as though I wasn't in the room. A touchier person might have taken offence, but it seemed to me that they probably knew what they were doing, so I had a little snooze. I was dreaming of this and that, when I distinctly heard the word 'Harbottle'. I spun in my seat like a conditioned rat that's been given an electronic ping in the brain.

'What was that you said?' I asked Mr Rabin.

'I was saying that they might very well take out an injunction against you.'

'No no, before that. Who might take out an injunction?'

'Harbottle.'

ZOWIE-*Ping!* Hell, there it was again.

'I say, you've gone very pale,' said Mr Rabin. 'Are you feeling all right?'

'I'm not sure. What's this got to do with Harbottle?'

'He's representing Tynan. I was just explaining to Mr Clowes that Tynan seems to have heard about the deal with Packer and is now threatening, through Harbottle, to take out an injunction against you, to prevent you disposing of the film rights.'

My God, all we needed now was Oscar Beuselinck to be called in to hold the coats and sweep up the bits and pieces. I said as much to Mr Rabin.

'You've been involved with them before?'

'I should say so, though not, as it happens, always on the losing side. On one memorable occasion I had the better of the pair of them, and in front of Lord Goodman too. It was back in the Swinging Satires, don't you know, when something called the Shrimp was on the throne, Mary Quant had six records in the top twenty, George Harrison had just been appointed Grote Professor of Mind and Logic at London University and a designer of ladies' underwear was awarded the Nobel Peace Prize. I expect you remember?'

'No, I don't think I do,' said Mr Rabin.

'No? Too young, I expect. Anyway, I had a lease on the Comedy Theatre at the time and I let it for a season to a banker called Wagg. Well, he proceeded to put on the mother and father of all turkeys, did this Wagg. It was a catastrophe. An outrage. You had to pay extra to sit behind a pillar, and on the first night the ingénue's mother booed. It was as bad as that. At the end of the week Wagg withdrew the play, owing about £5000 in rent and wages. I'd have put on a false nose and left at once for the Balearics, but this Wagg preferred to take legal advice. Something to do with the cloakrooms at the Comedy not having been decorated for a year, or some such nonsense. The dispute eventually went to arbitration before Lord Goodman. At these proceedings Wagg was represented by Harbottle *and* Beuselinck, but I made do with David Jacobs.'

'David Jacobs eh?'

'That's right. Lord Goodman was at the top of the table, Harbottle and Bumscratcher were on one side, and David Jacobs on the other. I tell you, if a bomb had gone off, there wouldn't have been a theatrical lawyer worth his fees left in London. The next time I saw him, strangely enough, it was as Mr Grant the visiting masseur.'

'Great heavens! David Jacobs a visiting masseur?'

'No, no. *I* was the masseur.'

'I wonder if we could get back to the business in hand,' said Mr Clowes. 'Len Deighton's coming to my office at four-thirty and I'd like...'

'I got this call one day to visit a Mr Howard in Chelsea Cloisters. I trotted off with my little bag of tricks and you can imagine my surprise when he opened the door stark naked.'

'Good lord!' said Mr Rabin. 'Harbottle?'

'*No*. You're becoming confused.'

'Look,' said Mr Clowes, 'this is fascinating, but...'

'Not Bumscratcher, surely?'

'No no no. David Jacobs. I took a pace back, I can tell you. It was a damn awkward moment. I mean, I hadn't seen him

163

since our victorious appearance before Lord Goodman, and here I was revealed as Mr Grant the visiting masseur. Mind you, he didn't look too clever either, stood there in his socks. But he didn't bat an eye-lid. "Ah Mr Grant," he said, "do come in, my dear."'

'Warner Brothers,' said Mr Clowes, 'are offering...'

'And did you?'

'I most certainly did. I needed the money.'

'How much?'

'Two thousand pounds,' said Mr Clowes, 'against two per cent of...'

'Two guineas. Those were the days. I used to advertise in *The Kensington and Chelsea Post*. Did very well for about two months. Thought I'd cracked it at last, in fact.'

'I really think we ought to get down to the...'

'Were all your clients men?'

'Alas yes. Except, that is, for a French lady who should have known better, but you know what the French are like. She lived in Wimbledon and I visited her three or four times. Then I worked out that the taxi fare to Wimbledon and back was costing me more than I was charging her. In fact, David Jacobs was one of the last clients I saw. My business suddenly stopped like a tap being turned off. Very bewildering. One week I was earning about eighty pounds, the next nothing. Must have been doing something wrong, I suppose. I'd just married Mrs Mouse, so I buried my pride and took a less prestigious job. I became a teacher at...'

'Now look here,' said Mr Clowes decisively, 'I've really got a lot of other very important things to do. Could we return to the subject of the meeting, do you think?'

It was finally agreed by two votes to none (it being taken for granted that my opinion didn't matter either way) that Mr Rabin should write to Leighton James, informing him that the document signed at the Savoy wasn't worth pussy. When I nervously pointed out that, shameful though this might seem, the balance of Packer's money wouldn't altogether come amiss, Mr Rabin silenced me with a wave of the hand.

'Peanuts,' he said.

I hope he won't mind if I say the same to him when he sends me his bill.

❊   ❊   ❊

Tea with my sister Bobo in an old ladies' cake-shop opposite Harrods. She had her dog with her, so the manageress tried to deny us entry.

'I'm sorry madam,' she said, 'but we don't allow dogs in here.' She was a formidable looking woman but she proved no match for my sister Bobo.

'Balderdash!' roared Bobo, brushing her to one side with a magisterial sweep of the arm. The manageress, seeing she was out of her class, wisely withdrew to a neutral corner. From here she managed to transmit waves of starched outrage that were strong enough to re-establish a degree of gravitas with her staff, but not so strong as to re-arouse my sister Bobo's dreadful wrath.

'Seen the Major?' asked Bobo casually, once we were seated to her satisfaction.

'No.'

'You're a confounded liar, Button.' (As a child I used to fly into terrible rages which caused me to spin like a top, after the fashion of a bad-tempered character in a nursery book called the Little Green Button man. Bobo has called me Button ever since.) 'I happen to know for a fact that he visited your beastly brothel place after his Regimental dinner. He's made a full confession.'

'Ah, apart from that.'

'I'm disgusted with you! What about poor Diana? You didn't think of her, did you?'

'Oh come now, she wouldn't have enjoyed it.'

'Don't be pert with me, my boy! And who's this S. Z. Corbett creature? Fancy introducing the Major to a type like that! I knew you weren't to be trusted. And where are Diana's tomatoes?'

'Diana's *tomatoes*? What are you talking about?'

'You know perfectly well what I'm talking about. They've gorne.'

'*Gorne?* Well, I haven't got them.'

'That may be so, but you're behind it. Poor Diana, she got the most frightful shock. The morning after the Major arrived home with that ghastly friend of yours, she went out into the garden and found they'd all been dug up. Not a trace of them. It must have been your friend S. Z. Corbett, but why? Is he a tomato thief? Speak up! Has the cat got your tongue?'

I was trying to put together a plausible explanation when I was temporarily let off the hook by the arrival of two of Bobo's sons, Gerard and Simon. They'd been on a shopping spree, it seemed, to buy a white tuxedo for Simon. There was mention of a dance, whereupon Bobo looked most embarrassed.

'What dance?' I said.

'Oh, you know,' said Bobo, 'just a dance.'

'*Our* dance,' said Simon.

'Be quiet Simon!' barked Bobo.

Here was a stroke of luck. If I exploited this situation to the full, we'd hear no more of Diana's prize tomatoes.

'You're giving a dance?'

'No,' said Bobo.

'Yes,' said Simon and Gerard.

'Boys!' roared Bobo, 'for the last time, hold your tongues!'

'But Mummy,' said Simon, 'why can't wicked Uncle Willie know about the dance?'

Why indeed? We like a dance, do me and Emma Jane. I'd have to hire some pumps, of course, and, come to that, a dinner jacket too.

'Because he's not coming,' said Bobo, 'and that's all there is to it.'

'Why isn't he coming?'

'Because he isn't, and I don't want to hear another word on the subject. Is that clearly understood?'

'Yes Mummy.'

Bobo turned to me. 'Now don't be offended, Button,'

she said. 'You know it's not *me* who'd mind if you were there.'

'Who would? Your husband?'

'No, of course not.'

'Who then?'

'Don't be *silly*.'

'I'm not being silly, I want to know.'

'Our friends, of course. If you were there they'd be quite *hideously* embarrassed. Surely you can see that?'

'*Embarrassed?* Great heavens, why?'

'*Why? Why?* God, you can be so *thick*. Because of your beastly book, of course.'

Well, what a relief! I'm still waiting – albeit with ever decreasing hope – for one of my friends to call me a squalid rat, but to discover that the old standards, both literary and otherwise still hold good in Berkshire is something I suppose. My younger acquaintances, it's true, tend to be bored or disapproving, but the over-thirties consistently react as though living in a brothel were both clever and amusing. Were it not for my occasional meetings with my sister Bobo I'd think the war was lost.

'Look,' I said, 'you've got it a little wrong, you know. My life-style, I mean. It's not all black girls running through the door and people falling under one another in the sauna bath. Not by a long chalk. Oh dear me no. For instance, I quite often dine with my good friend Kenneth Tynan.'

My sister Bobo's pleasant features froze instantly into an expression of outraged incredulity from which it seemed possible they might never recover. She stared at me for seconds, utterly aghast, utterly lost for words.

'But my dear boy,' she said at last, 'can't you *see*? He's *worse*.'

My nephew Gerard has solved his career problem – rather provocatively, it seems to me – by joining the Police. He enlists next week at the training academy at Hendon. Here's food for thought.

❊   ❊   ❊

Further information concerning my nephew Gerard's decision to join the police will be available to us when he comes to dine in ten days time: an occasion cloaked in greater secrecy than the Allied Invasion of Normandy owing to the fact that Bobo's husband has just ruled my home off-limits to his children. Foolish fellow. Nothing could cast me in a more alluring light than to put me out of bounds. And what a sad misunderstanding of my life-style! Alas, an impressionable young man in search of dreadful pleasures would find them sooner in a laundry than in my cosy little home. Predictably enough, within an hour of the ban being imposed, my nephew Gerard phoned me from a call-box to make the date for dinner.

❊ ❊ ❊

Received a letter this morning from my son Charles. A much less clumsy effort than mine, I thought. He seems disposed to see me and suggests I go down to Eton this Saturday. He instructs me to be under the clock in the station at 1.30. Not having set eyes on him since he was three, how will I recognise him?

❊ ❊ ❊

Unless he's fallen apart tragically during the close season, I don't think the Leighton James who is advising Packer can be the Wales and Derby County striker after all. Having invited himself to a meeting at Mr Rabin's office this afternoon, he turned out to be an overweight gent of sixty with a bloodshot left eye. I assumed he was present due to some familiarity with the law, but he made it clear at the outset that he saw his function more as that of literary critic. As soon as we were seated round the large table in Mr Rabin's conference room, he announced aggressively that £7500 seemed to him a grossly inflated price to pay for the film rights to a book like mine.

'I don't agree,' said Mr Clowes.

'Ah yes,' continued Leighton James, pausing slightly and allowing himself the superior little smile of a man with a hay-maker up his sleeve, 'but I've *read* it you see!'

Well, fancy that! Did he expect us to throw in the towel at once, mumbling through our displaced gum-shields some such grovelling excuse as: 'Golly, in that case the jig's up, of course. Had we known you'd read it, we'd never have tried to unload the beastly thing on your client.' What a prat! For half an hour or so, I struggled to disperse the red mists of rage that were hindering the composition of a statement of such annihilating properties that Leighton James would melt before it into a spot of grease, leaving only his false teeth as evidence of where he'd sat. While I framed and rejected a selection of ripe insults, I was dimly aware of legal mutter-ings in the background.

'Unconscionable.'

'Undue influence.'

'Nonsense. Over twenty-one, can read and write, I sup-pose, and seems not to have been drunk.'

'Balance of mind disturbed. *Nolle prosequi*.'

'*Mens rea*. Specific performance. Copyright Act 1956.'

'Harbottle and Bumscratcher.'

My riposte, when at last it came, struck me as being rather good.

'Buying litigation. Can't advise my client to proceed unless you can clear Tynan out of the way.'

'Burke v Worpleston, ex-parte Cockpride, 1924. Before Mr Justice Pipe.'

'Injunction.'

'Tort.'

'SHIT FACE!' I shouted.

'I *beg* your pardon?' said Mr Rabin. 'What did you say?'

'I said "shit face". Hullo, where's Leighton James?'

'He left ten minutes ago.'

'Oh. Dear me, I do apologise. My remarks were addressed to him, you understand. Was anything decided?'

'Not really. We're in a bit of a fix, I'm afraid.'

'Hell. Could you explain?'

'I'll try. While we're maintaining that Tynan has bought only the stage rights and that you are therefore free to sell the film rights to Packer or anyone else Leighton James has been sufficiently alarmed by the threatening noises issuing from Harbottle's corner to be reluctant to proceed unless we can get Tynan to agree to the deal which of course will be impossible which leaves us with no alternative but to sue Packer for specific performance of the laundry list which would take time and cost a lot of money and even if we were successful and there's no guarantee that we would be Tynan could then sue you for damages not that that would get him anywhere because you're a man of straw but such an action on his part would make it impossible for Packer to make the film so there seems to be a sort of stalemate with Packer holding on to the laundry list for dear life and Harbottle threatening to issue an injunction if anyone so much as blows his nose which is how the situation can remain till kingdom come as far as I can see it's a *fascinating* state of affairs quite unprecedented in my experience and you owe me five hundred pounds.'

Something like that.

'Don't despair,' said Mr Clowes, clearly moved by my stricken expression. 'I'll try to work out a formula that will be acceptable to all parties.'

I hope he comes up with a cracker.

❋ ❋ ❋

Down to Eton to visit my son Charles. I'd promised Emma Jane that I wouldn't play the heavy-handed father, but, debating the matter with myself in the train, I came to the conclusion that I'd be shirking my parental responsibilities unless I made it perfectly clear that his present plans to go to Sandhurst seriously displeased me. What was the the point of my coming all this way if I failed to give him the benefit of my experience? Resolved to speak my mind, I took up my position under the clock as instructed and cast my eye over the dozen or so little boys who were hanging about, hoping, I dare say, to make contact with *their* long-lost fathers. The question was, which of the be-tailed and top-hatted little fellows was mine? One of them had bushy eyebrows and looked more alert than the others, so I grabbed him by the ear and marched him down the street.

'Now then you young blighter,' I said, 'what's all this about your wanting to go to Sandhurst?'

'Please let go of my ear, sir.'

'Not until you explain yourself.'

'I don't want to join the army, sir.'

'Don't argue with me, my boy. I've received a letter from your mother in which she says you want to go to Sandhurst.'

'No sir. And please let go of my ear, sir.'

'What *do* you want to do then?'

'Please sir, I want to be a pop singer.'

'A *pop* singer! Goats and monkeys boy, take that!'

I boxed him to the ground, then, remembering my promise to Emma Jane, I decided to gain his confidence a little before pursuing this particular line.

'Are you hungry, my boy,' I said, helping him to his feet and dusting him down. 'Care for some lunch?'

The mention of tuck cheered him up so much that I made a mental note that I must have a word with Matron before returning to London. Clearly the school meals were quite inadequate.

'Oh yes please sir. Thank you sir.'

'Good good. Where do you suggest? You probably know this part of the world better than I.'

'There's an excellent Italian restaurant just round the next corner, sir.'

Sod. If I knew Italian restaurants, that would cost at least ten pounds and we'd be lucky not to be poisoned. Still, what was a mere ten pounds when one was seeing one's boy for the first time in nine years?

'That sounds fine,' I said. 'Lead on Macduff! Ha! Ha!'

I followed him into a wop establishment with all the characteristic trimmings – hams, plastic grapes and empty bottles hanging from the ceiling – and here, to my great dismay, he proceeded to order the most expensive items on the menu, together with the best wine in the evil place's cellar. If he finished the meal off with a brandy and cigar, we'd be doing the washing-up. I was so concerned, in fact, about the size of the bill we were running up (Emma Jane had capitalised the entire venture at a mouldy £15) that I found it increasingly difficult to make swift and urbane small-talk. Nor, it must be said, was my boy much help. Munching his way through soup, fish, escalope de veau and imported strawberries, he blocked my various conversational probes with monosyllabic grunts. I battled on, however, hoping that the wine would eventually loosen him up.

'It would be very jolly if you could come and stay with us during the Christmas holidays,' I said.

'Thank you, sir.'

'Your Auntie Emma Jane is particularly looking forward to meeting you, as are your Aunties Dawn Upstairs and Pretty Marie.'

'Why is she called Auntie Pretty Marie, sir?'

'Because she's so pretty, I suppose.'

'Aren't Auntie Emma Jane and Auntie Dawn Upstairs pretty, sir?'

'Oh yes, very. But not so pretty, perhaps, as Auntie Pretty Marie.'

'Do you by any chance have a photograph of Auntie Pretty Marie on you, sir?'

'Alas, no. I used to carry one in my wallet, but unhappily your Auntie Emma Jane found it during an R.S.C. when I was in the bathroom and...'

'R.S.C. sir? Does that stand for Royal Shakespeare Company, sir?'

'No, random spot check. It's a system much favoured by women, customs officers and policemen. She destroyed it, of course, and the incident was followed by ten days loss of privileges. You know what women are like.'

'I'd like to meet Auntie Pretty Marie, sir. Do you live with them all, sir?'

'Alas, no. Only with Auntie Emma Jane. But Auntie

Dawn Upstairs is, as her name suggests, only a few floors up, and Auntie Pretty Marie drops in from time to time.'

'What does Auntie Emma Jane do, sir?'

'Do? Oh, you know, bits and pieces. She's in the entertainment business, I suppose.'

'Is she a tart, sir?'

'What! A *tart*? Your Auntie Emma Jane a *tart*? Good God, never in all my life have I heard such . . . well yes, she is, as it happens.'

'And my Auntie Dawn Upstairs and my Auntie Pretty Marie too?'

'Well – er – yes, I suppose you could say that.'

'Please sir, I would very much like to come and stay with you during the Christmas holidays, sir.'

'Good, good.'

Now that we were hitting it off so much better, I decided it was time to return to the unfortunate business of his going to Sandhurst.

'Now look here,' I said. 'About this army idea. I'm really most distressed.'

'But sir, it's never crossed my mind to join the army. Honestly sir, there's nothing I'd like less.'

'I don't understand. Your mother definitely said that this was your one ambition. Are you suggesting that she made it up?'

'No sir, I'm not suggesting that. But why should my mother discuss it with you, sir? Are you the new Careers Master, sir?'

'No, of course I'm not the fucking Careers Master. I'm your father, and don't you forget it.'

'You're not my father, sir.'

'What! How *dare* you speak about your mother like that! She's a fine woman, your mother, with a *spotless* reputation. Not a whiff of scandal has ever attached to her name. Take that, you young scoundrel!'

I was so cross with him for saying this terrible thing about his mother that, even though we were in a public place, I once again boxed him to the floor. It was becoming more and more obvious to me that I had come back into his life in the nick of time. Quite clearly, the lad lacked discipline.

'Please stop boxing me to the floor, sir,' he said, climbing back on to his chair. 'I really do believe there's been a mistake. What's your name, sir?'

'What's my name? What sort of silly question is that? Donaldson of course, the same as yours.'

'No sir, my name's not Donaldson, sir.'

'No? Then who the hell are you?'

'I'm the Honourable Ned Footware-Fowler, sir.'

'The Honourable Ned Foot . . . Good God boy, stop eating those strawberries this minute! At *once*, do you hear?'

Too late. Half the plate had already gone and the head-waiter refused to put the rest back on the pudding trolley. Then the confounded fellow presented me with a bill for £11.89. I was very gradually recovering from the shock of this, when a pop-eyed old party in a loud check suiting waddled into the restaurant and up to our table.

'How dare you?' he spluttered. 'How bloody dare you?'

Who the hell was this?

'How dare I what?'

'Walk off with my boy. I've been looking for him high and low.'

'Who might you be?'

'I'm Lord Footware-Fowler, that's who I might bloody well be, and that's my son you've got there!'

'In that case you owe me some money. The young blighter just ripped into me to the tune of £11.89. In the circumstances, I'd be grateful for it back.'

'Why you . . . you . . .' There seemed a considerable danger that a cerebral haemorrhage might cause the silly old fool to topple into the pudding trolley, and since I didn't want to be charged for the loss of any more strawberries, I tried to calm him down.

'Sorry to hear about your wife,' I said.

'Eh? Eh? What about the wife?'

'Young Ned here told me everything. It's always sad when the children find out. People should think of these things before embarking on small adventures. I don't pretend to be blameless myself in this respect, but...'

'*What?* You're mad, sir! If you were a younger man, I'd punch you up your nose!'

'Why, you cheeky old bugger! I'm young enough to be your son. Begging your pardon, Ned.'

'I've had enough of this,' said Lord Footware-Fowler. 'Come along Ned. And as for you, sir, I've a mind to put the police on your tail.'

He started to drag Ned towards the door, but before they reached it, Ned broke free and ran back to my table.

'Please sir,' he said, 'does this mean that I can't come and stay with you and Auntie Emma Jane during the Christmas holidays and meet Auntie Pretty Marie, sir?'

'No, of course it doesn't, my boy. Here's my phone number. Give me a ring and I'll fix you up. It'll be my pleasure.'

'Thank you sir.'

What was I to do now? It was already 3.30 and unless I caught the next train back to London, I wouldn't be home in time for *The Generation Game*. And even if I were still able to find my son, I no longer had enough money on me to put up any sort of show. In the circumstances, there was nothing for it but to return to London.

'How did it go?' asked Emma Jane, when I got home.

'Not at all badly,' I said. 'Of course there were a few sticky moments, but that was only to be expected. I think I coped pretty well.'

'You hit it off well together did you? You and Charles?'

'We didn't, altogether, no.'

'Oh dear, what went wrong?'

'Well, I didn't actually see him.'

'You didn't *see* him? What the hell are you talking about?'

'There was a slight mishap. I got conned by this young blighter, you see. He pretended to be my son. Cost me £11.89. Could have happened to anyone, I suppose, but can you beat it?'

'My God, you're *impossible*. You go all that way and...'

175

'Here, don't go on at me. It wasn't my fault. And the day wasn't entirely wasted. The Honourable Ned Footware-Fowler is going to ring us up during the Christmas holidays and . . .'

'The Honourable Ned Footware-Fowler? Who the hell's he?'

'He's the young shaver who conned me into taking him out to lunch. It seems his mother's been playing around a bit. It turns out that his father isn't really his father. Very sad business. I met his father, in fact, and I can't say I altogether blame his mother. The man was most uncouth. Threatened me with violence, he did. Anyway, he's going to be a punter, so at least we'll get the £11.89 back.'

'Who is? Lord Footware-Fowler?'

'*No*, his son Ned.'

'His *son*? You're mad! How old is he?'

'Great heavens, how should I know? Fourteen, fifteen, I suppose. Something like that. I gave him our number and he's going to ring us during the Christmas holidays. He particularly wants to be fixed up with Pretty Marie. You should be delighted with me. He'll hand the number round and you'll have little Etonians swarming through your door like ants at a picnic. Best day's business I've done since I moved in.'

To my amazement, Emma Jane didn't seem delighted at all.

'You're the fucking limit,' she said. 'And poor Charles! How *could* you let him down like that after nine years? You ring up his housemaster this minute and offer some explanation! Go on!'

'After *The Generation Game*.'

'No, not after the fucking *Generation Game*, now.'

'Okay, okay, keep your wig on.'

As it happened, I didn't have to offer any sort of explanation. As soon as I got through to Charles's housemaster (who is called Mr Altham, oddly enough, just as mine was) the fellow started to apologise. It seemed that Charles had been up to some sort of mischief, which had caused him to be confined to barracks. By the time it had been established that

176

he was supposed to be meeting his father, it was too late for him to go to the station. Mr Altham then invited me down to Eton at half-term, to see the school play (in which Charles has a small part) and to take a drink with him beforehand. I foolishly agreed to this without first establishing what the play in question was. It turned out to be *The Duchess of Malfi*, of all unsuitable choices. Had I known this in advance, I think I'd have cobbled together a quick excuse.

❀ ❀ ❀

My Mr Clowes has worked out a most cunning solution to our problems. It has already been accepted by Harbottle in practice and by Leighton James in theory, and it is now on its way by telex to Packer in Wagga Wagga. The formula is as follows. Packer immediately pays me the balance of the £7500. This, for the time being at least, secures him the film rights. Tynan then has until the end of the year to produce the play. Should the play turn out to be such a success that a film company is persuaded to bid a substantial sum for it, Packer has fourteen days in which to match the offer. If he does, the film is his for the making and he also gets the benefit of Clive's script. If, however, he wishes to back out, his £7500 is returned to him immediately, plus interest for his trouble and a small profit participation in the film. The balance of the new and substantial offer would then be split between the Tynan group and me. In principle, this formula should suit everyone. Tynan is no longer excluded from the film rights; I'm getting my money, with more to come if the play is a success; and, as Leighton James admits, Packer can't lose. He might still get the film at the original price and should he find himself gazumped it will only be because the success of the play has boosted the value. A cunning formula indeed, the only snag being that I don't for a moment imagine that Packer will accept it. It is built, I think, round a colossal misunderstanding of his present fantasies. He's driven at the moment, I'd say, by a wild desire to be a film producer, not a cunning business man. What he wants is to chat up starlets, fly to L.A. (or the Coast, as *Variety* has it), negotiate with sun-tanned distributors, talk balls at breakfast conferences and ponce around a set. All that old-time stuff. Mr Clowes's formula says that he can't do any of this for at least a year, and perhaps not even then.

If it comes off, Mr Clowes is a genius. If it doesn't, I'm in deep snooker. The ubiquitous Mr Pulley is, like a heartless bird of prey, circling ever closer, picking off ponces before breakfast and causing havoc among their benefactors. Dawn Upstairs has made good her threat to become a hairdresser, her new young man Des the Dealer has gone home to his mummy, Black Danielle has become a teacher at a nursery school, and Emma Jane will see only regular customers. Since she hasn't got any, we've been on cod fingers for more than a week. To cap it all, my firmest support in times of trouble, Lord Dynevor, won't speak to me. This follows my inadvertently losing him his job at Hatchards. Amazingly, my client, the Sikh's mistress, has, ever since the debacle in the sauna bath, been trying to arrange a repeat performance. At least once a week, the Sikh phones, asking to speak to Lord Dynevor. Usually Emma Jane or I say that he's abroad, in Wales, indisposed or otherwise unavailable for immorality. Two days ago, however, he caught me unawares and without thinking, I said:

'Lord Dynevor? He doesn't live here. You can get him in the children's department at Hatchards.'

The Sikh trotted off to Hatchards and found his way to the right department.

'A very good morning to you,' he said to the manageress of children's books, 'and if you would be being so very kind, I'd like to be having the word with the Lord Dynevor, his highness.'

'Just a moment, sir,' said the manageress, 'I'll go and fetch him.'

She disappeared and shortly returned with Lord D.

'This gentleman would like a word with you,' she said.

'Yes, sir,' said Lord D, 'what can I do for you?'

'No, no, no,' said the Sikh, 'we seem to be having some

of the cock-up here. This is not Lord Dynevor, oh dear me no. Lord Dynevor is a much older man and has the head like the bald egg. He has been giving my mistress Shrimati the severe seeing to, for which I pay £25, but this is not the gentleman.'

'But I *am*,' insisted Lord Dynevor. 'I mean, I'm not the man who's been – er – ah – um – the – with – er – what? But I *am* Lord Dynevor.'

'No, no, *no*,' insisted the Sikh, becoming quite excited, 'this is not the man who's been attending to my mistress. This man is the imposter! He is the Lord Dynevor, my donkey!'

'Arse,' said the manageress of children's books, 'oops, do excuse me!'

The upshot was that the management at Hatchards chose to believe the Sikh, and Lord Dynevor has been sacked. He holds me responsible and has broken off diplomatic relations. This is very serious. Now, when Mr Pulley strikes, there'll be no one to stand bail for me, since my other guarantor, my friend Scott, has just flown off to L.A. to make some silly film.

❋ ❋ ❋

My nephew P.C. Downes to dinner. He's now been at the Police Academy in Hendon for a week and he's looking rather stunned. The popular theory that policemen are not people too honest to be criminals but that criminals are people too short to be policemen seems to be confirmed by the fact that half the recruits have spent the first week burglarising the valuables of the other half. P.C. Downes has so far lost his watch, wallet and gold cuff-links. To cheer him up, I appointed myself as his snout. With me behind him, I argued, he'd rise to the top like a bad apple in a cider vat. All he had to do was get himself appointed to B division, and he'd be in a position, thanks to information coming from me, to arrest half Chelsea in his first week.

❋ ❋ ❋

I have applied for a job in publishing. A large organisation whose fortunes had hitherto been based on the manufacture of detergents, has recently invaded the paperback market with an imprint called Climax Books. They have been advertising for enthusiastic young editors with experience of detergents, and last week I wrote off for an interview. This morning I received a letter from the managing director, inviting me to attend on him next Tuesday. I will go along, even though I haven't much faith in my ability to secure a position. The last time I applied for a job was in 1966, when I offered my services to the BBC. After a series of interviews with well-mannered rowing blues and out-of-work headmasters, at which it seemed to me progressively more obvious, I must admit, that I was about to be rewarded with a position commensurate with my special gifts and experience, I was offered a job in the accounts department. Since I'd just produced four West End hits in a row and yet managed to go bankrupt, this seemed a rather eccentric move on the BBC's part and one which would have resulted, no doubt, had I accepted the challenge, in the Corporation's hitherto rock-solid gooses bouncing like Rumanian acrobats all over London. Things are so bad at the moment, that should Climax Books, after careful perusal of my *curriculum vitae*, decide to offer me the post of Finance Director, I shall be tempted to accept it.

❊ ❊ ❊

Mr Pulley of the Morals Squad has netted me at last, and let it be said at once that if I've ever written, spoken or otherwise published an offensive, superficial, woolly-minded, glib or irresponsible hearsay innuendo against the Metropolitan Police, I here and now irrevocably withdraw it. Mr Pulley is the most civil, cultured, perceptive, charming and kindly gentleman it has ever been my privilege to meet.

The phone rang at six o'clock yesterday evening. Dr Bryson, who had been staying for the weekend, was watching *Magic Roundabout* and I was doing my pantry accounts.

180

Emma Jane had gone to Newmarket, I'm glad to say, so I answered it.

'Frank Pulley here,' said an educated voice. 'May I speak to Mr Donaldson?'

'Oh hullo Mr Pulley,' I said, thus making my first mistake, 'how *are* you?' That I'd been expecting him to call was all too obvious. A reputable rate-payer would have said: 'Frank Pulley? Who the hell are you? If you wish to speak to me, make a date with my secretary.' With me, however, it was 'Yes Mr Pulley', 'No Mr Pulley', 'If you say so Mr Pulley', 'Kick my arse Mr Pulley', – just like any petrified minor villain in *The Sweeney*.

'I thought we might meet,' said Mr Pulley.

'I'd be delighted to, of course, but why?'

'I'd like a chat.'

'How nice! What about exactly?'

'Oh, this and that.' He really sounded very cordial. 'You seem to be very well connected and I thought you might give us some information. Would you like to come down to West End Central?'

'I'd rather not.' I had visions of never getting out again, and the Doctor and I were due to attend a meeting of The Aristotelian Society, at which Quinton was to read a paper on Social Objects.

'Just as you wish. Where would you prefer to meet?'

'Do you know the Goat and Boots?'

'I certainly do. See you there in half an hour?'

'Fine, but how will I know you?'

'Don't worry, I'll recognise you. See you there, then.'

At that moment Emma Jane returned from Newmarket and, on hearing of my date with the Vice Squad, went into an immediate tail-spin. I tried to reassure her, pointing out that they'd be unlikely to arrange a meeting in a pub with a man they planned to collar. They'd much prefer to kick his front door down at five o'clock in the morning. Such a procedure would be more fun and, what with the price of alcohol these days, cheaper. Emma Jane was beginning to see the sense of this, but then she rang everyone up – as the girls always do on these occasions – and was advised by a predictably helpful Dawn Upstairs and Dopey Linda that meeting their victims in pubs was frequently the Yard's practice. What the reason was, they didn't know, but both had ex-consorts, they were quick to point out, who had walked cheerfully into just such a trap. Emma Jane started to blub, and even the Doctor began to show symptoms of unease.

'Oh dear,' he said, 'we seem to be in some sort of snooker here.'

Then, to my great surprise, he produced a timetable from his briefcase and started checking on the trains to Warwick.

'You clearly imagine,' I said, 'headlines of the order of "Lecturer in moral philosophy held in Chelsea vice swoop".'

'I'm not a lecturer in *moral* philosophy,' he said testily, his commitment to precision getting the better of him even in this trying situation. 'And this isn't Chelsea, it's Fulham.'

'It's bloody not!' said Emma Jane, her indignation at being downgraded in this way causing her blubbing to cease abruptly. 'I'll have you know that I pay my rates to the Royal Borough of Kensington and Chelsea.'

'I do beg your pardon,' said the Doctor. 'No insult was intended, I assure you.'

This small misunderstanding seemed to have cheered them up, but I was beginning to feel a trifle shaky. Meetings with the law always go to my legs, for some reason, but after a quick smoke and a couple of valiums I felt steady enough to walk down the road to the Goat and Boots. I had assumed that Mr Pulley would let me stew on my own for a while, but he arrived after only a few minutes.

He was one of the most unmenacing looking policemen I'd ever seen. He was about forty-five, with the rather reassuring, next-door neighbour good looks that advertising agents believe sell pipe tobacco well. I had him down as someone's favourite uncle; reliable at parties, but with a twinkle in his eye and likely to tweak his niece's knickers when her mother wasn't looking. I offered him a drink, but he refused.

'I suppose if you allowed me to buy you a drink,' I

said, 'you'd technically be living on immoral earnings. Ha!
Ha!'

'That's right,' said Mr Pulley. 'Ha! Ha!'

Having set off on this note of cheery banter, we never
looked back.

'How's Emma Jane?'

'In the pink, thank you Mr Pulley.'

'And Dawn Upstairs?'

'Fine, just fine. She's a *sweet* girl. She's a hairdresser now,
you know.'

'Yes, and not a moment too soon, as it happens. She's been
a very naughty girl, has Dawn Upstairs.'

'What! She's practically an angel!'

'I could tell you different. She can count herself very lucky,
in fact, that we didn't pull her in a year ago. We were all
set to, but then we got put on to something more important.
You can tell her that from me. I'm Knights or Mason, by
the way. Whichever you prefer, I suppose. Ha! Ha!'

Good God, this was a bit of a bomb-shell, and Mr Pulley
looked thoroughly pleased with himself as he casually tossed
it across the table. In *Both the Ladies and the Gentlemen*, how
offensive had I been about this alarming couple who, with
their prolonged investigation into immorality, had caused us
to take off in all directions in search of cover? I must have
been fairly offensive, else why had I given them, or me, the
protection of pseudonymity? There had certainly been
something about their threatening Big Elaine and some un-
pleasantness involving Scotch Anna, but the details refused
to come to mind.

'Oh dear,' I said, 'you've read the book then?'

'Indeed I have, and that's why I'm here. In a semi-official
capacity, you might say.'

That was encouraging. Surely one couldn't be semi-
officially arrested?

'I see.'

'Yes,' continued Mr Pulley, 'I wanted to congratulate you
on it. It's been keeping West End Central in stitches.'

'I'm so glad.'

'Yes. When I said I was going to meet you, half the station wanted to come along.'

'That's most gratifying.'

'Mind you, I don't wish to imply that it's a frivolous book, a mere literary romp. I take it to be a serious and highly moral document.'

'My own feelings precisely, Mr Pulley.'

'Your analysis of the relationship between the Vice Squad and *The News of the World*, for instance, is most thoughtful, and, as it happens, largely correct.'

'Thank you.'

'Your suggestion that the police at all times know the names of London's top madams is, of course, perfectly true. You are also right in saying that we only take action against them once they have been exposed in *The News of the World*. But you are wrong to conclude from this that there's some reluctance on our part to prosecute. It's simply a question of time and manpower. We can't justify the time and trouble it takes to bring a fairly harmless madam to court. This doesn't mean that we approve in any way of her activities.'

'Of course not.'

'If, for instance, I now devoted three months to building up a case against our friend Dawn Upstairs, my Commander would ask me what the hell I thought I was doing. He'd want me out chasing the bigger villains, right?'

'Right.'

'But once she'd been exposed all over *The News of the World*, he'd have to let me get on with it.'

'I see.'

'The same applies to you, I may say.'

'Oh?'

'Yes. We could pick you off any time we felt like it.'

'Golly.'

'But what would be the point? You'd draw a £25 fine and be handed a clip round the ear. Waste of everyone's time. We've got better things to do. Of course, if Chelsea wanted to nick you, that would be their business. And don't think it would break my heart if they did.'

184

'No?'

'No. Let's face it, you're well overdue.'

'You're absolutely right, Mr Pulley.'

'I mean, what's a man of your education doing living off a brave little girl? Not that we really think of you as a ponce. More of a parasite, really. We're after the bigger fish.'

Why would no one take me seriously?

'Anyway,' continued Pulley, 'I'm really here, as I say, to congratulate you on the book. Quite the best on the subject I've ever read. Would you consider coming down to West End Central some time to sign copies for my colleagues?'

'I'd be delighted to.' For an author to sign copies of his work at West End Central was surely a greater honour than to be invited to do so across the road at Hatchards. 'I think I must tell you, though, that your boss, Sir Robert Mark, fails to share your favourable opinion of my work.'

'Is that so? You surprise me.'

'Yes, in a letter to a relative he described it as badly written and only of interest to the intellectually perverted.'

'How extraordinary. I wouldn't, of course, want to say anything against Sir Robert...'

'Of course not.'

'... but I do think that judgement shows how well advised he was to opt for a career in the police force rather than in literary journalism.'

'Delightful! May I quote you?'

'No.'

'I thought perhaps we might put Sir Robert's comment on the cover of the paperback edition, with yours underneath.'

'No.'

'Oh well.'

'Now then. While everything I've said about the book has been sincere, there is something I want from you.'

'What's that?'

'Information.'

'*Information?* Good heavens.'

How was it possible that I'd know something that the Vice

Squad didn't? It's never been part of my case against the police that they're ill-informed.

'You surely don't expect me to put up a friend, do you?'

'Goodness no!' Mr Pulley looked comically shocked at the very idea. 'We're after the big villains.'

'*I* don't know any big villains! What sort of circles do you think I move in?'

'You might have heard something.'

'I'm sure I haven't.'

'Come on, think. You never know what might be useful.'

Oh dear, what a predicament. Mr Pulley had been so cordial about my work that I felt I couldn't let him down. It was like the nightmare of being tortured for information you haven't got. Suitable candidates for framing passed quickly through my mind. Richard Ingrams? Harbottle and Bumscratcher? Patrick Cosgrave? Lord Hailsham? Sir Robert Mark?

'I have heard something,' I said.

'Yes, yes, what?'

'There may be nothing to it.'

'Never mind. Let me be the judge of that.'

'Janie Jones is no better than she should be.'

'Ha! Ha! Come along now, you can do better than that.'

'Let me think. Ah yes. James Humphries is a bit of a Jack the lad.'

'Come on William, you're not trying.'

Suddenly I had an inspiration.

'I don't think I can help you,' I said. 'It wouldn't be ethical. You see, I'm already P.C. Downe's snout.'

'P.C. Downes? Who the hell's P.C. Downes?'

'He's my young nephew. He joined the force a week ago and I'm his snout. The last episode of *The Sweeney* showed us all too clearly what happens to a promiscuous snout. He gets totalled in a phone-box.'

'A disgusting programme, glamorising mindless violence.'

'I do so agree with you.'

'Look, I'd be delighted if you'd dine with me this evening. There's an excellent Chinese restaurant down the road. What

186

do you say? We could continue this discussion over a pleasant meal.'

'That's awfully good of you, but it so happens that I have a house-guest at the moment, Dr Bryson, a lecturer in Philosophy at Warwick. He and I – with your permission, of course – are off this evening to a meeting of the Aristotelian Society. Quinton's reading a paper on Social Objects, in which he argues a middle line between those who take an almost Hegelian view of a social object's existence and those who want to deny that a social object (The Aristotelian Society itself, would be a happy example, or the British Nation, if we want to operate on a larger scale) has any existence apart from the existence of its constituent parts.'

I sat back feeling thoroughly pleased with myself. Now perhaps Mr Pulley would appreciate that he was dealing here with no ordinary bawdy house piano player, to be hauled at short notice into pubs and quizzed as to the company he kept, but with a thinking man. Game, set and match to me, unless I was much mistaken.

'Quinton, eh?' said Mr Pulley.

'Yes, he's...'

'I'm quite well aware who he is, thank you. I was going to say that I've always found him rather too *urbane*. A nine-to-five philosopher, if you know what I mean. He gives the impression that he's constantly on his elegant way to or from a wine tasting party. He spends far too much time on *Any Questions* and light-weight nonsense of that sort. For a philosopher to keep the company of the likes of Enoch Powell and Jimmy Saville is unbecoming, in my opinion, and it should be no part of a serious teacher's function to answer the trivial questions of plain men. One wouldn't be flabbergasted if he cropped up with Shirley Bassey as a guest on The Parkinson show.'

'Hell.'

'I'm not denying that he's got an encyclopaedic mind. He seems to have read everything, and, what's more, he remembers what he's read. But he can be accused, I think, of ignoring difficulties. You've read his book *The Nature of Things*?'

187

'Indeed.'

'Then you'll know what I mean. Take his chapter on mind, for example. At no point does he tell us what empirical evidence he'd accept as corroborating or refuting his thesis that minds and brains are identical.'

'Nor he does.'

'Does the thesis rest on the theory that mental and physical states are perfectly correlated? And what, in that case, would be needed to turn this correlation into an identity? Is it just a *decision* to call them the same? Until these points are cleared up, the thesis, I think you'll agree, can hardly be assessed.'

'Bless my soul.'

'And what about the chapter on value?'

'What indeed.'

'Quinton's position is, as you may remember, strictly utilitarian. From the premise that all desire is for satisfaction – which he treats as a tautology – he concludes that value judgements state the conditions of satisfaction with reference to people in general and in the long-run. But he nowhere shows us how this principle applies to the assessment of particular actions, nor does he look at those difficult cases where the principle of utility appears to be incompatible with our intuitions about freedom and justice. He prefers, as I say, to skate urbanely round these difficulties.'

'Tell me. Have you ever arrested someone called One-Eyed Charlie?'

'What! I should say so. A most engaging fellow.'

'Spend much time with him, did you?'

'Indeed. On one occasion it was my privilege to interrogate him for three days.'

'What happened?'

'I had to let him go. He was able to convince me of certain elementary fallacies in my case. He made quite an impression on me.'

'I can see that.'

'Thank you.'

'Look, I've got an idea. Why don't you come home with me? I know Dr Bryson would like to meet you. You could dine with us – it's only cottage pie, I'm afraid – and then we could all go on to the meeting. What do you say? I'm sure the Doctor could smuggle in another guest.'

And thus it was that an evening that had started out so unpromisingly ended with Dr Bryson and I escorting a member of the Morals Squad to a meeting of the Aristotelian Society. Quinton read his paper on Social Objects and then the Secretary stood up.

'Since there are so many unfamiliar faces here tonight,' he said, 'I'd be grateful if, before addressing a question to Mr Quinton, you'd first announce your names and teaching posts. Thank you.'

Mr Pulley immediately rose to his feet.

'Pulley,' he said, 'Vice Squad, West End Central,' whereat a little old philosopher in the third row fell off his chair, another bolted for the exit and Quinton went white as chalk. He was so relieved to discover, however, that Mr Pulley was here, not to arrest him, but to accuse him of nothing more criminal than a lack of logical rigour, that he took his mauling in good part.

❊    ❊    ❊

Inasmuch as he's ignored it, Packer seems to have rejected Mr Clowes's cunning formula. It's a month now since it was sent to him by telex and we've heard nothing. This afternoon I had a most unsatisfactory telephone conversation with my Mr Rabin.

'What do we do now?' I asked.

'I suggest,' said Mr Rabin, 'that I write to Leighton James, informing him that we are prepared to go back to the original agreement, as outlined in the Savoy Hotel laundry list, and asking him for the balance of the money. We'd better write to him at Loftus Road, since he's now moved from Derby County to Q.P.R. Ha! Ha!'

'Ha! Ha!'

I can't be doing with people who make silly jokes at serious moments.

189

'What will happen?'

'Absolutely nothing,' said Mr Rabin cheerfully. 'He'll ignore my letter entirely. So we'll write to him again, saying that we take his silence to be a repudiation of the laundry list. He'll ignore this too.'

'What could we do then?'

'Sue Packer, either for specific performance or damages.'

'What would that cost?'

'If you won, between two and three thousand pounds.'

'And if I lost?'

'You'd go bankrupt, I suppose.'

Good grief, I only wrote a book. It took me *five years* to go bankrupt in the theatre and I had a couple of laughs along the way. The first night of *The Three Musketeers*, for instance, when the Alberts blew up the Arts Theatre just as the critics were taking their seats. They'd left their explosives stacked by the window in their dressing-room and the heat of the sun had eventually detonated them. The bang was terrific and that excellent mime Stratford Johns, who'd been crouching in the karzi at the time doing his number 2's, emerged as white as a sheet and didn't speak for three days. As soon as he got his voice back he cancelled all his bookings and checked into a health farm.

'What if Packer *were* to sign the original contract and cough up the balance of the money?'

'Ah, in that case you'd be sued by Tynan.'

'Good morning.'

So: in a moment of insane greed at the Savoy Hotel I handed Packer the freehold of a film he'll never make and at the same time scotched Tynan's plans. A good night's work.

> The desires of the heart are as crooked
>    as corkscrews,
> Not to be born is the best for man;
> The second best is a formal order,
> The dance's pattern; dance while you can.

I'm no gonk, but I am a dancing man – or, to be more precise, a man of the theatre – and it's a well-known fact that when despair visits a man of the theatre he will not be comforted save by a stage production of such definitive excellence that the memory of it will stay with him for the rest of his days. There are five hundred balloons left in the black bag and after my interview next Tuesday with Climax Books, I intend, whatever the outcome, to repair with these straight to the Hilton Hotel, there to invest every last one in a small private production of such perfection that I'll continue down the greasy pole with a smile on my face proof against all life's insults. After careful study of Bamber Gascoigne's fine book *Twentieth Century Drama*, I have selected *The Killing of Sister George*, from a short-list including *The Maids* and *The Balcony*, as the play that best lends itself to the kind of staging I have in mind. My budget, I regretfully decided, wouldn't stretch to a satisfactory production of *The Balcony* (unless I played the Queen, the Judge, the General and the Chief of Police), and *The Maids*, in so far as Madame is off-stage whenever anything immoral occurs, contained no worthwhile part for myself. *The Killing of Sister George*, however, might have been written with Pretty Marie, Scraggy Janet and myself in mind. After a series of eye-ball to eye-ball negotiations, compared with which dealing with Irving 'Swifty' Lazare would be like looting a nursery school, I have been able to secure Pretty Marie for the Susannah York/Eileen Atkins role and Scraggy Janet for the part previously played by Coral Browne and Lally Bowers. I myself will appear – not for the first time, I may say – as Beryl Reid.

If everything goes according to plan, then, my programme for next Tuesday is as follows:

8.30. Rise, bathe and shave. Trim eyebrows. Emma Jane will notice this small cosmetic touch, but I'll say it's for the Managing Director of Climax Books. Over breakfast (a cup of coffee) notice with annoyance that *The Sun* still hasn't printed my sensible letter to Claire Raynor.

9.30. Get to work on household duties. Clean bathroom and kitchen and dust in sitting room. Can't Hoover yet or will wake Emma Jane. Squeeze oranges for Emma Jane's breakfast.

10.00. Take Emma Jane her breakfast on a tray. Also her mail (only twenty letters today) and her copy of *The Guardian*. 'Good morning, my dear,' she says, 'why have you trimmed your eyebrows? Are you planning to mount a production of *The Killing of Sister George* at the Hilton Hotel with Pretty Marie in the Susannah York role, Scraggy Janet in the part previously played by Coral Browne and with yourself as Beryl Reid?' 'Good heavens no,' I say, 'I'm off to an interview with the Managing Director of Climax Books.'

10.15–11.00. Finish the housework.

11.00. Sign *exeat* book and leave flat with half an ounce of soft drugs, three copies of French's acting edition of *The Killing of Sister George* and five hundred balloons stuffed up my shirt.

11.30. Arrive at Climax Books. Astonish the Managing Director with my qualifications. I am offered the post of Finance Director – or not, as the case may be.

12.00. Leave Climax Books, confused if I've been offered a job, but cheered by the prospect of the theatrical production to come.

12.00–13.00. Purchase cheap suitcase and several copies of *The Evening Standard* to put therein as simulated night clothes. The management of the Hilton quite rightly look askance at punters who arrive without luggage.

13.15. Check into the Hilton, where I have taken the precaution of booking myself in as Lord Dynevor. Not, I may say, in order to land him with the bill, but merely to secure the suite in the first place. At such times I've always found a title helps.

13.30–14.00. Fiddle with the lighting, rearrange the furniture, dress the set, read through the play, work on my interpretation (a shade less butch, perhaps, than Beryl Reid's? Leave the heavy stuff to Scraggy Janet, that's best), roll a couple of joints, bathe and rest.

14.00. Pretty Marie and Scraggy Janet due to arrive.

14.30–15.15. Pace up and down in a fury brought on by non-arrival of Pretty Marie and Scraggy Janet. Rehearse suitably sarcastic speech about unprofessionalism of artistes who fail to turn up by the half.

15.15. There's a knock on the door. Thank goodness, and about time too. I open it and in strides an officious little pansy with carrot-coloured hair.

'Who the hell are you?' I say.

'I'm Bent.'

'I can see that.'

'What? I don't get it.'

'I'm not surprised.'

'No, no. Mr James Bent, an Equity theatre representative. Word has reached us that you – a long-standing entry on our list of struck-off impresarios – plan to mount in this suite a production of *The Killing of Sister George* in which scenes of simulated sexual intercourse may take place involving one of my members. It's my duty to tell you that unless an Equity observer is present throughout and unless you lodge the customary deposit with the Theatre Council, I'll have to pull my member out. What do you have to say to that?'

'You keep it where it is, you daft little pouff, that's what I've got to say to that! It so happens that I'm not using any of your grotty members, so get on your bike! How dare you!'

'What about Miss Doreen Sopwith?'

'I've never heard of her. Now on your way! You're exhausting my patience.'

'She's in the play.'

'The devil she is! Doreen Sopwith indeed! Now lose yourself you interfering little pip-squeak before you get the toe of my shoe up your backside!'

'Mr Plouviez will hear of this!'

'Mr Plouviez can fuck himself!'

I've always wanted to say that. Mr Bent looks thunderstruck at such blasphemy, but he backs out of the suite (a wise precaution) muttering threats.

'We'll be back.'

'Sod off!'

The cheek of these union officals! Why can't they get their

own scenes together? Still, I'm pleased with the urbane way I handled the incident. As soon as Pretty Marie and Scraggy Janet have arrived I'll push the wardrobe against the door as a barricade against the lascivious Mr Bent.

15.30. Pretty Marie and Scraggy Janet arrive at last. Pretty Marie looking so exquisite that I quite forget my speech about unprofessionalism. Get straight on with script conference, rehearsals and technical run-through. Iron out difficulties, correct faulty interpretations, soothe first-night nerves, cope with last minute manifestations of artistic temperament etc. etc.

15.45 Curtain up.

17.00. Curtain down. Pay artistes. Return to flat, leaving suitcase and copies of *The Evening Standard* at the Hilton (to be retrieved the following day, when checking out and settling my account).

I'm sure I'm doing the right thing. As the day of my big theatrical come-back draws near, I feel the familiar adrenalin pounding in my ears. My return to the laughter and heartbreak of the live theatre! The smell of the greasepaint, the roar of the crowd, the flickering footlights, the carriages at eleven, the bouncing gooses, the repossession men coming for the set! This will be my final throw, my last offensive, my Battle of the Bulge.

✳  ✳  ✳

Behind an enormous desk made of black glass, Mr Zapper, the Managing Director of Climax Books, lounged dynamically.

'Mr Dickenden!' he cried, bouncing to his feet as I entered his office and macheted my way towards him through the undergrowth of potted plants. 'Hi there!'

He was nineteen or thereabouts and had the demented zest and curious mid-Atlantic twang of a disc-jockey. I'd supposed that the cult of nappy-capitalists had died a death along with the fringe banks and paper real estate conglomerates to which it had given birth, yet here it was flourishing still in – of all places – the world of letters. Faber and Windus would be turning in their graves.

'Doddledon,' I said. 'I'm afraid I'm a little late.'

This was so. In my excitement (not so much at the prospect of my interview with Mr Zapper, I'm afraid, as with the thought of the matinée to follow), I'd left home without the five hundred balloons. Returning home, I'd been horrified to find that Emma Jane had already started her Captain's rounds. Unable to extract the balloons from the black bag under her beady eye, I'd been forced to set out again with the black bag itself under my arm. Emma Jane had been suspicious, but carrying a brief-case, I'd argued, made me seem more serious. Emma Jane's radar eyes had scanned me up and down for clues, but I'd got away with it.

'Yeah,' said Mr Zapper. 'Well, what can I tell you? Do you watch much television?'

'I do indeed. Is that bad?'

'Bad? *Bad?* It's terrific. Look, let me tell you something. TV's the name of the game, baby! The only thing worth publishing these days is a spin-off from a TV series. Would you believe that nowadays I read nothing but *The Radio Times* and *The TV Times?*'

'I would, yes.'

'Just to check on the up-coming shows, you understand. Yes sir, that's where it's at. TV. Oh, and really high-class erotica, of course that always sells. But only the very best. Look, I don't want to hold you up, Mr Dickenden...'

'Doddledon.'

'Yeah, so I'll give you the bottom line. Can you come back this afternoon?'

This was a ballbreaker. Obliged to choose between a casual sexual escapade that would probably end in bloody recriminations and a business appointment that might have a decisive bearing on my whole future, I would normally, of course, opt for the casual sexual escapade. But what with one thing and another, I was at such a low ebb at the moment that for once I hesitated.

'Ah well, the thing is...'

'Look, I'll give you the deep background to this, Mr Dick-enden . . .'

'Doddledon.'

'Yeah. I dig your track-record, I really dig it. It's exactly what we're looking for.' He picked up a piece of paper and began to read from it (with a certain amount of difficulty, I couldn't help noticing). 'Left school at fifteen with an 'O' level in industrial riveting, a couple of years as roadie for Goldie and the Gingerbreads, a year as Pete Murray's body-guard, two years diving for North Sea Oil, a spell as leader writer for *The Daily Telegraph* (we'll overlook that), three years doing PR for the National Front, six months writing dirty jokes for Esther Rantzen and another six months for smuggling watches. Exactly the sort of background we want our senior editors to have if we're to give Penguin and Pan a run for their money.'

My own credentials suddenly seemed lamentably thin compared to this fellow Dickenden's, so I made no further attempt to establish my true identity.

'But here's the hang-up,' continued Mr Zapper. 'Just half an hour ago, a face ran through the door that really fitted, and I've got to move fast because Simon and Schuster have asked him to take over their operation in L.A. You may have heard of him. Name of Pardoe.'

'Not *Ken* Pardoe, by any chance?'

'Right on!'

'An Australian?'

'No, I don't think so. He struck me as being from the States.'

Great heavens, Ken the Australian Horse Player was about to pinch my job! This was the second ballcrusher in two minutes and in my agony – not to say surprise that he wasn't still in the boob on the pebble-dashing caper – I'm ashamed to say I nearly blew it for him.

'I thought he was still in the . . .'

'L.A.? No, he told me he had been our there for a few months finalising some deal with Peckinpah, but he flew back to London last week for the opening of *Jaws*. It was his prop-

196

erty originally, you know, and he sold it to Twentieth for a big profit. He's certainly got bags of editorial clout, this Pardoe, and it's editorial clout we're looking for here. I was lucky to catch him before he flew back to L.A. to take up this job with Simon and Schuster. There's no way I can let that happen, no way.'

'No way.'

'But – and it's a big but, I'll admit – the Chairman really likes your qualifications too and he'd dig to see you both before we make the final decision. What do you say? He'd see you now, but at the moment he's down in the gym working out.'

'Working out what?'

'Right! Fittest man of twenty-three I've ever seen. So can you tough it out until this afternoon?'

Should I? With a little thought I could roast Ken's chances, the manic Mr Zapper's present infatuation with him notwithstanding. And yet...Pretty Marie and Scraggy Janet...the sawdust and the tinsel...the laughter and heart-break...the flickering footlights...the carriages at eleven...no, the show must go on. First things first.

'Alas,' I said, 'that would be quite impossible. Anyway, I knew Pardoe when he was Chief Story Editor at Warner Brothers and I have to admit he's the better man. In the circumstances it's honour enough to have come second. I'm most grateful to you for having seen me. And now it's back to the oil-rig, I suppose.'

'Well, that's the way it goes. What can I say?'

'Some you win, some you lose?'

'Some you win, some you lose! I like it!'

'You're welcome. Right on?'

'Right on!'

The next stage in the game-plan (Mr Zapper's style was catching) went more smoothly. I bought a suitcase in the Strand and – a spur of the moment impulse buy – half a dozen pairs of Army surplus winter longjohns, which would provide more realistic ballast, I decided, than fifty copies of *The Evening Standard*. I then checked into the Hilton, without

197

mishap, as Lord Dynevor. Installed in my suite, I carried out certain alterations to the lighting (these days one likes others to see just a mere outline of oneself indoors in the afternoon), fiddled with the layout of the set, bathed and then grabbed forty winks.

To my great surprise, Pretty Marie (looking so exquisite that my throat tightened and my knees dipped slightly at the prospect of the play to come) and Scraggy Janet (looking sterner, but that was all to the good) arrived together promptly at 2.30.

'Here,' said Pretty Marie, 'does Emma Jane know about this?'

'No, I thought it best not to tell her. Not being of the live theatre herself, she might not have appreciated every aspect of the situation.'

'Well, I don't know. After all you said in that book thing of yours! About gonks and that. You gave gonks a hard time in that book of yours, you did. And look at you now!'

'We won't go into that, if you don't mind. By the way, what's your name?'

'Here, are you all right? I'm Pretty Marie, me, as well you know.'

'Yes, yes. I mean have you got another name for when you're working?'

'I'm working now.'

'I'm well aware of that, thank you. I mean for when you're doing film work and so forth.'

'Oh, I see. Yes, my real name – don't laugh now – is Doreen Sopwith.'

'Good lord. So you're a member of Equity?'

'Of course. But why?'

'Never mind, it's not important. Anyway, you're looking very tasty, if I may say so.'

And indeed she was. Risking the ridicule of the fashion conscious the enchanting girl, aware of an old man's preferences, had dared cross London in a white mini-skirt and bottle-green thigh boots.

'How's the film career going?'

'Ooooh it's all happening! I've just had some smashing new pictures done and next week I'm meeting Polanski!'

New pictures and meeting Polanski! The perennial double-strength specific to boost any would-be starlet's confidence. Nothing changes.

'That's nice.'

'And I've got this amazing new gonk, haven't I? Here, who's Mrs Scratcher then?'

'Not *her* surely?'

'No silly, not *her*. But who is she?'

'Well, if you mean Mrs Thatcher, she's the leader of the Tory Party.'

Pretty Marie looked disappointed. 'Oh,' she said, 'is that all? I thought she might be quite important, like.'

'No, I'm afraid she's not important. But why do you ask?'

'Well, this new gonk of mine writes speeches for her.'

'Really? What's he like?'

'*Old*, you know, and very English, with beautiful manners and that. Always running around after me picking things up and opening doors, so it's all getting a bit heavy on my head. Still, the bread's good. He gave me a thousand pounds the other day. Well, I had to spend the whole night with him, but even so, I mean that's as much as some people earn in a whole week. Right?'

From now on I expect the standard of Mrs Thatcher's speeches to rise spectacularly. With her stomping the country at the next election saying things of the order of 'Hey, that Jim Callaghan's getting a bit heavy on my head,' the Tories may be in with a chance after all.

'Here,' said Scraggy Janet, who was beginning to show signs of impatience, 'about this Sister George number. I'm not doing a moody or anything, but do you plan to do the whole play? I haven't got all day, you know.'

'I realise that. I thought we'd concentrate on that telling scene towards the end when...'

'Yeah,' said Scraggy Janet, 'I saw the film, didn't I? I quite reckoned it, as it happens. You mean the one where the old dyke from the BBC...'

199

'Hey, that's you darling,' said Pretty Marie. '*Perfect!*'

'Do you mind? I'm well aware it's me, thank you. As I was saying when the charming lady from the BBC shows the girl what it's all about and the other old tart walks in and catches them at it. That one?'

'Precisely. I myself will be playing the other old tart, as you put it.'

'Here, it didn't last very long. In the film, I mean. And nothing much happened. Not that I'm complaining, of course.'

'Oh *charming*,' said Pretty Marie. 'Thanks very much.'

Excellent! A degree of atmosphere was building up already and Pretty Marie had assumed an adorable expression from those unliberated days when it was still permissible for girls to pout provocatively at some imagined slight to their seductiveness.

'In fact,' I said, 'being something of a student of these things, I will let the scene run its course for rather longer than the British Board of Film Censors deemed artistically viable.'

'Yes, I thought you might,' said Pretty Marie. 'Okay girls, here we go! Let's get cracking!'

'Let's get *cracking*? Do you think you could be a little less hearty? It's not exactly the right tone, you know. What we're trying to create here is a mood of unbridled sensuality, not the atmosphere of novelty night at a Pontinental holiday camp. Let's get *cracking*! And what the hell do you think you're doing now?'

'Taking my clothes off.'

And indeed she was. She'd already unbuttoned her blouse and her exquisite, provocatively tanned breasts were promising to spill forth.

'*Taking your clothes off?* Great heavens, whatever next? You're the sort of person who on the day of the Cup Final wouldn't switch their television on until three o'clock! It's the *build-up* that counts. The mounting excitement. Breakfast with the stars. The road to Wembley. The interview with Kevin Keegan's mum. Taking your clothes off! The lady from the BBC does that. What on earth's the matter with you?'

'Look,' said Pretty Marie firmly, 'I don't know about breakfast with the stars and Kevin Keegan's mum and that, but this blouse cost me sixty-five pounds, didn't it? I've got the receipt in my bag. Would you like to see it?'

'That won't be necessary.'

'Well, I don't want her tearing it off, do I? I mean it's an expensive blouse, this.'

'She isn't going to *tear* it off. She's from the BBC for goodness sake! She's going to ease you out of it as lovingly as a voluptuary peeling a grape.'

'Oh yes? Well, I don't know. Look, can she hang it up in the wardrobe, then? Once she's peeled me out of it as lovingly as what you said? I don't want you trampling all over it in your excitement, do I? I know what you're like.'

Honestly, if Pretty Marie hadn't been looking quite so lovely, I'd have been tempted to call the whole thing off. I'd had less trouble with Warren Mitchell and Peter Bayliss in *Council of Love*, and that's saying something. In the circumstances I persevered, which is more than I did with *Council of Love*.

'Okay, okay. Now, at the beginning of the scene, you, Marie, are alone in the bedroom. You're lying on the bed playing, if I remember right, with one of your silly dolls. The stage management have failed to provide us with any dolls so you'll have to use your imagination. Improvise. After a while, Scra – er – Janet comes in and sits down on the bed next to you. She takes your . . . and then . . . you . . . well, I'm sure I don't have to go into detail. Right? Then I come in, watch with mounting dismay and then I . . . got it?'

'Got it,' said Pretty Marie. 'It starts with me lying on the bed improvising. That'll be good. Okay, let's go. Ooooh sorry, that's too hearty, isn't it?'

'Never mind.'

Pretty Marie lay down on the bed as instructed, taking exaggerated care, it seemed to me, not to damage her sixty-

201

five-pound blouse, while Scraggy Janet and I made to leave the room.

'Here,' said Pretty Marie, 'where are you going?'

'Next door. We'll wait till you're ready.'

'Ooooh, just like charades! How super! Do I have to guess what you are? That won't be difficult! Sorry, I'm being hearty again. It's nerves, I should have taken a mandy. Here, Jan darling, you won't mess up my hair, will you? I've only just had it done. And don't forget to hang my blouse up.'

'Blimey,' I said to Scraggy Janet, once we were in the adjoining room, 'is she always like this?'

'Oh, she's very professional once the whistle goes.'

They don't believe in letting you keep your illusions, these girls. We waited for a minute or two, then I opened the door and tipped Scraggy Janet back into the bedroom. I had intended to be patient, but my self-control, never remarkable when this side of myself is off the leash, snapped in no time. I stepped into the bedroom, only to bump into Scraggy Janet coming back.

'What's up?'

'She's not quite ready.'

'Oh? Still trying to get into the mood, is she?' Bless the dear girl, at last she seemed to be taking the whole thing more seriously.

'Actually she's on the phone.'

'On the *phone*? Christ, whatever next?'

This was really too much and I stormed into the bedroom, where Pretty Marie, instead of reclining dreamily on the pillows, had indeed picked up the phone and was in the process of dialling a number.

'What the hell do you think you're doing?'

'Ringing Central Casting,' she said. 'Do you mind?'

'Central *Casting*? Why? We don't need anyone else.'

'I'm not ringing about *this*, silly! I'm ringing about a commercial I'm meant to be doing tomorrow. I've forgotten where to go.'

'Can't it wait till later?'

'I suppose so.'

202

'Okay, let's try it again.'

Scraggy Janet and I withdrew once more to the sitting-room, and after another short interval I pointed Scraggy Janet back to the bedroom. I gave them a couple of minutes to sort themselves out, then I opened the door carefully and crept into the bedroom. This time at last the scene was being played in accordance with the script. Pretty Marie was lying on the bed without her clothes, eyes closed, sighing with pleasure through ecstatically parted lips while Scraggy Janet stroked her lovely thighs. False starts and hang-ups quite forgotten, all disbelief willingly suspended, I swayed, a great balloon of lust, unsteadily towards the bed, realising as I drew near that Pretty Marie's sweet sighs of pleasure were in fact the whispered murmurings of rapture. It was not until I reached the bed, however, that I was able to share the dear intimacy of her actual words.

'I wouldn't mind,' she was saying, 'but he keeps his socks in a bucket in the kitchen.'

'Cut!' I screamed. 'What's your game?'

'Oooh fucking hell!' cried Pretty Marie, sitting up in startlement. 'I didn't think you'd come in yet. You shouldn't creep about so quietly. I was telling Jan about my new guy. He's not very good round the house yet. Well, he's Capricorn and they're not very domesticated, aren't Capricorns. I'll get it right this time, I promise.'

'Well do try. This is really most off-putting.'

I retired once more to the sitting-room, but no sooner had I closed the door than Pretty Marie called me back to the bedroom.

'What's up now?'

'Look, I'm sorry about this,' she said, 'and I'm not doing a number or anything, but you remember what happened last time. At that funky flat you took for parties and that? Remember?'

'Yes. What about it?'

'Well, you didn't have any money and poor little Emma Jane had to pay me and French Simone. Remember? After we'd done our thing and you'd fu...'

'All right, all right, I don't need reminding.'

'Look, I'm sure the same thing isn't going to happen this time, but just to be on the safe side, do you think we could have our money like in advance?'

'My dear girl, the situation's entirely different! I was a low pander in those days trying to scratch a living by staging shows for jaded business men, whereas...'

'The only fucking jaded business man that night was you as I remember.'

'But now, as I was saying, I'm a distinguished author. Great heavens, only the other night I took dinner with the Tynans and I've been on the Epilogue!'

'Oh I know, I know, but we'd still like our money now. Wouldn't we Jan?'

'Yes,' said Scraggy Janet.

Really, this was intolerable! Still, they'd be looking very silly in a minute.

'It may interest you to know that I've just sold my film rights. I've got *five hundred pounds* in that black bag!'

'What black bag?'

'The black bag over there.'

'Over where? I can't see no black bag.'

'Over th...Hullo, somebody's pinched my black bag! Jumping Jesus, where have I left it?'

At any point along the route between Climax Books and the Hilton Hotel, that's where I'd left it, and my brain went ahead of me into some black hole in space. Pretty Marie, wearing the slightly silly expression of someone who's slipped twice on the same banana skin, got dressed most thoughtfully, and then, since I was in a state of shock, she and Scraggy Janet helped me down the passage to the lift, across the foyer and out into Park Lane.

'Don't worry,' I said. 'Tomorrow I'll retrace my steps. The black bag must turn up somewhere.'

'Yeah yeah. Sure. Poor Emma Jane.'

If it didn't, Pretty Marie and Scraggy Janet would be the least of my problems. In the morning, the management of the Hilton would be most distressed to discover that Lord

Dynevor had done a bunk, leaving only a cheap suitcase and six pairs of army surplus longjohns as collateral against his debt. As I'd already cut short his promising career at Hatchards, bringing about his arrest for attempting to gain a pecuniary advantage over Conrad Hilton might be considered unforgivable. On top of which, I could already feel the sharp edges of a painful confrontation with Emma Jane.

'I say, Emma Jane, would you consider advancing me a few hundred? Just till my deal comes off, you understand. Got myself into this silly scrape, do you see? I blame my deep attachment to the live theatre. I mounted this small private production of *The Killing of Sister George* with Pretty Marie and Scraggy Janet, and when the time came to pay the cast, well bless my soul if someone hadn't pinched the wages! Can you beat it? It's quite a lot, I'm afraid.'

Oh dear, I'm up the spout this time.

❊   ❊   ❊

Down to Eton to see *The Duchess of Malfi* and to call on Charlie's house-master, Mr Altham. This acting business is a doddle. Though I say it myself, I scarcely put a foot wrong. If you hired some silly old piss-pot of a mime to play the part of a concerned parent, a pillar of the Middle-Class Association much exercised about the current form of his young son, he'd want a script, a decent rehearsal period, a run of the play contract, a dressing-room, star billing and at least a hundred and fifty pounds a week. And then he'd cock it up. Yet here was I, concussed on my feet by the events of the last few days, but word perfect and doing it for nothing. I should have received sixteen curtain calls, the kind of notices mimes only dream of and *The Evening Standard* award for the best supporting actor of the year.

We were sitting in Mr Altham's large, leathery study under the intimidating gaze of ancient wet-bobs clutching oars, photographed in groups: mustachioed, muscle-bound old parties with tiny heads under schoolboy caps. From the business quarters of the house there wafted the faint but unmistakable aromatic blend of damp towels, cricket bat oil and tuck from home now being brewed on Primus stoves. A man could get the horrors here.

'Care for a sherry?' said Mr Altham.

He seemed a shade less obviously mad, I thought, than many of the breed, his upright bearing and crisp manner suggesting a remaindered military man rather than one of the jittery misfits into whose care Public Schools in my day put their charges: Doggart, the Corinthian Casual, who never went anywhere without his football and dribbled it even to morning chapel; Ridgeway with his frightful rages (he had to go); Colonel Ronnie Hamilton, O/C the Corps, but a *bon viveur* and light comedian *manqué* of the Jack Buchanan school, who once a year put on a funny hat and did a one-man show; 'Hearty' Hodges, the PT master, who had an IQ of 43 and jogged on the spot while chatting; and 'Sponge' Walker who swam in the nude and goosed the boys who were bent over about to dive.

'Do what?'

'I said "care for a sherry?"'

Oh dear, it was going to be one of those conversations. I hadn't been offered a sherry since my own dear Mr Altham had sent me and the other school leavers out into the world some twenty years before. Any minute now I'd be told the facts of life. Not that this delicate task had fallen to my Mr Altham. No, Mr Paterson, the Head of Woodcote House, my private school, had undertaken this and a dog's dinner he'd made of it. If Jinx Grafftey-Smith, a most sophisticated boy who sang *basso profundo* in the school choir at the age of thirteen, hadn't marked my card during my first week at Winchester, goodness knows how I might have ended up. Jinx Grafftey-Smith! What on earth had become of him? Probably married now with a boy of his own and on the board of a merchant bank. Yet he wouldn't mind my mentioning that he used to break wind a lot. Tremendous blow-outs which had put an end to our promising careers as burglars since the worst attacks used to bring the house down at moments of the highest tension. Hell, I was wandering already. In the last forty-eight hours, this had been happening more and more. The black bag had vanished from the face of the earth, any day now Scraggy Janet and Pretty Marie would be putting final demands through our letter-box, Lord Dynevor would have his collar felt for fraud, Tynan would sue me for illegally disposing of his rights and Emma Jane would elope to L.A. with Leighton James. True, a meagre shaft of light had just been shed on an otherwise grim horizon by Toby Danvers the Impresario. Perusing the 'Jobs Vacant' column of *The Times*, he'd come across an opportunity which seemed more or less up our street. The management of St Paul's Cathedral were seeking two new vergers and Danvers had written to the Dean (on writing paper selling shares in his new musical *The Christine Keeler Story*) advising him to search no further. The Dean had written back most civilly – taking up two units in *The Christine Keeler Story* each carrying ten per cent of the net profits – inviting Danvers and me to attend on him shortly. Still, with my luck at the moment, it was odds on we'd turn up for the *viva* only to be told that the positions had just been filled by my friend S. Z. Corbett and Honest John the Thief.

'May I be blunt?' said Mr Altham.

'Please do be. Take the bull by the horns.'

Perhaps I should try and interest him in *The Christine Keeler Story*. I must remember to mention the matter before I leave. Come to think, I should have sold a few units to unwary little boys when down here the other day. They all have trusts. 'Tell me my boy, do you have a trust? Excellent! Perhaps you'd care to invest in my new musical *The Christine Keeler Story*. Sir Alec Guinness, Lesley Anne Down and Fink's mules. You would? Splendid! Make the gooses out to me.'

'Your boy's a pest.'

'Oh dear.'

What a pillock Zapper of Climax Books had been! God forbid the black bag and its precious contents had fallen into his manicured claws. No, my only wish now was that a man of the theatre like myself had come across this sudden windfall and was even now using it to fund a tasteless act in a rented room.

'Plenty of brains, do you see, but the lad won't use them.'

'Have you thrashed him?'

Mr Altham looked comically shocked. Here was progress. My Mr Altham would have taken the suggestion in his stride.

'We don't do that any more. *Nous avons changé tout celà.* Ha! Ha!'

Hell. You're on your own, Magdalene, no conferring.

'Molière? *Le Medecin Malgré Lui,* if I'm not mistaken.'

'Quite so. And more's the pity, I sometimes think.'

Even as he spoke, the dismal background noise of chapel bells and piano practice was sharply broken by a shrill squeal of protest, suggesting that a group of younger boys were about to launch one of their number down the stairs boxed in a laundry skip. So violence still took place, though less ritualised, apparently, than in my day.

'To be blunt,' continued Mr Altham, 'it's his attitude out of the classroom that troubles me more.'

'Yes? Why's that?'

As though I didn't know. I could have played both these parts and done the pools at the same time. How lovely Pretty Marie had looked, how *unnecessarily* nude! In green thigh boots only, and a gold chain. As disturbingly, as shockingly sensual as a photograph by Henry Newton. What an excellent photographer! Ambiguous, perverse without ever being tasteful, obsessed by a story he read at the age of fourteen called *Fraulein Else*, the erotic content of which he's been trying to photograph ever since. It is about a banker who loses all his money. He has a daughter of seventeen who is as beautiful as she is innocent. In desperation, he seeks the help of a rich friend, a banker too. His friend listens to him sympathetically and then makes him an offer. He will be taking tea the next day, he says, in the vast, ornately decorated hall of Berlin's grandest hotel. If the banker can persuade his daughter to come to the hotel, walk slowly up to him and remove her coat, he will give her father one million pounds. The only other condition is that under her coat she must be naked. The girl loves her father and she agrees at once to do as his friend wishes. Coolly threading her way through the rich decadence of the crowded hall, she approaches her father's friend, and, when she reaches him, she very slowly removes her coat and stands before him. He doesn't touch her and he saves her father. Henry Newton? That sounded wrong. Henry was Derby County's donkey surely, their clogger and ball-winner, soon, alas, to lose his abrasive mid-field role to young Stevie Powell. *Helmut* Newton, that was it. Get a grip on yourself, Winchester.

'The boy can't accept discipline. One set of rules for the rest of the school and one set of rules for Charlie, that's his attitude. I confess I don't understand the lad. It's not merely that he breaks the rules, all boys do that. It's a healthy sign. Within reason. To be blunt, we like boys with spirit. No, it's more that he doesn't seem to recognise that there *are* rules. He doesn't seem to appreciate the need for them.'

As perplexing a characteristic this to schoolmasters as to the Conservative Party Conference. People unable to respect the conventions in theory mess up the whole system in practice. One-Eyed Charlie would have been enjoying this.

'That's bad,' I said. 'Could you give me an example?'

'Yes, I think so. If, for instance, he's playing soccer, he picks the ball up and runs around with it, by no means always in the right direction; but if he's playing rugger, he refuses to touch the ball except to kick it.'

Very irritating, no doubt of that, and eerily familiar too. At Winchester the playing fields had been so small that it had been only too easy to become involved in the wrong game. Once, when playing cricket for my house, I'd grown bored with fielding cover-point and had discovered that by turning round I'd become an acceptable extra mid-wicket in the next-door game. I'd made some spectacular stops and then I'd run a fellow out. By the time it had been discovered that 'C' house had been fielding an extra man – and he a stranger – four more wickets had fallen, I'd bowled a couple of tidy overs and the fellow I'd run out was half a mile away having an ice-cream in the tuck-shop. There'd been the devil

209

of a row. My Mr Altham had had me on the carpet and had then sent me along to the head of the school (Godfrey Hodgson, incidentally, who crops up in an investigative role from time to time on television and whose hair, I'm glad to see, has turned prematurely grey) to be caned for general attitude.

'It's particularly disappointing,' continued Mr Altham, 'since he was highly recommended to us by Paterson, the Headmaster of his private school. Woodcote House. You know it, I expect.'

'Never heard of it.'

'Oh. Well, anyway, the point is that Charlie came to us as a promising scholar and, which is more important, of course, a fine athlete.'

'Mens san – er – etc. etc. in corp – er – '

The aged wet-bobs looked down from the walls, I felt, with a degree less disapproval. You're doing better Winchester.

'Precisely. At first, everything went according to plan. His work was satisfactory and he won the under-fifteen hurdles. Then he caught this pop music thing.'

'Hell. He caught that, did he? We know where that leads.'

'We do indeed. Er – where?'

'May I be blunt?'

'Please do be.'

'Drugs and nudity.'

'My fear precisely. Another drink?'

'Not for me, thank you.'

'I find I need a little pick-me-up at this time of the day.'

'Of course. Care for a smoke?'

'Thank you, no.'

'Mind if I do?'

'Not at all.'

Thank goodness I'd taken the precaution of bringing my gear with me. While Mr Altham poured himself a stiff slug of gin, I rolled myself a joint.

'Well, anyway, now he sits in his room all day strumming his guitar and lounging around with an older boy who plays the drums.'

210

Oh sod, an older boy who played the drums. That sounded bad. Was my Charlie about to be accused of beastly Ericing? Keep a stiff upper-lip now Winchester.

'Ned Footware-Fowler. The two are inseparable.'

Thank God for that. Nothing fishy about young Ned. But what a strange coincidence. And how odd of Ned not to have twigged that I was Charlie's pater. Common name Donaldson, I suppose. Still, it was good grass, this. Not your homegrown rubbish. After a few puffs I'd be able to handle the situation with relaxed aplomb.

'It might be thought,' continued Mr Altham, 'that young Footware-Fowler, as the older boy by nine months, is a bad influence on Charlie, but it's the other way round in my opinion. And, to be blunt, I've told Ned's father as much. Lord Footware-Fowler, that is. You may have heard of him.'

'I have indeed. In fact I've met the old fool.'

'You have? How interesting. When was this?'

'When I was down here the other day. The family seems to be having problems.'

'Problems? The Footware-Fowlers having problems? I knew of no problems.'

'Oh dear, haven't you heard? Perhaps I shouldn't have mentioned it.'

'But they came to see me just the other day. There seemed to be nothing wrong.'

'Putting a good face on it were they? How courageous. Well, that's the tradition, I suppose, but it's very sad none the less. Young Ned told me everything. It seems that Lord Footware-Fowler isn't his father at all. God knows how the lad found out. It seems that Lady Footware-Fowler – well, I'm sure I don't have to go into the sordid details. Let's just say that she went slightly off the rails some years ago. Now it looks as though it's all going to come out into the open like that squalid Ampthill case. It's such a tragedy when the children become involved.'

'Yes indeed. Oh dear, I hardly know what to say. Ned told you all this?'

'Yes, but in the very strictest confidence, you understand.

I'm sure he'd be horrified to think I'd told someone else. But perhaps you ought to have a word with Lord Footware-Fowler next time you see him. Just to set the record straight.' That would scupper the old maniac, and it would scupper Mr Altham too. 'Let him know you appreciate the terrible strain he's under. Man to man.'

'Yes, you're absolutely right. He and Lady Footware-Fowler will be down here in a week or two and I'll mention it to them then. Oh dear, how very sad. Still, to get back to Charlie.'

'Of course.'

'As I say, all was going according to plan until a year ago. Then he came back from the summer holidays having caught this pop music thing.'

'Yes, from Ned Footware-Fowler.'

'No, in fact he'd been staying with his other great friend, Kim Kindersley. His father's Gay, you know.'

'How sad.'

'Yes. I mean no. Gay Kindersley, that's what he's called.'

'I'm not surprised. Are you sure you won't have a pull on this? It's good stuff.'

'Er – thank you, no. Well anyway, from that moment Charlie seemed to chuck it in. Hardly went near the gymnasium or the running track. I tried talking to him.'

'Yes?'

'I sat him in that very chair you're sitting in now. "What's got into you, Charlie?" I said. "Why have you given up the ghost? If you won't try for your own sake, try at least for the sake of the house." I appealed to his sense of honour, do you see?'

'What did he say to that?'

'Nothing. Absolutely nothing. That was what was so bewildering. He just set his jaw and stared back at me with a sullen expression.'

'Did you tell him to take that expression off his face?'

'I did. "And take that expression off your face," I said.'

'Dumb insolence.'

'"It's not good enough, Charlie," I said, "it simply isn't

212

good enough." Night after night I used to say it, and he just sat there where you're sitting now, staring back at me with that peculiar expression on his face.'

'Oh dear.'

'It's such a *waste*. That's the tragedy of it. He's a first class gymnast and he can run extremely fast.'

'It sounds as though he may have to.'

And I'll come with you Charlie. Back to the Balearics, if need be, with the proctors, Mr Pulley, Lord Goodman and the Fraud Squad puffing after us. Not that I'd keep up for long. Could have done once, of course, but not any more. Been something of a hurdler in my day too. No form in the gym to speak of, but a bit quick over the high hurdles. Until I started running into them. Seemed easier than jumping them, somehow. Emma Jane would hand me my head this time, that was for sure. If she didn't throw me out. And where would I go then? To the Basil Street Hotel, where they have a copy of the bible by the bedside? More than you can say for the Hilton.

> The Bible is a goodly book
> I always can peruse with zest,
> But really cannot say the same
> For Hilton's *Be my guest*.

If she eloped to L.A. with Leighton James, of course, she might leave me the flat and its contents too. Then at least I could pop one of the colour television sets for marching money. If you're living alone, you don't really need two colour television sets. Or do you? You might, after all, have guests whose viewing tastes were not the same as yours. How sublimely fatuous Parky had been on Saturday, though, fawning in crazed admiration at the feet of Paul Simon, the pop musician. 'That's fabulous!' Parky had babbled after Simon had done a number, 'that's poetry set to music!' 'No it isn't,' Simon had said, staring at Parky in pop-eyed wonderment, 'it's a song.' Funny thing about Emma Jane: she had her standards, but if you were up for something you hadn't done, you'd want her on the jury. And of how many people could you say that these days? Damn few, alas, damn few. I'd over-stepped the mark this time, though, no doubt of that. Still, playing in the wrong game of cricket and running out Reggie Bosanquet, that had been fun. No great achievement, I suppose. A bit stiff in the joints even then. What would happen to me now? Probably be sent along to see Hodgson for a thrashing. Hell, Mr Altham was still rambling on.

'I'm so sorry. What was that you said?'

'I said "I suppose you think that's funny."'

'I think what's funny?'

'What you just said. "It sounds as though he may have to." Is that supposed to be funny?'

'No sir.'

'Well, it isn't. And don't answer back. That's the trouble with you, isn't it? You won't answer at all except to answer back. It's a way of drawing attention to yourself. Is that all we've managed to teach you here? How to draw attention to yourself?'

'No sir.'

'Don't interrupt. Have you any idea how many members of this house gave up their lives in the desert for your generation?'

'No sir.'

'None sir, that's how many. And do you know why? Because they obeyed orders, that's why. They were fighting for freedom so they did as they were told. That's what Winchester is supposed to teach you. To obey orders, to keep your head down, your trousers up and your eye on the ball. Not to go lounging about the place with your straw hat at a facetious angle. You insist on popping your head up, don't you Donaldson?'

'No sir.'

'Exactly. Well, one day someone's going to shoot it off. Then you won't be able to answer back, will you?'

'No sir.'

'No you won't. And what did you think you were doing

214

playing in the wrong game of cricket? I suppose you thought that was funny too?'

'No sir.'

'Well it wasn't. You let yourself down, you let the team down, you let your captain down and you let young Dynevor down. I thought he was meant to be a friend of yours?'

'Yes sir.'

'Well, was that the act of a friend? Making a nonsense of the whole game? Reducing it to the level of a silly joke? Running out Bosanquet when he wasn't even playing in the same game as you? Bosanquet's all right, a sensible boy. He won't come to grief in later life. Let me put it this way. Suppose you and Bosanquet were out at sea in a small boat and it capsized. What would happen? You'd panic, wouldn't you?'

'Yes sir.'

'Yes you would. But Bosanquet wouldn't. No sir. He'd drown. For the sake of the school. That's the difference. You'll have to be thrashed, you know. Do you want to be thrashed?'

'No sir.'

'Don't try that silly bravado with me! Just as soon as I've finished with you here, I'm sending you along to see Pulley. Another sensible boy. He'll do well in life. But what will become of you? Your sister Bobo's very worried about you, you know. She says that all you do in the holidays is mooch in your room dreaming about Virginia Mayer.'

'Mayo, sir.'

'No you may not. Not until I finish with you here. You'll be leaving soon, going out into the world, standing on your own two feet. And what will become of you then? Have we taught you nothing here? I sometimes wonder. Society, the fabric of the world outside, is a magnificent tapestry, you see, made up of many different strands and Wykehamists, by tradition, are the tailors and darners of this social fabric. Let me put it this way. Winchester is like a sturdy bridge over fast-running rapids. The rapids are life. Eventually, we all have to leave the bridge and take our chances in the un-

215

friendly water. Now, what happens to an ordinary common object, a crude piece of metal, say, if you throw it off a bridge?'

'It gets wet, sir.'

'No it doesn't, it sinks. But if it's been moulded into the right shape, if it's been to Winchester, it floats. The river's natural, you see, but the bridge is man-made. It represents everything that's most worth preserving in our heritage. Our heritage, I sometimes think, is like a length of silken cord stretching back to the dawn of civilisation. It grows stronger and finer over the years, which isn't to say that it never becomes tangled or is in danger of being severed altogether. Certain envious elements with vested interests devote their entire lives to a carefully orchestrated attempt to sever this fine silken cord. This is why moderate people, of whatever colour, race or creed, must be forever watchful. Not everyone using the bridge, you see, is a friend to civilisation. And if we voluntarily let go of that fine silken cord or have it prised from our grasp by sophisticated men of violence, what happens to us? The turbulent rapids smash us against the rocks of chaos. Empty out your pockets, boy.'

'Why sir?'

'Because I say so, sir. And because your Auntie Emma Jane thinks you may be hiding incriminating evidence. Ah! What have we here? What are all these stamps? The Leeward Isles? Fiji? Trinidad and Tobago? Six penny reds? What's going on here? How did you get hold of these?'

'I swapped them for my grandfather's gold half-hunter, sir.'

'Oh? With whom?'

'With Tynan of the sixth, sir.'

'Tynan? A difficult boy, a bad influence. Got a few brains, there's no denying that, but most unstable. No sense of the proper balance of things. Obsessed with matters appertaining to the water-works. You know your sister Bobo wishes you to have nothing to do with him. These are his stamps?'

'No sir.'

'Whose then?'

'Packer's sir.'

'Packer? I've not heard of him. What house is he in?'

'He's not a member of the school, sir. He's a common boy I met in the town, sir.'

'In the *town*? You know you're not supposed to mix with town boys! This is more serious than I thought. You swapped your grandfather's watch twice?'

'No sir, six times, sir.'

'The same watch *six* times?'

'Yes sir.'

'So how many people think they own it?'

'Seven, sir, including my grandfather.'

'Great heavens, boy, that's tantamount to fraud! They'll be on to me again!'

'Who will, sir?'

'The Fraud Squad, that's who! They were down here last week, you know, following a complaint from the Dean of St Paul's. It seems that you and Danvers – another unsatisfactory boy – sold him shares in *The Christine Keeler Story*.'

'A good show, sir. Sir Alec Guinness, Diana Rigg and Fink's...'

'That's as may be. But two units of £250 could hardly carry thirty-three per cent of the net profits. To say nothing of the Vice Squad. Yes, they were here too, you know. After that squalid business involving your so-called friend, young Dynevor. First you lose him his holiday job at Hatchards and then – as if that wasn't bad enough – you book a hotel room in his name and use it for monkey-business below the belt. In *his* name? What would happen if everyone got up to monkey-business under someone else's name? Utter chaos would ensue. Fortunately for you, your Auntie Emma Jane managed to straighten that one out. She paid the hotel bill and also, I regret to say, the two – er – trollops whom you involved in the squalid episode. She's practically an angel, that poor dear lady, but she's got her own life to lead as a social worker and she can't go on getting you out of silly scrapes forever, can she?'

'Yes sir.'

'No sir! Right, cut along now, and remember this: life, I sometimes think, is like a game of football. But do the players in a game of football make up their own rules as they go along? Does each player have his own whistle? No, only the referee is supplied with a whistle and the others, by common consent, play to its command. Morality, you see, must have its basis in the rules. So what happens if we don't heed the referee's whistle? We have a crisis of authority, leading to civil disorder.'

'Delightful! SOCIETY, Civilised: The greatest of virtues in a civilised society, greater even than freedom or justice, is order.'

Well interrupted Winchester.